NO WAY BACK TODAY

ERIC SHOARS

Copyright © 2019 Eric J. Shoars
All rights reserved.
Print ISBN: 978-1-54398-541-2
eBook ISBN: 978-1-54398-542-9

For
Generation X

TABLE OF CONTENTS

	ACKNOWLEDGEMENTS	9
1	KISS AND T.E.L.L.	11
2	CHIVE TALKIN'	35
3	SPRINGING A LEEK	62
4	BACON AND ONIONS	163
5	COME ON, GET ONIONS	185
6	LIGHTS, CAMERA, ONIONS	208
7	WILD SCALLIONS	257
8	THANKS, SHALLOT!	288
	NO WAY BACK TODAY LYRICS	313
	AND NOW FOR THE LEGAL STUFF…	334
	ABOUT THE AUTHOR	336

ACKNOWLEDGEMENTS

Writing a book is always a journey without a map or directions. Along the path of every journey are people who make the trek even more memorable and special. I'd like to thank the people who were with me on this particular excursion.

Thank you to my wife, Julie, for her support, encouragement, and belief in my art. I'm so blessed you are on every journey with me.

Thank you, Aniko Eastvold, for being the little sister I always wanted and for being a constant source of positivity. This book would never have happened if you hadn't invited me to speak to your English classes so I could share my stories with your students. You have my never-ending gratitude.

Thanks to my collaborator Lisbeth Tull for working with me on the lyrics for the Onions At A Crime Scene album **No Way Back Today.** You helped create the emotional impact I envisioned for each song.

Thanks to my editor Judi Blaze for not being afraid to take a red pen to my work and for helping me make a good story an epic one.

Thanks to the publishing team at Book Baby for getting this story reader ready.

Thanks to James Sturm, author of Unstable Molecules. The way you told that story was the inspiration for how I'd bring the legend of Onions At A Crime Scene to the world.

And, most of all, thanks to the members of T.E.L.L. for the opportunity to complete some unfinished business. I wish you all the best in the next chapters of your lives.

CHAPTER ONE

KISS AND T.E.L.L.

January 12, 2018

It's been more years than I care to remember since I was in a high school classroom for any reason. It is 8:05 on a Friday morning and this will be the first class of three grades I will address today. My appearance here is at the request of my sister Aniko who is their English teacher. A sea of 20 faces examines me with curiosity and suspicion, not sure what they are about to experience. The students - tenth, eleventh, and ninth graders in that order - will be the fortunate recipients of my wisdom about storytelling.

This sampling of the digital generation that communicates in short bursts via emoji or abbreviations is having a difficult time grasping how to write stories that are more than 140 characters. Ani asked me a couple months back if I would come in and do a presentation about the storytelling process. Of course I said yes.

The room is very much a classroom. Light blue, cement block walls are two sides of the room that are covered with motivational posters. The wall to my right is interrupted by windows that run nearly the entire length of it. Aniko is seated at her desk which is tucked into the corner to my right. The door is to my left opposite of Aniko's desk. Behind me is the Smartboard. Sophomores are in front of me.

The tardy bell sounds alerting everyone in the school that if your butt isn't in a chair, you're late. I look over and nod at Aniko letting her know I'm all set to go. She smiles and rises from her chair.

Aniko and I look like we're brother and sister with our brown hair, blue eyes, and glasses. The main difference is that she's a pixie, almost seven inches shorter than me. Her blue eyes are kind whereas mine are mischievous. Her demeanor is more laid back and studious where mine is more in your face and impulsive. We are opposite sides of the same coin; her introvert to my extrovert.

"Good morning, class," Aniko begins walking around me to get to the dead center of the room. "Today I have a special guest, my brother Eric, who is going to help you become better storytellers. Eric owns his own marketing company. His job is to help businesses tell stories about their products and services so people will buy them."

The faces looking at me change again. The looks are a mixture of curiosity, amusement, wariness, and outright defiance. *What could this guy possibly tell us that would be of any use?* Then the mixture of expressions among the kids unifies when they realize a substitute teacher is here and they're not going to have to do a thing. The feeling of jubilation is almost palpable.

"I expect you to pay attention because when we start our next section on Monday you'll need to be able to do what Eric is going to share with you today. Okay?" Aniko reminds. A classroom full of nods comes back at her. "Great. Well, then, let's welcome my brother Eric." My sister returns to her desk and takes a seat. The group greets me vocally instead of clapping. I'll take it.

"Good morning," I greet with enthusiasm. "When Mrs. Eastman asked me to talk with you today I thought a lot about how I could best help you without lecturing you. Is it okay if I don't lecture?" The room is filled with bobbing head dolls; emphatically communicating a lecture-free hour is totally fine with them. I smile. They have no idea what they're in for.

The next thirty-five minutes are spent telling stories from my life growing up through adulthood. Every story has a purpose and every story has a moral. Out of the corner of my eye I catch Aniko smiling. She knows what I'm doing and she approves. The kids, however, haven't caught on.

"All right, my friends, that wraps up our storytelling lesson," I say with about 15 minutes until the bell rings. My audience, however, is openly bewildered. Everyone is looking around at everyone else wondering if he or she is the only one in the group that has missed the lesson somewhere; wondering if he or she had fallen asleep at some point and not realized it. The head turning is replaced by buzzing as people are trying to figure out what just happened.

"This is a storytelling lesson, isn't it?" I ask. "All I've done is tell you stories, see?" The buzzing stops and I have everyone's complete attention. They don't know it but I'm having a blast.

"Here's what storytelling is," I begin explaining a joke no one got. "There are four parts." I hold up my right index finger. "Once upon a time..." My middle finger joins my index finger. "...there was a person who encountered conflict. Conflict just means something happened to him or her. It doesn't mean a fight." Third finger goes up. "Here's what the person did about it." Pinky finger rises. "And he or she lived happily ever after or didn't or here's the moral of the story. That's it. Nothing magical. All stories have those four components. The only difference is the length of the story it takes to tell the four parts."

Eyes widen and jaws drop. They just got the joke. I had been teaching them while entertaining them and none of them had caught it until now and they are bobble-head dolls once more. They get it and understand. Each of my stories wasn't merely entertainment. Each had purpose. Each had substance.

"Let me tell you one more story before the bell rings. I glance at the clock by the door and turn to Aniko. "Ten minutes till the bell, right?" Aniko nods. "Outstanding. Here we go."

I pause for dramatic effect while returning to the front of the classroom making sure everyone can see me. "When I was in fourth grade," I start, "I wanted to be in a rock and roll band. I had it all figured out." With each word my excitement grows as I recall how my nine-year-old self felt that October day on the playground.

"Three friends and I were going to be in the band and we were going to call ourselves T.E.L.L. - Todd, Eric, Laurie, and Lori. I was going to play drums and sing, Todd would play bass guitar, one Lori would play keyboard, and the other Laurie would play lead guitar." Smiling faces look at me with expressions of amusement trying to picture this old guy in a band.

"Oh, we had it all figured out," my eyes widen like a mad scientist about to bring forth something that will change the course of history. "Now, there were two problems - I couldn't sing and I didn't know how to play drums. But those were just details because I knew that in sixth grade we'd have music class focused on singing and in seventh grade I could take band and learn how to play drums. I just had to get to those grades and it would be full speed ahead." I pause to look at the group and study their faces. I have their full attention. How would this story end? What would the moral be? What happened with the band?

"When I got to sixth grade my music teacher Mrs. Schmidt told me - in front of the whole class - that I couldn't sing. I told myself that was okay. You don't have to be able to sing to be in a band. You do need to know how to play an instrument. The dream is still alive." I pause again for effect.

"Then I got to seventh grade and was so excited that after all these years of biding my time I was finally going to learn how to play the drums. A week into band class everyone in my grade had their instruments - even the drummers - except me. I sat in class watching everyone else play. I was confused and frustrated for sure. I walked into Mr. Tripolino's office after Friday band class one day and asked him when my drum kit was going to arrive."

I break off my story momentarily to make eye contact with every student in the room. All eyes are on me. No one makes a sound. No one moves. I take a deep breath and fully exhale before continuing.

"Mr. Tripolino looked at me and said, 'Well, I didn't think you'd be any good at it so I didn't bother ordering any for you'."

A collective gasp of horror fills the room. Of all the possible outcomes this one was not on their radar. Some kids have a look of dejection as if those words had been directed at them not me. A few girls have tears of empathy in their eyes that a teacher would be so cruel to a kid.

I lift my right hand and move it through the air mimicking an airplane making an appropriate jet sound only to be replaced by the sound of a whistle of descent; my hand now in a sharp motion toward the floor accompanied by a vocal effect of a crash and explosion. "Rock and roll dream crashed and burned. Done." I punctuate the end of my sentence with a shoulder slump. "I quit band and that was that. I never did learn how to play a musical instrument."

A collective shoulder slump mirrors mine as this group is reminded how awful some people can be. Tears are flowing down half a dozen cheeks.

"I didn't tell you that story so you'll feel sorry for me or to bring you down. You're in a time of your life where people are trying to tell you what you can or can't do or who you can or can't be. Don't do like I did and let someone - anyone - who really doesn't know you end your dream. If you want to do it, take a chance. Don't be afraid to risk. You find out if you can do it by giving it your best shot. Don't let someone's opinion determine your reality."

Aniko rises from her seat with the speed as if she'd sat on a tack. She quickly moves in beside me. "Let's thank Eric for sharing how to tell stories. Be sure to write down some thoughts in your notebooks or your devices so we can hit the ground running on Monday."

The bell rings. The students scramble to gather their gear to get to their next class. Each one thanks me for telling sensational stories as he or she walks by. I thank each student for the opportunity to share them.

The room is empty for a few moments before the juniors come in for their storytelling lesson. I'm satisfied with how this first hour went and how well I was received. A positive omen for the next two grades I'll address.

"Is that what you're looking for?" I ask Aniko seeking an assessment of my performance.

"Yes, that was perfect," Aniko replies almost giddy. "I wasn't sure how they would act, if they'd pay attention or not but they were spellbound. Wish I could get them to do that."

"Oh come on, sis. I'm the substitute teacher. Everybody loves the substitute," brushing aside an assertion I did anything special.

"I had totally forgotten about your rock and roll band," Aniko tells me with more than a hint of bemusement. That band was all you'd talk about when we were kids. Tripolino was such a jerk. I hated band until I got to high school." Aniko, three years younger than me, had played clarinet all through school and still plays on occasion. Apparently Mr. Tripolino had seen more ability in her than he had in me. She got her instrument almost immediately.

A new crowd rushes in to fill the seats. The expressions I received from the previous group are the same ones I'm getting again just on different faces.

The second bell rings and round two of Storytelling 101 begins.

* * *

If tossing and turning were an Olympic event I'd have won a gold medal two hours ago. A check of the clock reveals it is three in the morning. Haven't slept much all night. My wife Julie enjoys a peaceful slumber beside me. Thankfully my restlessness has not prevented her from having a restful sleep.

Sleep continues to elude me because the gears in my brain won't stop turning, working on a problem that has no solution. I should be feeling triumphant. My guest-speaking stint before Aniko's students was an undeniable hit. All three classes I spoke to reacted almost identically to my stories, my lessons. It was an enjoyable experience and every minute was gratifying for me. If it's one thing I love, it's a good story...especially when I'm the one telling it.

Triumphant is not the word to describe my mood at this point in time. The word is troubled. Or sad. Or disturbed. Take your pick.

The story of my band that never was has weighed on me since departing the high school this morning. Memories came back with a weight I hadn't felt since I was a teen. That weight is something I'm wrestling with in between brief interludes of sleep. What eludes me is why this story is so bothersome and why now? What is so special about sharing the story today that produced this evening's toss and turn fest?

Suddenly the answer lands. October 1977. January 2018. Forty years. October 2017 marked 40 years since the conversation on that elementary school playground among four friends of a dream never realized. The underscored point my brain is making is that it has been 40 years since the young me had a dream that others had crushed like a bug.

It's only five months till the big five-oh would be attached to me, till that AARP card arrives in my mailbox. AARP card. How did I get this old this fast? It doesn't seem like 40 years since we were on that playground together.

October 18, 1977

"Are you going to play football?"

I look up from my staring contest with the asphalt that is the elementary school playground. We're at recess after another disgusting lunch. Standing over me is my best friend in the whole wide world, Todd Kane. I've known Todd for as long as I can remember. Our dads work together at the local seed company.

"No, not this time," I reply.

"How come?" Todd inquires taking a seat on the swing beside me. "Are you feeling okay?"

"I'm fine. I just can't stop thinking about something."

"A problem?"

"No. KISS."

"KISS?" Todd responds. "Gene Simmons is great. I'm hoping to get their album Destroyer for Christmas."

Todd and I had discovered KISS almost exactly a year ago. They performed on The Paul Lynde Halloween Show. Todd and I watched the Halloween TV special together at his house and we were stunned by what we saw that night. The costumes, the music, the energy hit us both like we had touched a live electrical wire.

We became fans from the first time we saw KISS on TV. Todd's a Gene Simmons guy. Me, I'm an Ace Frehley guy. Beyond that, I saw four people having a blast playing music and entertaining people. That's not a bad life.

"No, I'm thinking about the band idea," I tell Todd.

"Still? You haven't given up on that idea yet?" Todd acts with more than a hint of incredulity.

Two girls in our class approach us before I can respond. Todd and I are the only kids who are in this area of the playground so the girls' curiosity has gotten the better of them. Laurie Laning and Lori Politis are two of our friends and classmates. Laurie has short, sandy blonde hair and is one of the smartest kids in our grade. Lori has long, brown hair and is one of the most popular kids in our grade.

"What's going on, guys?" Laurie asks. She's wearing her green jacket and blue jeans. Lori is in jeans also, but her jacket is brown.

"Eric's decided not to play today," Todd tells them.

"What's going on, Eric?" Lori asks me. No matter what Lori says it sounds like she's singing.

"I'm thinking about our band," I reveal.

Todd shakes his head upon hearing my admission a second time. Laurie scrunches her eyebrows and the corners of her mouth turn down. Lori cocks her head to the left pausing for more information before committing to any reaction.

"Are you kidding?" Laurie asks. "We're nine-years-old. How are we going to form a band?"

"We aren't going to be nine-years-old forever," I fire back. "We have to think about the future." My voice is stern and certain like I'm trying to inspire an army before a battle.

"You're my best friend but you're nuts." Todd, clearly, is not taking that hill.

Lori is at least courteous if not curious. "Tell us what you're thinking."

I reach into my back right pants pocket and pull out a folded up piece of paper. I unfold it as Todd leans next to my left shoulder while Laurie and Lori walk around my swing to look over my right shoulder. On the paper is a drawing I made and colored.

Pictured on the page are four figures - two boys and two girls - in a band. I'm behind the drums triumphantly raising drumsticks in the air. Todd is standing in the foreground to my right playing guitar. Lori is near the drummer's left standing behind a keyboard. Laurie is in the foreground with a guitar.

Laurie's arm extends over my shoulder almost touching the paper itself. "What is tell?"

At the top of the drawing in all capital letters are the T, E, L, and L. Each letter has a period behind it. I have been waiting for this question most of all. "It's the name of the band as an acronym - T.E.L.L. It's us. Todd, Eric, Laurie, and Lori."

"The name is catchy," Todd thinks aloud. Laurie nods in agreement adding, "I don't know, though. Seems like a long shot."

My mind brings me back to the present, Laurie's 4th grade assessment echoing in my head. It does seem like a long shot even more at this juncture as thoughts come back to the now.

Maybe sentimentality is getting the better of me. Or regret. When you're 9, 19, 29 or even 39 you have so much time ahead of you so many things to do so many possibilities.

Fifty, though, is a different ballgame. Not that 50 is death but there feels a certain finality about more years being behind you than lie ahead; and there remains unfinished business. So much unfinished business and a race against time to tie up the loose ends before you run out of time, opportunity, or health.

This piece of unfinished business seems destined to remain unfinished which probably is why the gears keep grinding in an effort for a solution that remains elusive. How can a nine-year-old boy's fantasy become a reality at the age of 49? Impossible. Isn't it?

What about my bandmates, their interest in this rock and roll fantasy, and their whereabouts? Laurie, no, Laurel as she prefers to be called now, graduated with me so I can find her.

Lori and Todd? Lori moved away after 5th grade and Todd after 8th. I hadn't seen or heard from them since then. They could be anywhere in the country now.

The gears in my brain are spinning as fast as a centrifuge. More information, more variables flood my mind with still no solution, no resolution on the horizon. There is only one thing I can do and that is mentally run toward the impossible and see what happens.

I can't sing or play an instrument but is it too late to teach this old dog some new tricks? Is that impossible? No.

Where are my bandmates? Laurel is in Ames. Todd and Lori are who knows where but in our internet age nearly anyone who has even a tiny digital footprint can be located. Would it be impossible to find them? No. Challenging but not impossible.

Then there's the idea itself. Would Laurel, Todd, and Lori be interested in reviving T.E.L.L.? Would they embrace the implausibility of reviving the dream of getting the band together?

Gears start to slow down. Clarity is coming. Implausible is a long way from impossible. Getting the band back together becomes an extremely intriguing thought as I consider implausible. A long shot is a better than no shot. Long shot or not, why does a band get back together including a band that never was one in the first place? Why do they go on tour?

KISS, REO Speedwagon, .38 Special, and Van Halen – to name four - have all gotten back together in recent years and done reunion tours. My thought path comes to a screeching halt at an answer stumbled upon. What if T.E.L.L got back together for a reunion tour?

But how can a band that never was have a reunion tour? What if the reunion isn't about the band but about a reunion of four people who had a Once Upon A Time but never had An Ever After?

What if?

Then something I once read on the wall at a Caribou coffee shop pops into my head. One of the lines in their mission statement is: *"It's where What If meets Why Not?"* Why not? Why the hell not? Impossible becomes implausible. What if has become Why not. Could this actually happen?

The gears in my brain kick into solution mode and start working. The rest is just details. There's the matter of songs, venues, interviews, websites, promotion, all the rest of the things a band needs. This is the digital age, for crying out loud. What can't be accomplished with the tools provided by the World Wide Web? That stuff is just marketing and that is all about storytelling.

And if there's one thing I love, it's a good story...especially when I'm the one telling it.

* * *

Hours following sunrise I'm sitting at the kitchen table contemplating over oatmeal. Slept like the proverbial infant once my brain had put forth a satisfactory solution. I managed to get five hours sleep before the sunlight squeezed between the curtain and the window frame nudging my eyes open.

A sea of glistening white blankets everything as I gaze out the sliding glass patio door and into the backyard. Minnesota winters are cold, yes, but between the snow on the ground and frost covering the empty tree branches, they are a thing of beauty. Somehow the answers I seek lie somewhere between my oatmeal and the snow outside. My quiet contemplation does not go unnoticed.

"Whatcha thinkin' about?" Julie, the light of my life, asks. She checks on the pot of coffee brewing as she passes by my place at the table. Julie is rocking her baby blue winter robe which covers a figure that shouldn't be covered. Ever. Her curly brown hair looks barely disturbed as though she hadn't moved all night which is in sharp contrast to my hair that is going every which way imaginable. Her hazel eyes are clear. My baby blues not so much.

"My morning with Aniko's students," I answer. "Didn't sleep well for most of last night as my mind was unsettled."

"Unsettled?" Julie repeats, pouring herself a cup of coffee then pouring one for me placing it next to my bowl. "Why? I thought you said your talk went well yesterday."

"The morning went amazingly well. Glad I did it. One of the stories I told involved my rock and roll band dream and how it never came to pass. My brain wouldn't let it go and wouldn't let me sleep till I had figured out why it bothered me so and what I'm going to do about it."

"Do about it?" Julie questions me, leaning back against the counter while bringing the cup to her lips.

"Yeah. It occurred to me that it's been 40 years since I first had the rock and roll dream with Todd, Laurel, and Lori. And I'm hurtling headlong toward 50 and feeling like I have some unfinished business."

"Unfinished business?" Julie repeats before her second sip. A feeling of annoyance at her repeating the last part of my sentences begins to rise within me.

Looking her in the eyes with my most serious face, letting my spoon rest in the bowl in front of me, I say it aloud for the first time: "Boo, I want to get the band back together. I want Todd, Laurel, Lori, and me to do a little reunion tour. Just a few dates."

There. I said it. Out loud. It's a real thing now.

Julie's eyes narrow. She holds back, wondering if I'm pranking her, bracing for a punchline or a Bazinga or something. The room remains silent. Then a verbal game of Ping Pong ensues.

"You want to get a band together that was never actually a band?" is her opening query.

"Yes."

"You don't sing or play an instrument."

"No, I do not."

"Do you know where the other three people are?"

"Laurel, yes. Todd and Lori, no."

"Do you think they remember they were part of this band or have any interest in pursuing this now?

"Maybe. I don't know."

"And you say this is a reunion tour? For a band that never existed? For a band that has no songs, no albums, never played together?"

"The reunion isn't about the band; it's about the four of us. The rest can be overcome. We'll be a sensation."

The gears in Julie's noggin are grinding as the questions that came to me last night are coming to her now. I sense she's trying to figure out how to ask these questions in a way that doesn't come across as unsupportive or that she thinks I've lost my mind. She takes a deep breath and asks, "What if I said you could build a baseball field in the backyard instead? Would that help?" Julie takes another sip.

My eyes narrow no longer able to hold back the annoyance that has been working its way to the surface. "No," comes out flatly accompanied by a slow, determined head shake. "I know how this sounds..."

"Do you?" Julie leans in toward me. "Because I don't think you do."

I throw my hands up in exasperation. "Okay, sure. Maybe this is a mid-life crisis. Maybe this is crazy. But maybe it's so left field-off the wall-ridiculous that it just might happen. How do I know this isn't something the other three would jump at if they had the chance?"

Julie walks toward me and pulls the chair opposite me away from the table. A small squeak comes up as the feet of the back chair legs are dragged against the linoleum. She sets her coffee cup on the glass top table and sits down.

She studies me. Part of her remains on alert that the other shoe is about to drop and I'm going to spring a "just kidding" on her. I let the silence stand as a testament to the seriousness of my intent. Minutes pass.

"You really want to do this?" she asks breaking the non-verbal stalemate.

"I do."

"Are you going to leave your company?"

"No, no. Nothing like that. Our lives don't change. We still do what we do but, in the meantime, I'm going to pursue this in my free time. Getting T.E.L.L. back together isn't going to happen overnight and neither is the rest of it. It'll be like a hobby - like woodworking or gardening or putting puzzles together. That's all."

Julie sighs. I can't tell if she's disappointed this isn't a joke or concerned her husband has separated from reality. "Rock and roll band, huh?"

"Yes."

"You're sure?"

"Yes."

"Okay," Julie tells me. "If you're going to do this, now's the time to do it. Our girls are grown and on their own, your parents are gone, and we're stable. If you feel this strongly about putting your band together, you should do it...with two conditions."

I sit straight up in my chair, in front of my oatmeal that has long since gone cold. "Anything. What?"

"No groupies. And do change the name of the band. It does nothing for me." Julie gets up, takes her coffee with her, and leaves me with a room temperature cup of coffee and a bowl of cold oatmeal.

And I couldn't be happier.

* * *

January 19, 2018
The house is mine tonight. Bixby – my faithful little Cairn Terrier – is curled up on his pillow a couple feet behind my chair. His is the only other heartbeat under this roof. Julie is off with her friends Becky and Emily for their monthly topless pillow fight. Or - as they call it - Ladies Night. The three take turns hosting each other once a month. It's a night filled with rich food, a few bottles of wine, giggles, and the aforementioned topless pillow fight. That's my belief anyway. Tonight Becky is hosting so I have the evening to myself until I am called to go pick up my bride when she's ready to come home. Since she's drinking, I'm driving.

I'm at my desk ensconced in front of my 19-inch monitor. The two wall sconce lights provide the only illumination. I could turn on my track lighting but I'm feeling much more comfortable in dimly-lit surroundings given my task at hand. The search to track down my three bandmates begins now. No reunion can occur till I find them.

I'm feeling like a film-noir detective trying to track down some long-lost relative or missing spouse...someone out of a Humphrey Bogart movie or Mickey Spillane novel. That's why the half-light seems the way to go as my skulking begins behind the keyboard.

My fingers lace and I crack my knuckles shaking them out before deploying them to the keyboard. Momentum is a key so let's start with easy and work toward difficult. Chrome comes up on my computer as the exploration begins with a trip to America's News Source - otherwise known as Facebook. Once logged in, I bring up the group where my classmates virtually gather to organize our class reunions. It takes only a few moments of scrolling to find Laurel. I click on her name to bring forth her profile. Laurel Connor's life appears before me. She and her husband Seth, who graduated a year after Laurel and I did, have three sons - Christopher, Colin, and Cole.

Laurel lives just outside Des Moines or about three hours from me down I-35. She's a financial advisor. The years have been kind to Laurel. Her hair is still the sandy blonde it always has been. Her face shows that Laurel has taken care of herself. Not a wrinkle to be found. She's put on a couple of pounds but, hell, who hasn't? We're almost 50 and our metabolisms aren't what they used to be.

My scrolling pauses at her interests. A smile parts my lips when I see Laurel plays guitar. A key part of the band getting together is that we keep the members who can't play a musical instrument to one. I add Laurel as a friend before I get so caught up in my search that I forget to do so.

That's one.

Todd Kane is next up. It becomes very clear very quickly that he will not be easily located here. At this moment I can't pinpoint his footprint on Facebook. Logging out I go back to Google and type in Todd Kane Iowa. A page full of options appears in the proverbial blink. Scanning the options, I single out the one who appears to be my former best friend. Clicking on it brings another smile to my face. The age, middle name, parents are all a match. It is my Todd Kane. He is in Boone, Iowa, and owns an implement dealership. Of course he does. His love of tractors makes it a natural path for someone who collected toy tractors as a kid. His tractor collection is just larger in size than the ones he kept on the shelves in his room back in the day.

My head shakes in wonder at my quick success in locating two of the three long-lost bandmates. A flash of memory reminds me of a comic book I read as a kid. In the story, a hero is trying to find someone and, at one point, holds up a phone book. The hero calls it the "world's greatest tracking device". If that was true 40 years ago, what would you call the Internet...the world's greatest tracking device or the world's greatest stalking device?

An emotional wave of filth flows over me making me feel more than a bit slimy about what I'm doing. Poking around other people's lives, peering into their privacy, just seems wrong. Sure, it's all out there online but does that make it right for me to be compiling it? It's all public record - I get it - but am I a step or two away from being the bad guy in the next Lifetime movie?

A lone bark from Bixby jolts me out of my internal debate. I look at him. Something has disturbed him. I pause, cocking an ear. Then I hear it. A neighbor dog down the block is barking at something which led to Bix' response. I tell Bix it's okay. He looks up at me before corkscrewing himself back into a curled position on his bed. All is quiet once more.

Todd's home address and phone number are before me on the screen. Google has become room service bringing what I need to my office. An option exists on the website allowing me to order a background report that would provide me with financial reports, arrest records, everything anyone would ever want to know about Todd. A shudder nearly topples me out of my chair.

Bix's head pops up, his ears perked, wondering what I've sensed that he hasn't. I shake any potential remaining shudders out of me and reassure Bix nothing is amiss. I've found where the line between searching and stalking is and this is it. No thanks. I'll pass on the background report.

While my search for Todd is successful there are a lot of questions that remain unanswered: Is he married? Does he have kids? Does he still play bass guitar? I'll find out eventually because I'm confident we'll have an opportunity to talk face to face. Part of my curiosity also lies in the fact that I wonder why Todd stepped away from our friendship. We were close friends but when he moved away that was the end of our friendship. I wrote a few letters but he never responded. More unfinished business, I guess.

The Google home screen pops into view again. I exhale. Laurel and Todd were quite simple to locate. Even though my emotion is running high with optimism and satisfaction, nagging doubt is not far in the background. Unlike the others locating Lori is going to be tough. What if I can't find her? It has to be the four of us if any reunion is going to take place.

My left hand cups my mouth, dragging itself over my chin, stroking my five o'clock shadow. My brow furrows and the corners of my mouth turn down. My lips purse. I fidget in my chair. Hesitation isn't my thing but it is at the moment. It's all of us or none of us and suddenly I'm psyching myself out. I place my elbows on the desk and rest my chin on my hands. Paralysis has overcome me. Fear of failure slinks through me. A sigh comes out.

Doing my best Taylor Swift impression, I shake it off, jumping out of my chair and walking around my office, wiggling my arms as I move around. Bix, wondering about the suddenness of my movement, begins following me so he doesn't miss out on any potential excitement. Gotta get out of this doubt funk.

Nothing is stirring on a Saturday night as I peer through the window looking out upon the neighborhood. Whatever had the attention of the neighbor's dog is long gone. One advantage of living on the end of a dead-end street; no one comes down this street by accident. Quiet is the norm in this neighborhood. Looking out into the night I wonder what can I do to get myself back on track. Then the idea hits me.

I walk briskly out of my office, through the kitchen, and through the hallway until I come to the door that reveals the staircase taking me - and my faithful sidekick Bixby - up to the attic. Julie has never been up here. I've been keeper of all things stored here and most of the reason for that is to protect her sanity. Of the two of us I'm the sentimental one, the one who can't stand to throw anything away. It's a trait I picked up from my parents who grew up during the Great Depression and were married during World War II when there was no extra, when you didn't throw anything away because you might be able to reuse it somehow. The word "re-purpose" is in vogue today but my parents' generation invented it.

When Julie and I were first married there were about four dozen boxes of stuff up here and four boxes were Julie's. She would pitch a fit if she had seen all those boxes of stuff. No fit pitching necessary now. Over the past few years, I have been able to get over my pack rat tendencies and divest myself of the clutter. Now only one dozen boxes remain and four are still Julie's.

Bix sniffs around the attic on the trail of who knows what. The trail takes Bix in the opposite direction of me as I make a beeline for the box I seek. It is a box full of childhood memories, of photographs, school assignments, all of the mementos my mom saved that are now mine to safeguard.

I pull the top off one particular cardboard box, my fingers work through it like I'm flipping through a file cabinet. My School Years book presents itself. A spiral bound testimony of all that was worth remembering from each year of my K-12 life, grade by grade.

My photos, report cards, noteworthy assignments, accomplishments, friendships, and my vital stats for every grade stare up at me. I set the book aside briefly while I replace the top on the box and put it back where I found it.

I call out to Bix to come with me as it's time to go back downstairs having found what I need. He turns on a dime and trots over to me, on my heel as we make our way down the steps and back to my office. I plop down in my high-back chair and lean back slightly. Bix stands dutifully next to me awaiting further instructions. "It's okay, Bix. Go back to your pillow." Bix turns around and corkscrews himself onto his pillow once more.

My page flipping through the book stops at the page pocket holding my fourth grade memories. I pull out my report card which not only holds my grades but also my class photo and a few pieces of paper. I set the papers aside while I gaze upon the photo. There's my class section assembled on the risers with Mrs. Johnson standing on the floor on the right side of the photograph. I always thought she was old but as I look upon her now, she wasn't any older then than I am now.

I tear four small pieces of tape from the tape dispenser on the desk, rolling each into a circle and put them on the back four corners of the photo. I'll find a frame for it eventually but, for now, I tack it to the wall behind and over my computer monitor.

My attention turns back to the papers I had set aside. I sift through them scrutinizing each one not knowing what I'm looking for...that is until I hit the motherlode with the last piece of paper in the pile. I'm as giddy as a kid Christmas morning who got the one present he wanted. I look at the paper that is creased in four sections and I'm beaming. I gently set it on the desk and smooth it out.

I'll be damned.

Honestly, I forgot I had it. In my hands is the picture I drew and colored. Four figures playing musical instruments in a band. Two boys and two girls...two guitars, a keyboard, and drums. A word with four letters each punctuated with periods headlines the top of the page. T.E.L.L. - Todd, Eric, Laurel, and Lori.

This is a sign. It's a sign! It's going to happen. This reunion is happening. I take the paper and jog out of the room, Bixby hot on my heels as I head to Julie's craft room. Throwing her supply closet open, I rifle through it till I find an unused document frame that will allow my drawing to fit without having to trim it. It slides in and fits perfectly. I go back to my office having grabbed a hammer and nail from the kitchen tool drawer and hang the picture on the wall. Bixby watches curiously.

I take two steps back to admire my handiwork. It's all in front of me now...the fourth grade photo and the drawing that started it all. Carefully stuffing the unneeded documents in my School Years book, I file it on the book shelf against the wall behind me.

Time to find Lori.

My phone buzzes just as my fingers are about to begin a Google search. A text from Julie. Topless pillow fight is breaking up. Time to go bring my bride home.

Locating Lori will be delayed just a bit longer.

This is so happening.

CHAPTER TWO

CHIVE TALKIN'

January 26, 2018

My frustration level has increased steadily in the week since the search for my missing band mates began. Laurel accepted my friend request four days ago. Todd's friend request acceptance has been pending for two days.

    The disquiet filling me is centered on who I haven't found - Lori. She is a ghost. It would be understandable if this were happening 20 years ago before the internet made finding people ridiculously - and scarily - easy. My frustration stems from the fact I've done everything I know how to do using every resource I can think of; minus shouting out across social media that I'm looking for Lori or hiring a private investigator to track her down. Social media isn't an option - yet - because this little endeavor is going to require some subtlety and finesse. Social media is many things but subtle it's not.

Private investigator? Creepy on all levels. But what are my other options? Lori is the linchpin. She must be found if this reunion has any chance of happening.

I rise from my chair and start bouncing like I'm a boxer in the corner between rounds of a prizefight. Shake out the bad juju. Loosen up. Let ideas flow. Look at the easily-solved issues and let momentum build. Also important to this reunion tour happening are the details including songs, venues, website, social media pages, radio interviews, not to mention the fact I still don't play drums. Little things.

I sit down again satisfied the bouncing around my office has sufficiently purged the negative energy. I pull up a different browser hoping it will yield different results. The surfing, admittedly, is a bit aimless at first. My fingers start idling just tapping on the keys without pressing them trying to determine what their next course of action is. Restlessness sets in. I turn and look out the window again. Something is missing. There is something I'm not seeing.

My head rests against the back of the chair which puts my eyes on the woodgrain of the ceiling above me. The mind begins whirling with thoughts that are about everything except the missing band member.

The band dream isn't the four of us playing in a garage. The band, at its foundation, is a business. Shouldn't I have a business plan then? If I put a business plan together that contains the elements I'm looking for, but in a professional manner, perhaps they'll truly consider my idea.

Dreams need money too. How is the band being funded? Am I asking them for money? Are they being expected to buy anything?

Are we playing for free? I've been focused on all the art aspects but have neglected to account for the Benjamins. Hmm.

The upside is I know how to put all those aspects together in one document. Bad news is that now I have another elusive thing to find. Funding. My face scrunches up at the thought of the task which is a clue it's time to focus on a less imposing aspect. What can I get accomplished at this moment? Finding a songwriter, that's what.

My body straightens up in the chair as my fingers have purpose again. They key in the URL for Fiverr, a freelancer website. Services on the site start at five dollars with thousands of freelancers peddling their services. In the search field goes *song writing*.

Dozens of options appear before me. The sifting begins as each seller gets their profile read and samples studied. It is tedious. A promising prospective songwriter named Lisbeth from England appears on my screen. I compose a note with details as to what I'm looking for in getting a project completed and ask if she'd be interested in taking it on. It's approaching 6 p.m. here which means it's about Midnight in England. Send button is hit and the message begins its journey through cyberspace. I ponder what the first song should be about when creaking from the door behind me interrupts contemplation.

Julie walks into my office and takes the two steps down from the kitchen to my office with a large manila envelope in her hand. "This was in the mailbox for you," she says, extending her right hand. "It's from Aniko."

"Thanks, boo," I reply, accepting the envelope. Julie returns to the kitchen as I open the envelope and examine the contents. There seems to be a bunch of index cards or something like them inside. I dump the contents onto my desk. It's a big pile of construction paper cut to the size of index cards. Grabbing a few at random it is immediately clear what these are - thank you notes from Aniko's students.

That's Ani all right. My sister is all about proper manners so she had her students write thank you notes to me for coming in and guest lecturing. Reading them brings a smile to my face, each smile different based on the thank you.

Some smiles are from amusement at the sentiment of a few summed up by the phrase *Thanks for not sucking and getting us out of a day of homework.* Other smiles are from students who were genuinely moved and shared how it applied to a situation they have gone or are going through. Some smiles were from aspiring writers or artists who don't always get positive reinforcement and were inspired by a story or two I shared.

One thank you causes my eyes to bug out and jaw to drop like some Saturday morning cartoon character. The construction paper is a black rectangle. Glued on it is a smaller white piece of paper with a drawing of Batman playing the drums. Written on it is simply, "To Eric. Good for one free drum lesson. From Nick".

The story of my rock and roll dream going down in flames had moved this young man to offer me a free drum lesson. I'm so excited I'm bouncing in an entirely different manner than I was earlier. All I had to do is pick a date and I'm playing the drums, baby.

This band thing? Totally happening.

* * *

Tonight is the mandatory Saturday night family meal. Even though our daughters Nicole and Ashley live in the same city as us they live on their own and have their own lives. Which means, like Julie and me, life is pulling them in eight different directions which can make it difficult to stay in touch beyond text. Julie and I made a pact with them that as long as we live close by we would get together one Saturday night each month for supper and games as a family. The four of us have kept that pact faithfully.

Supper is always simple. Tonight it's burger night. For us, it's not about the food; it's about sharing a meal and catching up. Tonight Julie has a stack of burgers she's seasoned and prepared in a cast iron skillet piled in a pyramid on a ceramic plate. Like an assembly line after it are the tomatoes, lettuce, red onions, pickles, ketchup, and spicy mustard.

We line up...Nicole first, Ashley second, yours truly, and then Julie. I'm the only one who likes onions so I pile a generous helping on my burger before adding pickles and mustard. No tomatoes and ketchup, thank you.

The four of us are seated and the conversation begins. I am content to eat and listen, joyful at the spirited exchange among the three women about the TV show America's Got Talent. My reality show involves a scoreboard so I am less interested in the content of their discussion as I am that they are here with me and how wonderful it is.

Nicole, 27, is the older of the two girls by 14 months. Her skin is flawless, a gift from her mother who she resembles. Her green eyes light up when she laughs which tends to happen at someone else's expense. A natural ginger, Nicole's shoulder-length hair is currently lavender. At times, it's fire engine red, other times it could be platinum blonde, black, or back to the natural. She does online hair and makeup tutorials on YouTube and hopes to make it her primary source of income.

She and I bonded over WWE and our taste in music. Each year the WWE makes a tour stop in a nearby city and we make the hour-long trek for father-daughter date night to cheer and boo and spend some quality time together. We also talk of our love of Disturbed, Five Finger Death Punch, and Foo Fighters. It gives me "at least you're relevant" credibility.

Ashley's curly blonde hair and blue eyes fit in very nicely with the Scandinavians of Minnesota though neither Julie nor I are of its descent. She looks more like me than Julie. Ashley cares about her appearance but is not as concerned about makeup as her sister. She has stomach issues so she is much more conscious about what she puts in her body and taking care of it.

Ashley and I bonded over our food choices and how we workout. She and I are both runners having completed numerous half marathons. We geek out over a new pair of running shoes and over our personal best running times.

She works in the health care industry as a roving home health care aide. She can't stand a job where it's the same stuff day after day. Ashley likes stability but doesn't do well with predictability. Her current job finds her helping a different person each week depending on the person's needs. She loves the elderly and finds the stories they share about their lives a big perk to her work.

Both girls take after us in that we *are* natural homebodies and they *can* be. That doesn't mean they don't enjoy going out. Nicole loves going to concerts while Ashley prefers live music in smaller, more intimate settings. Nicole's best friends are Jim, Jack, and Jose; Beam, Daniels, and Cuervo, respectively. It's not that Ashley doesn't drink but she is more subtle about it. Nicole is about as subtle as a nuclear warhead. They have a close relationship despite their definite differences.

I'm suddenly pulled out of my head when I hear my wife ask, "Has your dad mentioned his new project?" Both young women say no turning their eyes in my direction poised for me to share. All three women are now looking at me. The floor is mine.

"Well, it all started in fourth grade," I begin.

"I thought all your stories started 'back when I was in second grade'," Ashley teases, referencing a long-standing family joke that every story I tell begins from something in second grade. I am famous for my incredibly long, detailed stories. Julie snorts, Nicole's eyes light up, and I chuckle at the remark.

"Fair enough," I concede adding, "but not this time." I then convey the details of my rock and roll dreams to the girls and how they were crushed.

Nicole stiffens in her chair and her eyes flash red. "Is that Mr. Trampoline guy still alive? Cuz I'm going to punch him in the face!" Nicole has a short fuse and that is especially true when someone she cares about is mistreated.

"Mr. Tripolino is very much alive but is no longer a music teacher. I haven't seen him since he left to take a job at another school district after I finished 7th grade. Regardless, no face punching is necessary. But thanks."

Upon hearing my gentle stand down Nicole relaxes but adds, "He's an asshole."

No argument there. Picking up my story, I tell them about speaking to their Aunt Aniko's English students and about being disturbed afterward. The disturbance came from the realization it has been 40 years since the dream and that the four members are turning 50 soon. It's when the unveiling of the reunion tour idea occurs that the attentive faces turn into confused faces.

"Hang on," Ashley picks up, "you want to organize a reunion tour for a band that never existed?"

"Yes."

"But you don't play drums or sing?" Nicole adds.

"Also true," I confirm.

The next few moments I feel like I'm watching a tennis match as my head turns toward Ashley then Nicole as their alternating questions fire at me in rapid fashion.

"You don't know where these people are?"

"I have found Laurel and Todd. Lori, not yet."

"Are you going to be a cover band?"

"No. We'll have original songs. I'm going to have a freelancer to write them," I say.

"How is this a reunion tour when you were never a band to begin with?"

"The reunion is not about a band getting back together but the four friends reuniting," I answer.

"Where are you going to practice? Where are you going to perform? How are you going to play drums?"

"Not sure. Working on it. I actually have an answer to that," comes in rapid fire back at Nicole. "Whew!"

The girls pause for a moment allowing Julie to follow up on my last response. "You have an answer to playing drums?"

Julie's question allows my neck a respite as I look directly across the table at her. "In the manila envelope you gave me earlier were thank you notes from Aniko's students. One of the thank you notes was in the form of a gift certificate for a free drum lesson."

"Really..." Julie says not attempting to hide her skepticism.

"Really. I figure I'll take the free lesson and maybe hire the student to give me lessons. If not, there are professionals here in town I could go to."

Nicole, an accomplished singer, and Ashley, an avid guitar player, announce in unison, "It's not that easy."

Holding up my hands to pause their thought process from advancing any further I state, "No, it is not easy. But it's simple. At this stage I'm looking to line up all the simple I can because there's going to be a lot of complicated to overcome. But isn't it worth taking a risk to see a dream through?"

The question hangs in the air for a few heartbeats and then the girls' heads nod with Nicole's, "Hell, yeah," providing the punctuation mark. Julie and I smile.

"Hey, who's in the mood for seconds?" I inquire as I rise and move around Ashley's chair. She and Julie wave me off while Nicole gets up to follow me. Approaching the assembly line of meat, vegetables, and condiments, it is clear that the four of us left a bit of a mess in our initial wake.

What jumps out at me are the blotches of ketchup and bits of red onions co-mingled on the countertop. I've seen lots of dead bodies in pools of cinematic blood as a fan of shows like Criminal Minds and Law and Order. The ketchup and red onion carnage reminds me of it instantly.

"Good grief!" I exclaim. My utterance sounds so alarming that Nicole jumps to my side as Julie and Ashley spin from their positions to join me in front of the counter.

"What? What is it?" Julie asks, thinking I've been injured or something is on fire.

Eyes wide, I explain. "Look at this. It looks like a bloody massacre. The onions have been murdered. All that's missing is crime scene tape. Onions at a crime scene." I accentuate the assertion by extending my arms, palms facing the ceiling making me look like a magician who has successfully completed a trick.

The three women look at the countertop chaos then look at me. Head shakes and eye rolls commence. Ashley chuckles in a way that humors me in hopes it'll help end the weirdness.

I become a statue standing witness. Julie and Ashley return to their chairs. Nicole squeezes by me to get her seconds, popping a couple of pickles in her mouth like peanuts before grabbing her second burger. "Onions at a crime scene," I whisper to myself.

Sounds like a band name.

I smile.

It sure does.

* * *

February 16, 2018

It took some effort and a couple of weeks to get my free drum lesson scheduled. Not surprising given the fact that I'm trying to coordinate schedules with a high school junior who has a lot of commitments beyond homework. In the end, the solution is for me to show up at the high school band room after the pep band finishes playing prior to the girls' varsity basketball game.

Stepping into the band room is a surreal experience. It's been decades since I've stepped into one; maybe since my Freshman year of high school when the band room was utilized as a classroom for driver's education. Chairs and music stands are scattered as if the band left abruptly after the last practice. There are four tiers that provide the seating area for the band members. Cubbies for people to store their cases or backpacks are lined up against the wall behind the highest tier. Stationed on the highest tier is the reason for my being here tonight – the drums.

Nick greets me and extends a hand to invite me to take my seat at the drum set he's reserved for me. Nick is about two inches taller than me, heavy set with shoulder-length curly hair and stubble on his face that indicates he hasn't shaved for a couple of days. He's wearing a red and black flannel shirt, blue jeans, and work boots.

I take my place picking up the drumsticks, gently introducing them to each of the drums and the cymbals. It's the equivalent of pinching myself. This is happening. I'm going to play drums. It is challenging to stifle my giddiness. I am 12 again.

Julie and Aniko stand below in the front of the first tier of chairs; smiling at me upon seeing my excitement. They lean in to each other as they talk, arms crossed, keeping their thoughts between them.

"Okay," Nick says, breaking me out of my thought, "let's get started." He then advises me on hand and foot placement. It feels odd to play drums with my wrists crossed. Right foot is on the pedal. As Nick continues his initial explanation it becomes very clear the drummer is perhaps the most important person because the drummer sets timing and rhythm for everyone else. This means the drummer for Onions At A Crime Scene can't fake his way through and not affect the rest of the band. The first few drum strikes are tentative as though I may not know my own strength and fear I may damage the drums.

"Don't be afraid of breaking them. They can take it," Nick chuckles.

A hard exhale. More vigor in the striking. Better sound.

"That's it," Nick says approvingly. "Now try to keep this beat." Nick starts in on his drums and lets me hear the beat I'm to follow. "Jump in anytime and just do what I do."

I study his motion, hearing the cadence of the drums, keeping time with the tapping of my left foot. My hesitation is that of someone not sure if the water in the lake is the desired temperature before jumping in.

I begin striking my drums matching him beat for beat as best I can. The most difficult thing is trying not to overthink it. There are stops and starts as my brain tries thinking rather than feeling through the lesson.

"Arrgh!" I exclaim in mild frustration. "I get in a groove and then my brain gets involved and it all goes south." Even at that, I'm having a blast.

"You're doing great," Nick encourages. "Now let's try adding the foot pedal."

Great. Let's add another limb. Piece of cake.

Nick again starts in on his drums with hands only and then adds the foot pedal to the mix. Might as well try to rub my belly and pat my head at the same time. I try to mimic Nick and all is well for a few seconds at a time before I lose the beat.

Nick is as steady as a metronome which provides a guide so I can jump back in when I drop the rhythm. "Keep it up, Eric, you got this."

"I feel so uncoordinated," is my reply before jumping in again. My brain shuts off long enough for me to stay with Nick for nearly a minute before crossing myself up again. I laugh but it is a laugh of triumph not humor.

"Yeah!" Nick punches the air. "That was great!"

"I guess we're getting a drum set," Julie says from the peanut gallery.

A perfectly-executed rim shot is my reply. All assembled start howling.

Yeah. I'm getting a drum set.

* * *

Julie and I arrive back home at 8:30. She brought my drum lesson to an end after my rim shot by pointing to the clock and saying over an hour had passed since starting. Maybe people had other things to do on a Friday night. I agreed but couldn't believe time had gone that quickly. Felt like 20 minutes.

"Did you have fun?" Julie asks. Our ride back had been in silence. I was digesting the lesson and needed time to process. She knew that and gave me the mental space.

"You know I did. I could have stayed the whole night."

"That's why I had to remind you of the time," Julie acknowledges. "How do you feel about being able to pull off being a drummer for your band?"

An exhale of mixed emotions is the preamble to my response. "Overall, I feel fine. This doesn't seem impossible. What was brought home is how important it is for me to be more than competent. I have to be sharp."

Julie and I exit our SUV and walk through the interior door that gets us in the house via my office. Julie continues to the kitchen as I take off for my desk, plopping down in my chair. "I have to check on a couple of things and then I'll be in and we can watch some TV," I say.

"I'll go put on my pajamas and be ready when you're ready," she answers without slowing down.

I bring up my web browser and log in to Facebook. I've tried everything I can think of to find Lori and I guess it's time to do what I didn't want to do – involve another person.

I click on the Facebook Messenger icon and begin a new message. This missive is to my classmate Sara. Sara and I have stayed in touch over the years especially when Facebook made it easy to link with one another. Sara and I were in the same homeroom all during high school so we know each other quite well. Sara's been able to keep tabs on the whereabouts of our graduating class and some classmates who moved away before 12th grade. It's that expertise I require.

The reason for not wanting to involve anyone else is I don't want to divulge why I'm looking for fear that Sara might share this tidbit of information with others; information that could take on a life of its own. But she may be my last hope in finding Lori.

My message to Sara is a simple one. Does she know Lori's given name and maybe married name, where Lori moved after 5th grade and – most importantly – does she know how I can find her on Facebook or anywhere else for that matter? Luck seems to be solidly in my corner as Sara is online and gets my message immediately. She messages me back nearly as swiftly.

"Hey, Eric," she replies. "I think I can help you. BRB."

My stomach flutters that it might be just that easy. A stare down with the Messenger box ensues. The whole "watched pot never boils" axiom walks across my mind. Distracting myself with other thoughts doesn't work. Does Sara have the missing piece to this missing person puzzle?

The notification ding announces Sara's reply. "May have something helpful," her message begins, increasing my hopes. "I can't tell you where she went or is BUT in my classmate files I found that her given name is Lorelei Rae Politis. Can't help you with a married name but she might be using first and middle name as many women do to try to keep themselves anonymous."

"THANKS. That is a HUGE help!" I reply. This is the first solid breadcrumb I've had to follow. "Appreciate you looking this up for me. Now let's see if I can find her."

"You're welcome. GOOD LUCK."

Exhaling a combination of relief and nervous anticipation, I back out of Messenger to do a Facebook search for Lorelei Rae and cross my fingers for the nanosecond it takes for the results to appear. Or, should I say, result. There is precisely one result and I click on it. This woman lives in Pella, Iowa. I know Pella. Been there. One of the most iconic Downtowns I've ever seen.

Pella is a Dutch community and years ago its city council passed an ordinance that all buildings built in the Downtown stretch must have Dutch architecture. When McDonald's wanted to put a store in their Downtown the city council denied their request until McDonald's agreed to build their store to conform to the ordinance. The city council won. The end result was astonishing. It's one of my favorite McDonald's in the country.

Squinting to get a better look at her picture – trying anything that will help me positively identify her – 50-50 is as sure as I can be. Nothing in the Facebook profile leads me to believe this isn't Lori but nothing leads me to believe it is her either. Coin flip. Nothing ventured and all that, the mouse clicks on Messenger and I try to compose a message that is heavy on re-introduction and sentiment while being light on creepy.

Another deep breath to make sure every word hits the precise note. A chuckle. *Hits the precise note.* That's funny.

The message is posted and now I cool my jets for Lorelei's response to let me know if I've found her or if my search hit another speed bump. I log off and leave my office. Time to Netflix and chill with my wife.

* * *

Saturday finds me in an upbeat mood. Last night's drum lesson was a highlight. Even if the reunion never happens, the kindness of a high school kid will always be remembered fondly. It's the kind of stuff that restores one's faith in humanity.

I stroll into my office while the coffee maker is working on preparing my morning cup of giddy up and Julie is making me blueberry waffles.

Firing up my PC I check to see how my freelancer Lisbeth is coming with the songs I've asked her to write. Lisbeth answered my message a couple days after I posted it and we found ourselves to be a creative match. I gave her an idea for the first song with a couple of lines to use and gave her a direction the lyrics should take.

She did such an amazing job with the first song that I asked Lis to write the entire album with me. She accepted without hesitation. Each opening of my email from Lis brings with it anticipation to see what she's done with my musings. My Inbox reveals a note from Lisbeth with attachments. Songs are ready to review.

I do a quick scan for first reaction and then go back for a more thorough examination. A big smile appears as I look over the lyrics. Lisbeth took the ideas and turned them into some damn fine songs. I see a couple tweaks for her to make but they are minor adjustments. These songs will do just fine. She captured my thoughts turning them into legit songs for an honest-to-goodness band.

A quick reply is crafted that is part instruction and mostly gratitude on a job well done. My attention returns to Facebook now that my message in on its way through cyberspace and across the pond.

I've been busy relationship-building with Todd and Laurel since both accepted my Facebook friend requests. What I share is strategic – no cute animal videos or quizzes – in order to lay a relational foundation and bond with them emotionally again. I log in to Facebook now to see if my morning is going to get even better.

A couple days ago I jumped on YouTube and found the clip from Paul Lynde's 1976 Halloween special where KISS made their network TV appearance. This is what got Todd into KISS and got me into thinking of starting a band of our own.

My posts to Laurel have been in the realm of parents of twenty-somethings and how impossible it seems that so much time has passed so quickly that our kids are the ages they are. The number 8 appears on the notification icon. Clicking on it, the drop down window shows me some people who have replied to me or tagged me. Todd and Laurel aren't among them for now. Then I see it. *Lorelei Rae has accepted your friend request.*

A triple-take to ensure I'm not hallucinating and then my chair becomes an ejector seat as I launch myself up and out. A wild dance of fist pumping and spastic jumping is accompanied by me shouting, "YES! YES! YES! YES!"

I'm caught in a massive adrenaline rush and I'm riding the wave. The biggest hurdle to clear was finding the other three and being able to establish contact again. The most elusive of the three is now my Facebook friend.

A casual observer would think I am Tigger after drinking a forty of Rock Star. Julie has heard the commotion and comes running in to the room to see what happened during her absence.

"What the heck is going on?" she inquires, doing a visual sweep for any obvious clues as to what has caused my sudden outburst.

"It's happening! It's really happening!" I exclaim, still jumping around my office. "Lori accepted my friend request! Onions At A Crime Scene is happening!"

At this point I'm leaping in a circle around Julie grabbing her hands to bring her in for a 40-something version of Ring Around the Rosie. Julie indulges me in one rotation before letting my hands go.

"You've had a lot of positive things happen the past two days, sweetie." Julie pivots to leave the room. "I need to get back to my waffles. They'll be waiting for you once you've settled down." I watch as she tightens the belt on her baby blue bathrobe and walks back to the kitchen.

You might be waiting awhile I think as my impression of Tigger continues.

* * *

February 24, 2018

The Internet is a beautiful thing. All those beautiful ones and zeroes bring the world to my door. Finding old friends, finding someone to write songs, and finding a used drum set.

After becoming Facebook friends with Lori, I mean, Lorelei last Saturday, this Saturday has me behind my own drum kit which is set up in the family room.

It was ridiculously easy getting the drum kit. I went on Facebook and looked on the Stuff for Sale group. It's a rummage sale without having to leave my humble abode. Three kits were for sale and this one was only $350 and is in exquisite condition.

Contacting the seller, telling her I wanted the drums, meeting her at the local strip mall parking lot, then paying for and picking up the drums all happened before one in the afternoon. My wife is gracious enough to allow me to set up in the family room in our basement. It was like Christmas morning once the drums were unloaded from the SUV, lugged down here, and set up.

I'm sitting like Nick taught me. My sticks are raised in position ready to make a sound I should have made decades ago. For all my anticipation the sticks will not move. The drums are a temple; the drumsticks about to touch something holy and should do so with proper reverence. This is about more than a hobby or setting right a wrong by a 7th grade music teacher. This is about a second chance for a band that never existed. Doesn't that deserve more than just diving in?

Sticks come down and are gently laid across the snare. A sigh comes out. This rock band thing isn't all glamour; it's going to be work. Glamour. Glamourous. Glamourous life. That's it.

Jumping from the drums, I grab the remote for the smart TV from the side table next to the couch. The television comes to life and I bring YouTube up on screen and search for Sheila E.

The video I'm looking for loads then paused until I'm ready to watch it in the proper mindset. I take a deep breath. The year is 1985. American Music Awards. Sheila E and her band are going to perform her hit single "The Glamourous Life".

The pause turns to play and the song begins. I am 17 again, sitting in the living room at the farm, a senior in high school. The performance starts. Sheila E is wearing what would be called leggings or tights today with a very low-cut teal bodice and a black jacket with lace sleeves. Her band dances as they play, Sheila E playing her drums as she sings. It is fantastic.

Upon further examination, Sheila E isn't playing the drums; she's making those drums sing. I am transfixed in front of the screen. The last time I felt this way about a television music performance was a particular Halloween special that featured KISS.

Toes tap in time with the drums. The melody reaches my ears and then courses through my body as a massive adrenaline rush. Then it happens just as I remember: Sheila E thanks the audience of her peers; a band member eases a white fur coat over her shoulders as she waves and walks away from the audience. She suddenly stops between the risers supporting the band's two keyboard players. Sheila E drops the fur coat and picks up a couple of objects. The lights go down and then a 17-year-old's mind gets blown as he sits watching in stunned amazement.

Sheila E is playing her drums in the darkness but her drumsticks are plugged in and light up in various colors. All that can be seen are the drumsticks tracing light patterns at light speed. Drumsticks are a blur as light and sound meld in one of the most sensational things I have ever seen. In that instant, Sheila E cements herself as my favorite drummer ever.

The song ends. The 17-year-old leaves the near 50-year-old body but the adrenaline rush stays. Snapping the sticks off the snare, I now christen the drums with Sheila E's virtual benediction via YouTube. The next Sheila E video plays as I try the basic beat Nick modeled for me. Sheila E and I aren't in sync and it doesn't matter one bit. This is probably the only way I'll ever play with her. I'm okay with that.

After playing along with a few songs – that's being kind – YouTube and the television go dark as I focus on my drum playing only. My beats are far from perfect but they're a start. Still having some challenges in my mastery of the drums. The coordination from head to hands isn't perfect but perfect isn't required.

Nick agreed when I asked him to be my paid instructor. I insisted on paying him. His time and expertise are worth the money and it'll give him some extra cash to put toward college. His tutelage of me begins Tuesday.

I've been practicing for over two hours before I know it. Tempering my expectations on the new-to-me drum set has helped my overall experience. There is no frustration at the many mistakes, fits and starts, to my striking. Pausing after the latest mistake, it occurs to me that it might be time to call it a day. Sticks are returned to a cloth pouch mounted on one of the cymbal legs like a pistol being returned to a holster.

A spontaneous urge to sing overtakes me. Spinning the stool around brings me in front of the audio entertainment unit. I pluck a Charlie Daniels greatest hits CD out of the rack and then go to the turntable/CD combination. The CD goes in the slot and the advance button is pressed to track 7. *Drinkin' My Baby Goodbye.* The first notes play then Mr. Daniels and I begin our duet.

"Sittin' on a barstool, actin' like a durn fool, that's what I'm a doin' today...I'm sittin' here drinkin' trying to keep myself from thinkin' I'm boozin' my troubles away..." I belt out.

I match Mr. Daniels note for note with volume and joy for the next three-plus minutes. I've never been in the position of the person being portrayed in the song but you couldn't tell it by my singing. The last few notes fade away. My shoulders slump and a few long, slow breaths help me slow my heart rate. A satisfied smirk forms. That was fun.

"Holy crap," my oldest daughter exclaims, "that was fierce!" A wave of self-consciousness reddens my cheeks in a way that appears I've been caught doing something I shouldn't have upon realizing there are two more people in my makeshift practice studio.

Hitting stop then eject on the CD player brings the disc out and is returned to its case and placed in the rack. Both my daughters have left their positions on the staircase so now my drums are the only thing separating us. Looks that convey, *we have so many questions* are all over their faces.

"What the heck?" Ashley asks as she sweeps a few curls from her face, her eyes running over the drums. "When did you get these?"

"How long have you been able to sing like that?" Nicole inquires.

"Hi, girls," I greet. "Got the drums today off the Facebook Stuff For Sale page," in answer to Ashley's question and then, "I've always been able to sing along with artists like Charlie Daniels, Jim Croce, and George Strait. Singing on my own has been problematic. How much did you hear?" I reply turning the questioning back on the girls.

Nicole smiles. "We heard nearly the whole thing. You were excellent." Coming from Nicole that is quite a compliment. She was part of Honors Choir all through high school. This girl can sing. "If you get this band thing going, you should sing harmony and let the others sing melody. You need someone to follow so you have a guide on range and pitch. It's the reason you can sing along with certain artists because they're in your natural vocal range and you can mimic their delivery."

"You got drums on Facebook? *On Facebook.*" Ashley's astonishment is in full view. "You are serious about this reunion. You're actually doing this." Her attitude is not one of discouragement or disapproval but of recognizing the inevitability of what has been set in motion.

My mouth opens to answer but the voice heard is not my own. "Come on up for supper you three!" The voice is Julie's. It is family supper night.

Nicole and Ashley are reassured all of their questions will be answered as I rise and move around the drums. My hands make motions to guide them upstairs. Single file, Ashely first, we go up the stairs and enter the kitchen. The smell of Julie's skillet meat loaf fills the room.

"Everybody wash up and get back here," Julie tells us. The girls head for the bathroom while I take a shortcut and use the kitchen sink.

Soon we are all at our places at the round, glass-top table. The only thing missing is the entrée as the Caesar salad and breadsticks are already on the table. Julie approaches us with the skillet. A triangle spatula is underneath the first piece of meatloaf that will be claimed.

"This skillet meatloaf is ah-mazing!" Nicole exclaims, grabbing the spatula and removing the first piece as soon as Julie places the skillet on the hot pad in the center of the table.

"Thank you," Julie says, "but you could have waited a minute before pouncing on it." She chuckles at her oldest daughter's enthusiasm. Ashley takes the spatula when Nicole offers it to her and removes piece two. Pieces three and four are taken by yours truly and my wife in turn. Nicole's assessment is spot-on. This meatloaf is indeed ah-mazing.

"I can't believe you're eating meat, Ash," I observe. "Aren't you a Presbyterian these days?"

Ashley fires an annoyed glare in my direction. "Pescatarian," she corrects. "It's okay for me to cheat once in a while...especially for this meatloaf."

Julie and Nicole shake their heads at my teasing of Ashley's eating habits. She'll probably outlive us all. My mood is upbeat and exchanges like this lift my spirits even more.

"So you saw your dad's new toy, huh?" Julie asks.

"Yeah, it was a shock," Ashley answers, taking advantage of Nicole's mouth full of food. "I didn't realize Dad was so urgent about his band idea. But it's dope." She cuts off another piece of her portion and takes a bite.

"How exciting will it be when he pulls this off?" Julie adds.

My arms are flailing overhead. "Hello? I'm right here." The ladies are talking like they're the only ones at the table.

"Girls, did you hear that?" Julie asks her eyes darting around the room as her head follows where her eyes are tracing. Picking up on her cue, Nicole and Ashley begin looking around the room.

"Yes," Nicole answers. "It's a disembodied yet familiar voice. Where do you think it's coming from?"

"Probably where all strange noises come from," Ashley chimes in. "Nicole's butt."

"Hey!" Nicole protests, looking across the table at her sister.

"How droll," I assert. "You're all comedians. You'll be relieved to know I am not in Nicole's butt."

Julie snorts and the laughter begins anew. Family suppers are the best.

"Dad was singing when Nicole and I went downstairs," Ashley says between bites. "We haven't heard him actually play the drums yet."

"Yeah, Mom, he didn't suck," Nicole adds.

"There's more news too," Julie shares. "He found Lori and is Facebook friends with her."

Both girls stop mid-chew, eyebrows raised. Nicole quickly finishes the bite. "Seriously? You found her?"

My head bobs. "Sure did. Broke down and asked one of my old classmates for some help. She was able to provide a given first and middle name. That did the trick. Sent Lori a friend request on Facebook and a week ago she accepted it. Though now she goes by Lorelei."

"So, Laurie and Lori are now Laurel and Lorelei?" Ashley asks, still chewing. "And Onions At A Crime Scene is happening?"

Setting my fork down and leaning back against my chair it seems I'm about to excuse myself from the table. Instead, it is me using the momentary pause to collect my thoughts. "Not yet. But certainly a step forward. Can't have a reunion without all the original members."

"Now what?" Nicole wonders. "You guys all buds again?"

"If only it were that easy," I reply. "I've mainly been sharing things with each friend that are of interest to them and are safe. Small steps."

Chive Talkin' | 59

"You know, you can take some salad too," Julie abruptly reminds us. "The main course doesn't have to be eaten before moving on to the next. You all need your greens."

My little Presbyterian takes her cue and snags a heaping helping of salad with the plastic tongs. Nicole follows by taking just enough to say she took some. I take a serving size that is a compromise between what my daughters have taken. Julie is satisfied and, before she can say anymore, the three of us each quickly grab a breadstick.

"It's all about a methodical, step-by-step approach," I continue. "It's been so long for us since we were part of each other's lives that dropping a bomb like 'hey, we're going to be a band' has to be put on ice until we re-establish relationships. No matter what I do this is going to be a surprise when I share the master plan with them."

"Where are you in that master plan?" Julie asks finally getting an opportunity to pose a query.

"Things are proceeding beyond my best hopes. It's not going to be all sunshine and roses," and at this moment I'm not sure if I'm trying to caution them or me regarding the difficulties that lie ahead. "But the victories to this point are worth celebrating."

Ashley jumps in before I can continue. "What's next?"

"What's giving you the most trouble?" Julie adds to Ashley's question, taking another fork full of salad off her plate.

"The money. The other aspects I'm trying to figure out are just details and logistics. Not worried about that. But I just can't figure out the money." My right hand rubs my forehead.

"Ah, don't worry about it," Nicole reassures. "You're too clever not to figure it out." She picks up her soda can and takes a swig. "My dad's going to be a rock star...just like my energy drink."

My fork drops, bounces off the plate, hops the glass top table, and hits the floor with a clang.

"Rockstar." I repeat. "That's it!"

Three perplexed faces stare at me. "Rockstar! Don't you see it? Rockstar Energy Drink sponsors concert tours all the time. I'm going to write a proposal asking Rockstar to sponsor the Onions At A Crime Scene reunion tour! This is perfect. It solves all the problems."

"I love you," Julie says, "but you're out of your mind." She calmly takes another bite of salad.

Perhaps. But that doesn't mean I'm wrong.

CHAPTER THREE

SPRINGING A LEEK

March 24, 2018

I've been the next best thing to perpetual motion since Nicole's accidental inspiration for me finding a corporate sponsor of the tour. A proposal has been crafted and submitted to the sponsorship division of Rockstar Energy Drink. It might be a long shot but I'll take any shot at this point.

Nick's tutoring of my burgeoning drum skills has been going well. My playing is steadily improving. It's certainly not at concert level but being performance ready is not such a far-fetched idea.

Julie has been incredibly patient and supportive through this process. Any spare time I've had away from work has been spent working the plan and I've spent a lot of time working the plan; a plan that goes next level today.

After months of Facebook sharing and communicating it's time for us to see each other in person. I extended invitations to my once and future bandmates for the first stage of physically reuniting the four of us: Coffee dates. Laurel and Todd have get-togethers with me today while Lorelei's chat is scheduled for tomorrow. I'm meeting each individually in his or her Iowa town - Ames, Boone, and Pella.

The weekend's coffee commiserating comes with plenty of risk. Every step, plan, strategy, and action has depended on *my* willingness to undertake it. I'm heading into a phase where everything I've put together can collapse. If even one of the three people I'm attempting to reunite says no, it will be the big no. This next piece will either build on everything done to this point or blow the whole damn thing to smithereens.

My watch reads 10:03. My first coffee date of the day is three minutes behind schedule. Laurel should be here literally any moment.

My cover story is that I am passing through the area and wanting to get together for coffee. Laurel said she'd love to meet and indicated this morning would work best while Todd informed me this afternoon at 4 would be his preference.

I'm seated in the middle of what I'm assuming is the usual Saturday morning coffee crowd. The table is nestled in the corner of Morning Bell Coffee. This vantage point gives me a clear view of the door so it is impossible to miss anyone who enters.

The smell permeating Morning Bell now isn't the coffee itself but the freshly-ground beans. That, in and of itself, is worth being here. Laurel has made a praiseworthy choice not just because of the smell but also because this is not a chain coffee place. I don't have a problem with chains but they can be found at home. When I'm traveling I like to get a taste of local flavor whether that's coffee or food.

The place is packed with a laid back crowd. The table closest to me has a few moms who are catching up while their daughters are at dance. On the other side of me are a table full of college students clad in the burnt cardinal and gold of Iowa State. All are working on their tablets, their silence intermittently interrupted when someone has a flash of inspiration and a conversation burst occurs.

In my day our tablet was an Etch-A-Sketch and we liked it that way! The old man rant in my head elicits an involuntary guffaw which earns me some irritated looks from the group of kids over my disruption. "Sorry," I apologize, "random thought amused me." The students smile, nod at me, and go back to work. All is well again.

Continuing my scan of the room, there are a couple of middle-aged men – okay, they're my age, but sometimes I forget I am that age, cut me some slack – deep in conversation at a smaller, round table.

Seated to their right are some college kids who appear to be in the middle of some Biblical discussion. I'm only able to pick out a word here and there at this distance. The rest of the patrons seem to be gathered here for the same reason as me – Saturday conversation catch-up with friends.

Wonder how many other people in here are trying to re-form a rock band that never existed? My right foot taps anxiously. Has Laurel changed her mind? Tummy tickles intensify to the point of near nausea.

Come on, Laurel, where are you?

Laurel and I graduated together though we were never as close of friends after fifth grade. For some reason sixth grade seems to be the point where friendships diverge. Laurel grew into the smart, pretty, popular girl while I grew into the smart, quirky guy who kept to himself. Our social circles did not intersect.

It was seventh grade when Laurel started coming into her own and it did not go unnoticed. I had the biggest crush on Laurel. She – nor anyone else – ever knew and I never did anything about it.

That same year the song "Every Little Thing She Does Is Magic" by The Police came out. I am reminded of Laurel to this day when I hear that tune. Funny the power that music has on us.

The bell atop the door rings as a familiar person walks in and makes her way toward me. Tummy tickles evaporate replaced by a child-like glee. She's here! The years have been kind. Her hair shows no shades of gray. It's the sandy blonde it always has been. Her skin is nearly flawless; her figure is still rockin'. She's wearing leggings with a turquoise blue dress over them, a little black sweater accompanies it. Tall, black boots and a little black purse on her shoulder complete the look.

Be cool, Eric. Be cool.

I stand and smile at Laurel. She returns the smile and opens her arms as she approaches me. We embrace and my body relaxes. It is such a relief to see her and to know that the dream lives another day or at least another few hours.

"Hey, Laurel, so good to see you," I greet.

"Good to see you too," she responds. "I'm so happy it worked out for us to get together."

"Please, sit," I invite then pull out a chair for Laurel. "What can I get you?"

"A cappuccino would be terrific. Thank you," she replies. The first few bars of that old Police tune spontaneously come from the speakers in my brain. I smile as I make my way to the counter, order

Laurel's drink, pause briefly, pick up the cup, and then return to our table.

"Here you go," I announce carefully setting the drink in front of her. I fight the urge just to blurt out the real reason for our meeting. Tiny hands in my brain push those thoughts into a tiny closet in the far corner and shut the door. Today is about quality time with an old friend.

"How is that brave new world known as 50?" is my opening question. Admittedly, it's a potentially dangerous topic – women and their age – for any conversation. Caution thrown to the wind, it's where we begin.

"Oof," Laurel responds with an accompanying widening of the eyes. "It's okay but very emotional. I thought turning 30 was tough – which it was – but turning 50 was tougher for a whole host of reasons. Different ones. It's been all right so far."

Laurel pauses to take a drink of her cappuccino. "Of course, I'm only a few weeks in so that could change." She chuckles at her own cautious pessimism. Laurel is the first of the four of us to turn 50. I'm neither excited nor dreading the big five-oh but am wondering how I got to it so quickly. My mind and body feel a lot younger than that.

"Think about when we were young," I say. "People who were 50 were old. Look at us. Who would look at us and think you're 50 and I'm about to be?"

"We would," say four voices in unison from the table full of college kids.

Laurel turns and gives them the disapproving mom look while I nearly fall off my chair laughing. The four are all smiling so there was no malice just a little generational teasing.

"Why is now the time they pick to listen to adults?"

I fire back. "Hey, I have your emoji right here." Lifting my right fist I pretend that they're about to be flipped off. It is their turn to crack-up.

"Reminds me of my boys," Laurel says shaking her head. "Those three would have said the same thing." Another sip is taken. "Maybe that's part of my struggle with 50...my boys."

My head tilts right and brows furrow. Laurel pulls out her phone and brings up a family photo from this past Christmas. All the boys have Laurel's sandy brown hair and facial features but are built like their dad was back in the day...all about six-feet tall and stout but not an ounce of fat.

Laurel sees the confused look and explains. "Not because of my boys. Christopher is 23 and out on his own. He's works in the loan department at one of the banks in Lincoln, Nebraska. He has a degree in Finance and has started his journey to work his way up his career ladder." Laurel stops for a moment and looks away from me as though she sees someone she knows but apparently doesn't. Her thought continues.

"Colin is 20 and is a junior at ISU majoring in Agriculture. He wants to create a better type of corn that can be grown in any environment. He wants to create a variety that can be grown in any part of the world – especially Africa – where there is less rainfall per growing season than is typically needed to grow corn."

"Wow," I interrupt, "that's terrific."

"Yeah, Colin's always been that way. Trying to help others. Then there's Cole. He's a senior at Ames High School. He'll graduate in May and then he's traveling this summer before starting college this Fall at South Dakota State for Mechanical Engineering. Then..." her voice trails off and it all makes sense.

"...it's just you and Seth. Empty nesters," I finish her sentence.

"Yeah," comes wrapped in a sigh. "I love my life but for the past 20-some years it's been about Seth and me being parents and raising the boys. Once Cole finishes high school and is off to college...I'm not sure what life looks like. Seth is a terrific husband and has a successful career as an architect. I think I'm an excellent wife and have a successful career as a retirement planner. We have a beautiful home, we travel. But isn't there more to life than that?"

The question hangs in the air. Laurel looks away, momentarily embarrassed, outwardly appearing she's shared something too personal too soon. The silence is a temporary buffer in the conversation.

"Haven't you and Julie faced this with your daughters?" Laurel inquires both because she genuinely wants to know but also because she's trying to get the spotlight off herself.

"To an extent, yes. The big difference for us is that neither left town. Nicole walked her own path that didn't involve college and Ashley got her two-year degree at the community college and went to work. Both girls live on their own. We see them once a month for our family supper," is my response.

"Even so," Laurel presses, "it's different. They're not under your own roof. It's just you and Julie in the house, yes?"

"True. Julie and I certainly had an adjustment period. I think the fact that she's a teacher and is around kids all day helps her to be a little less lonely without the girls around. Plus we do some volunteering. I believe having something bigger than yourself to focus on is important." I stop to provide an opportunity for Laurel to say something. She lets the opportunity pass.

I press on. "And, quite frankly, the tough part is that our identities get so wrapped up in our kids' lives that we lose ourselves in the process. We lose what we're about; who we are apart from being spouses or parents or someone whose identity is independent from those we love."

A quick sip of my lukewarm coffee. Laurel's face is one of quiet contemplation. My thought continues.

"Julie and I struggled mightily on that score when the girls were out of the house. Took us a year to put our fingers on why we were struggling emotionally. Once we figured it out, the process to resetting our identities made a huge difference in our marriage and in our lives."

"Interesting," Laurel says. Her tilting head putting her eyes on the ceiling. A server walks up to our table. Her name badge reads "Annie".

"Sir, can I freshen up that coffee for you?" she asks. The young lady is in a staff shirt and khaki pants with her brunette ponytail sticking out the back of her cap. She looks to be high school age but as I've gotten older it's hard to tell ages anymore. They all look young.

"Yes, please. Thanks, Annie," I smile. She takes my cup and walks away. Her ponytail sways back and forth like a pendulum.

"Makes sense," Laurel picks up where my last thought left off. "Nearly half my life has been spent being someone's mom and taking care of their needs first. Same thing for Seth as a dad. Never thought about my issue being an identity crisis. I'd saved that for turning 50," she teases herself. We chuckle. My words seem to have given Laurel a bit of relief. At least I hope so.

"Your coffee, sir." Annie is back with a refill of my medium roast. Then to Laurel: "Ma'am, is there anything I can get you?"

Springing a Leek | 69

"No, thank you, I'm fine," Laurel answers. Annie heads back to the counter.

"Wasn't 1986 just a few years ago?" Laurel tosses into the conversation in wonder.

"Yeah. And remember when everyone thought the sky was falling before Y2K?" I toss back. "It stuns me to think that was 20 years ago. The '90s don't seem that far away."

Laurel nods in agreement. "Scary to think Seth and I have been married 25 years. Those years went by in a blink."

"Speaking of your husband, what's he up to this morning?"

"We're remodeling one of the bathrooms in the house. He and Cole are hard at it this weekend. They were thrilled to learn that you and I were having coffee today. Apparently me not being in the house is an improvement." Laurel shrugs her shoulders and opens her eyes wide. "I don't get it. Why wouldn't they want me overseeing their work?" She chuckles at her rhetorical question and the obvious answer. "By the way," Laurel shifts the conversation, "what brings you this way today?"

"Okay, this is going to sound silly," I answer a bit sheepishly, "but the real reason I came down this way is to go to Mayhem Comics." Ah, the cover story. Simple is best and that's what I'm going with.

"Here in Ames? Still the superhero fan, huh?" Laurel buys it. Why wouldn't she? I will be going there after our coffee get together concludes it's just not the main reason I'm in town. "You must be in heaven these past few years with all these superhero movies and TV shows," she adds.

"It's a great time to be me, Laurel. When we were kids I kept my love of superheroes and comic book collecting a secret because I didn't want to get teased by the other kids. I think I was 30 before I stopped keeping it secret."

"Times have changed, haven't they? Laurel observes.

"And how. People come out of the woodwork now to ask me questions before seeing the films or want to see the movies with me because I know all about these characters, their history, and their backstories."

I take a triumphant sip.

"Isn't it funny all the things kids got teased about or were afraid to talk about back then?" Laurel observes. "Remember that librarian we had in high school? The old lady with the blue hair?"

I nod and smile.

"I swear, the other day I saw a third grader with hair bluer than hers! We live in a time when about anything goes. It's crazy," Laurel marvels.

"It is indeed," I concur. "I've lost count of how many times my inner 12-year-old has been freaking out in joy. Never thought I'd see this age of superheroes we live in."

"It's terrific that you still have that love for it. There's not anything like that from childhood that I'm still into today but I've become quite the foodie," she informs me.

"I would never have guessed that."

"That's because you've never been in my kitchen," Laurel says with pride.

"That's superb. Would you call it a hobby or an obsession?"

"Oh, definitely an obsession," Laurel answers in a deadly serious tone. "Once I get in, I'm all in."

Mental note made.

Laurel looks down at her watch. "Oh! Didn't know it was almost 11:30. A group of us moms are getting together to firm up plans for prom. Cole's last prom," she says wistfully. "Sorry to run off suddenly." Laurel grabs her purse hanging on the chair then stands.

"No, no worries," I reassure her as I rise with her. "This was fun. Thanks for taking the time out of your schedule to have coffee with me."

"Thanks for thinking to invite me," Laurel says. We move toward each other and embrace.

"Stay in touch, okay? Happy comic shopping." Our hug concludes and Laurel is out the door with a goodbye trailing behind her. I return the wave and the goodbye.

Annie the server walks up to me and says, "Your friend seems very nice."

"Every little thing she does is magic," I say making my own exit.

* * *

Comic book stores are my happy place, my candy store. Mayhem Comics is such a place. Every comic book store I visit represents one of the best parts of my childhood where I can walk in the present and the past simultaneously. A man walks around the store with the eyes of a kid. It's awesome.

A leisurely stroll through Mayhem Comics to get my bearings and then I begin searching for the book I'd been seeking - a hard-to-find, hardbound edition of collected comic book storylines from my youth.

I've been reading comic books since Elementary school but it dawned on me a few years ago that the current adventures of my beloved superheroes no longer resonated with me. Reality came crashing down when it hit home that today's comic book creators are not catering to a middle-aged audience. Go figure.

It was then my attention went back in time as it occurred to me there are a lot comics I never read growing up. Back then you got comics off the spinner rack at the grocery store or the drug store and getting consecutive issues month to month was nearly impossible. I thought: *Why not go back in time and read the stories I'd missed as a kid?* And that's what I did.

The major comic book publishers now offer hard bound editions that reprint runs of superhero stories from their earliest days. These collected editions are the perfect way for me to revisit the missed stories of my youth. As much as visiting a comic book store is about the present for me, it's also about revisiting some unfinished business of my youth. Unfinished business seems to be a theme with me at this stage of life. Or maybe I'm just too damned sentimental.

Instead of finding the one book I was looking for I find three gems – the one I was seeking plus two more. The remainder of my time here is spent doing laps around the store ensuring I don't miss a single action figure, statue, t-shirt, or other collectible. I pay for my books after lap four and I'm out the door.

I hit the highway for Boone at 3 o'clock. It's only a 30-minute drive from Ames to Boone so I have plenty of time but want to make sure I get a prime spot at the coffee shop. Todd recommended we go to Van Hemert's Dutch Oven Bakery. The name alone was all that was needed to convince me to go.

A quick drive later I'm parked at the destination and on my way in to wait for Todd. Van Hemert's Dutch Oven Bakery is a family-owned, scratch bakery and it isn't quite what I was expecting. A diner is what I was anticipating. It should have dawned on me by the name that Dutch motif would be part of the experience. The interior – like the exterior – is like being in Holland. I haven't tasted anything but I know I'm going to enjoy whatever treat I try.

The dining area is all wooden tables and chairs. Selecting a seat by the window, I take a vantage point that provides a perfect view of the door. A friendly, middle-aged woman - yes, she's about my age, why do I keep forgetting how old I am? - approaches my table and asks if I'd like a menu and something to drink.

"Yes, please," I say accepting the laminated menu extended to me. "I'd like a cup of coffee. A friend of mine will be joining me soon so could you bring another menu when you get a chance?"

"Sure thing," she tells me. An instant before she turns away I take note of her name badge - "Claire".

Looking down at the menu I instantly know the impossibility of the ordering task. Everything looks delicious. Choosing one thing is going to be tough. Claire comes back as the feverish study of the menu continues. She places the cream-colored ceramic cup at the 11 o'clock position of my place setting.

"Any suggestions, Claire?"

"Depends. What are you in the mood for?"

"Pastries seem to be calling my name," I respond.

"Ooh, that is tough." She starts tapping her chin with her left index finger, her right eye squinting. She is giving this question serious consideration. "You should order the Raspberry Almond Tart. Definitely."

My head nods as I close the menu and place it down in front of me. "Sounds like a plan. Once my friend has ordered, that's what I will have. Thanks for the recommendation, Claire. And for the coffee."

"You're welcome. You just relax. I'll be back when your friend gets here." With that she is on her way to help customers at a nearby table. There are two couples in the place. It is certainly not full. But, given the fact that the place closes at 5:30, it's not surprising. Mornings and lunchtime must be crazy here.

The clock on the wall behind the counter tells me Todd should be here in about 15 minutes or so. Social media surfing on my smart phone passes the time till Todd's arrival. It's tough not to be distracted by the smells wafting through the bakery. The smells permeating the place remind me of Mom's kitchen with pies in the oven while making a batch of cinnamon rolls. The two best places in the house growing up were my room when I played Atari video games and the kitchen when Mom baked or when we were making sauerkraut.

The front door chime yanks me from my mom's kitchen and back to the bakery. Butterflies release from my stomach like doves at the Olympics. Todd and I make eye contact as he walks toward me. If Todd's happy to see me, he doesn't show it. His hazel eyes convey a weariness that goes beyond a day at work.

At six-feet tall, he stands three inches taller than me. By the looks of it, he's got more than 40 pounds on me today. He's wearing a long-sleeved red flannel shirt, jeans, and Red Wing work boots. He is a big man. His hand extends to mine. We shake and say hello.

Todd motions me to return to my seat. He takes off his baseball cap with the logo of his dealership on it and sets it on the table next to his place setting. Todd runs his left hand through his blonde hair to fluff out the hat head then looks to the counter and calls out, "Claire, I'll have a Filled Dutch Windmill and my friend..."

"...will have a Raspberry Almond Tart. I already got his order, Mr. Kane. One ticket?"

"Yes. Thanks." Todd turns his attention back to me and takes the seat across from me. He grabs both menus and sets them aside.

"You didn't have to do that but thank you," I tell him.

"It's the proper thing to do. You had a farther drive than me so it's my pleasure."

His demeanor is taking me some time to get used to. As kids he was always good-natured and friendly. This version of Todd appears more guarded. More world-weary. There is a heaviness on his shoulders which I can't determine if it's the result of a tough day at work or the past 30-some years. This reunion isn't starting out as joyful as this morning's.

"Why are you here again?" Todd asks in a way that sounds more interrogation than inquiry.

"Had a book I'd been looking for that the comic shop in Ames had in stock so..."

"...you drove nearly three hours to buy it? You ever heard of the internet?" Todd certainly is not the easy-going guy I remembered. Screw awkward this is turning cringe-worthy.

A shrug starts my response. "Of course. But there are instances when old school is the most satisfying."

Todd shrugs off my reasoning. Claire is back with our order before either of us can say another word. We thank her, she tells us to enjoy, and is off to help other customers.

We immediately dig in and only one of us is surprised by what we taste. My eyes nearly bug out of my head, taste buds nearly explode. "Oh my goodness!" I exclaim my mouth still full of tart. "This is phenomenal!"

"Yeah, it's superb," Todd acknowledges as he takes another bite of his Windmill thingie. "Is that your SUV outside with the Chiefs decal on the back quarter panel?"

My fork gets returned to its original position. No hurry to finish this tart. It's okay if it takes me a while to eat it.

"It is."

"Thought you were a Vikings fan. You always were growing up." Todd takes another bite.

"I was. My favorite uncle was a Chiefs fan. He and my aunt would come up to visit every July. The last summer I saw Uncle Ed I was nine years old. I told him the Chiefs were going to win the Super Bowl as he and my aunt were preparing to go back to Kansas City. He dropped dead of a massive heart attack a few months later. Dead before he hit the ground. I picked up the Chiefs for him and became a diehard fan. I'm still waiting on that Super Bowl I promised him."

"Good story. You always did like a good story." Todd shakes his head.

"Take it you're still a Steelers fan," I state finally getting to ask some form of a question.

"Till the day I die."

What is going on here? I feel like I'm having an exchange with a hostile witness at a murder trial. Todd acts like this is the last place he wants to be.

"Owner of an implement dealership, huh? How'd that come about? Do you like it?" Hopefully by asking a few questions at a time I may get a bit more out of him.

"Graduated from Iowa State with a business degree. Worked for a few years in the dealership I now own. Bought it from Bob the

Springing a Leek | 77

original owner when he retired which was a great decision. I have the best toys on my lot. Never wanted to be a farmer because I don't have the temperament for it. I like to help farmers but I don't want to be one. Too many uncertainties, too many things out of my control."

I nod with understanding. Todd probably got most of the same stories from his dad I got from mine. Only difference was that years before I was born, my dad *was* a farmer. He tried his best but he wasn't able to get enough land to be able to scale a profitable farm business.

Dad went to work for the local grain elevator after selling off the farm and all the equipment. Mom told me that Dad was a mentor to Todd's dad, Mike. Dad was 20 years older than Mike so he looked up to my dad. The friendship of our fathers is part of what led us to become friends.

"How are your folks doing?"

"Livin' the life," Todd says. "They retired to Florida years ago. Dad took up fly fishing. Mom got into needlepoint. They don't miss Iowa winters that's for sure"

"Does your mom still suffer from migraines?"

"Actually, no. My mom found a new dentist who specializes in unique dental solutions for treating things other than teeth issues. Turns out Mom's jaw was out of alignment which caused a chain reaction that led to the migraines. The new dentist made a special dental appliance and she hasn't had a migraine since."

"That's wonderful. I'm so happy for her. What a miracle that is."

"What about you? What do you do?" Todd asks changing the focus to me.

"I own a marketing consulting business. A firm of one. My business helps business owners with their marketing and advertising strategies to bring in more customers," I reply.

"Sounds tedious," Todd declares.

"You said I like a good story. Marketing and advertising are all about telling stories. It's how people align with your brand. Stories," I emphasize trying not to feel insulted at this point. "It's nice too because it's just me so I can office at home. Flexible schedule."

"Guess we're both helping different types of business owners in our own way," Todd says. He takes another bite. I do too. He finishes the bite and asks, "Married? Kids?"

"Yeah. Wife, Julie. Daughters, Nicole and Ashley; 27 and 26. You?"

A head shake. "Nah. Never took the plunge."

"Didn't ever get bitten by the marriage bug?"

Todd's shoulders slump, the weight pressing on his shoulders getting heavier. He lowers his fork. His body language seems to soften. "There was a woman," Todd starts, "her name was Meredith. Loved her and she loved me. We were together for years. She wanted to get married and I thought we would be. Just could never pull the trigger and ask her. She could only wait so long so one day Meredith broke up with me."

"That's tough stuff. If you don't mind me asking, why couldn't you pull the trigger?" I lean in. If Todd answers this question what is said will be profound.

"Guess I was scared," he waves in a dismissive manner. "Not of getting married. I wanted to spend the rest of my life with Meredith. My fear was the change that would come from being married." He stops for a moment to notice another customer walk in. "Meredith moved on. Found another guy. Lived happily ever after."

"And you?" I ask.

"She was the one. I let her slip away. Never forgave myself." He snorts in disgust. "It's not like I don't take chances. I just couldn't take this one. This one. Kept every other woman at arm's length after that. Won't be hurt like that again."

Todd could use a moment after that admission so I give him one. Not sure where to take our conversation. Easy to see where most of the weight on his shoulders comes from. My attention turns back to my tart.

"Ask me," Todd says.

My brows furrow. "Ask you what?"

"Ask me the question," he demands.

Then it dawns on me. "Why did you stop being my friend?"

There it is. Out in the open now. No putting it back in the box. Todd's body slumps slightly once more. It occurs to me the cringe-worthy exchanges after he first sat down were partially due to his being on edge about this subject.

"We moved away. You and I weren't part of each other's lives anymore. We were in high school, had activities, and we were three hours away from each other. What...were we supposed to schedule play dates on the weekends?" He verbally pushes me away.

"I get it. It was the early '80s. Back then Mom and Dad didn't go very far from home because they were busy. There was no internet so it was either letters or phone calls to stay in touch. I get it. But you could have said something," my voice starts to get louder as emotion starts to get the better of me. I catch myself and take a drink of water to allow me to compose myself.

Todd waits for me to continue.

"You could have just told me the friendship is over because of the distance or whatever. But you didn't. You just dropped off the face of the Earth. Nothing. I've always felt that I did something that ended the friendship and never knew what it was." My voice ended at a higher volume at the end of the sentence than it was at the start.

Other patrons turn to look at us. Silence as we go back to our pastries. We consider what the other has said, not sure what the next words are.

Todd polishes off the final bite. "You didn't do anything. I just didn't know how to say it so I didn't say anything. Just avoided the situation. You'd figure it out. I'm sorry."

It's my turn to wave him off. "No apology necessary. It's not what I want nor what I came for but since we were going to be here I wanted to know so I can put it to rest and not wonder anymore." I polish off my tart.

"The KISS video you posted from when we were kids was outstanding. Can you believe that was 40 years ago?" Todd changes the direction of the conversation and that's fine by me.

"I just couldn't believe it was out there on YouTube. Talk about random. But, then again, it is KISS we're talking about so it does make some sense. You still a big KISS fan?"

"KISS army all the way, baby," Todd proclaims with a fist pump. "I go to one concert a year. Try to pick a different city every time. What a blast. Gene Simmons is still the man. You still a Joan Jett fan?"

"Blackheart Nation all the way," I pronounce proudly. Our conversation is relaxed for the first time since we sat down.

Claire breezes up to our table and places the ticket in front of Todd. "Gotta wrap it up, boys. We close in ten minutes. Mr. Kane, you can pay at the counter like always. Thanks for coming by." She returns to the counter.

Todd and I look at our phones. Sure enough, it's 5:20. We look across the table at each other exchanging a knowing look acknowledging our time is up.

"Guess that's our cue," is all I can say stating the obvious.

"Yeah. Guess so."

We stand as one. I extend my right hand and Todd shakes it. "Thanks for the invitation. Let's not let so much time pass until we talk again," he says.

"Agreed," I reply.

Todd and I step away from the table. He slaps me on the shoulder. "Have a safe drive home."

"Will do. Talk to you soon." I wave to Claire as I depart.

Rocky start, strong finish.

One more coffee date to go.

* * *

A few hours later I'm settled in at the Americinn Hotel in Pella, Iowa, lounging on the bed. Time to call Julie to check in.

"Hey, handsome, how was your day?" Julie answers her phone on the second ring.

"Marvelous. Exceeded expectations," is my answer as the cable channel flipping begins. It's not that talking to Julie isn't a priority it's just that my eyes need something to occupy them as my ears and mouth are doing their conversation thing. *Jackpot!* TBS is airing an old episode of The Big Bang Theory. Oh! It's the one where Sheldon misses out on meeting Stan Lee. One of my favorite episodes. The outfit Penny wears to court is exquisite.

"Hello? Are you still there?"

My attention snaps back to Julie as the realization hits that my internal dialogue has hijacked my verbal one. "Yeah, sorry. I was sitting here flipping channels and landed on The Big Bang Theory where Sheldon misses meeting Stan Lee..."

"...and the outfit Penny wears to court is exquisite. Yes. I remember," Julie finishes my sentence. "Anyway, tell me about how your day went."

"Met with Laurel which was fun. Getting together with her was not as nerve wracking because we graduated together and have seen each other at a few reunions. What surprised me about both of my coffee meetings is how real they were. Conversations weren't superficial, that's for sure."

"How so?"

"Laurel and I talked a lot about how goals change and how life changes when we become empty nesters. Life after kids and all that. With Todd, there was unfinished business with how our friendship ended which we worked through. I think." After completing the thought I stop and reflect on it to determine if my assessment is correct.

"Sounds like a rewarding day," Julie encourages. "What's your gut tell you about the band?"

"Not sure. Obviously it didn't come up. My gut says Laurel would be more open to it than Todd. Todd...has changed. He was much more affable growing up. A much harder edge now. Very blunt, very matter of fact now. He's going to be a tougher sell."

"Excited for tomorrow's meeting with Lorelei?"

"Nervous. Don't take this the wrong way but it kinda feels like a blind date."

"No, I get it. You haven't seen her since grade school and now you're meeting, pretty much, with a stranger. Could be very awk-ward."

Julie hits the awk hard. She's not wrong. The tenacious tummy tickle returns for an encore performance. Lorelei is a stranger and I'm a stranger to her. Only the little bit I've gleaned from her Facebook page – admittedly not much – is all I have. It's a bit daunting.

"On the positive side, we have so much to talk about since she moved away, there is a potential for us to discover a lot about each other," is my attempt to put a positive spin on it.

"Perhaps. You said Todd has changed a lot over the years and he was your best friend growing up. Do you think it will be easier with Lorelei?" Julie presses.

"Apples and oranges, boo," getting up off the bed I begin pacing around the room. Julie's line of questioning has given rise to a greater restlessness within me. Gotta get up and walk it off.

"With Todd there is an emotional layer from a friendship that abruptly ended and some unresolved issues. Meeting with Lorelei contains no emotional component except for the nostalgia of childhood."

"True," Julie's voice trails off as if her attention is being averted. "I don't mean to cut you off but your sister is here. She's joining me for ladies night with my friends so I have to get going."

"Understood. Didn't have anything to add. Tell Ani I said hello."

"Will do," Julie acknowledges. "Love you."

"Love you too. Bye." A quick tap of the red End Call button on my smart phone officially brings our call to an end.

The pacing path I've navigated brings me to the curtains on the far side of my room. Parting them gives me a scenic view of the parking lot lit by the lamps now that the sun has set.

It is a quiet night in Pella, Iowa. The serenity of the town is not exactly shocking given the fact that Pella's population is a little over 10,000. Pella is a shade off the beaten path – but only 40 miles from Des Moines – and is surrounded by many smaller communities. It is a fairly closed community if you're not of Dutch heritage.

Pella is the headquarters of the Pella Window company which gives the town a lot of economic advantages most towns of its size do not have. How many communities this size have a four-year college?

The curtains fall back to their natural hanging position. The feeling of restlessness refuses to subside. Grabbing my master planner notebook from my suitcase I set up shop on the bed. This notebook contains every thought, every plan on this reunion quest. It's a multi-subject notebook so each part of the process is in its own spiral-bound compartment.

The section markers are flipped till the desired one is before me. This section is titled "Band Members". In it contains notes on Laurel, Todd, and Lorelei. Things I know, things I've remembered, things I've learned through our interaction on Facebook.

That's so creepy, Dad. Ashley's voice whispers to my ear from inside my head. Not arguing with her either. When viewing my notes my feelings rotate from giddy to guilty...long-lost friend/detective/stalker.

Ash and I were out for a run the other day and we were talking about my "surveillance" and how the other three will feel about it when I reveal my plan and layout the details before them. Ashley was very frank – which is her natural state of being – about how she would feel if it were her.

"I'd be so pissed, sorry, angry with you. I'd feel manipulated, like I was a chess piece or something in a game you're playing and you're the only one who knows you're playing."

Can't say I disagree with her and – out of all of the things about my quest – it's the part that is the most problematic and has the potential for blowing up in my face.

Another voice whispers from inside my head and it is that of my late mother's: *Cross that bridge when you get there.*

Pages are thumbed till Laurel's name appears and the new knowledge gained today pour onto the page. Writing furiously my brain instructs my fingers to move the pen across the page in no discernable order of information. Whatever thought, quote, impression, or perception that comes to mind just spills onto the pages. I don't qualify or evaluate any thought as it comes out. Brain-spilling instead of brain-storming.

Once the last of my Laurel thoughts finish I move on to Todd. It's not long till my impressions of Todd are complete but then thoughts start to get tangled and my process gets blocked.

Maybe I need to steam out the tangle. A shower might dislodge the mental cork so I make a straight line to the bathroom. The television sound is left on to simulate companionship. I don't want silence now.

* * *

What is it about standing under a flow of hot water for ten minutes that is so relaxing, so calming? A sweeping motion with my right arm pushes away the shower curtain and my left hand grabs a towel from the wall-mounted rack. I move the towel around my body quickly. Even though I feel relaxed I am anxious to see if thoughts will move more freely. The towel is dropped to the floor. Steam hangs like a fog in the room and covers the mirror over the sink.

My head cocks to the right, my brow furrows, and eyes narrow studying the mirror intently. Instinctively, I bring my index finger to the mirror and trace the number 86 in the steam. I stand and stare almost mesmerized.

During the winter months back in elementary school the bus windows would have a layer of frost on them on frigid mornings. It took a long time for the inside of the bus to warm up so the frosty layer took a while to clear up. I'm not sure who started the tradition but we'd seen the older kids trace the last two digits of their graduation year in the frost.

Those digits were a numerical mantra reminding us the year we would be released from our educational prison. We would finally be free if we could only make it to that year. A lightning bolt of inspiration strikes causing me to fling the door open and make a mad scramble to the bed.

My notebook is thrown open to the tab marked "Songbook". Now what comes from my mind isn't a flow, it's a flood. My hand struggles to keep up with the speed at which my mind is working. No mental cork exists now.

A nine-year-old's memories fly out. His thoughts about what the number 86 means along with those long winter days, the bus rides, and the experiences are what land on the pages. My mind doesn't stop there as more song thoughts flow behind the one just finished.

It is only after I am satisfied I have written all my mind has to offer when I realize I am buck naked. A laugh of surprise and joy starts at my toes, seemingly following up a circuit, till it hits my mouth and becomes audible.

I wish Julie and the girls could see this. Okay, no. Not this. Not me naked. No, I wish they could see the joy of this creative process, of the element of surprise that continually sneaks up on me when I least expect it and without warning. I stop momentarily to put on my Batman shirt and a pair of cotton shorts before returning to writing. Pages flip again and I look at the notes I wrote about the coffee dates with Laurel and Todd.

The pen is set down on the page. *1986*, *Take the Day*, *All Those Ones and Zeroes* are the song titles. The goal of these songs is to resonate with the life experiences of my generation but also – hopefully – to feed the curiosity of those generations after us.

Todd's story about his finding "the one" and letting her get away. That's a damn powerful theme. A lot of people could probably identify with that.

Laurel's questioning her identity once the boys are all out of the house will ring true with people. Our generation now faces the reality of our kids leaving the nest and many of our contemporaries are struggling with that. Thankfully, those days are past me but it is no less gut wrenching for those who are going through it.

Everything Changed is the song title I come up with for the song about Todd's circumstance and *No Way Back Today* for Laurel's. An exhale of relief mixed with accomplishment feels much like the final exhale after completing a long run – satisfaction mixed with exhaustion. Pen dropped and notebook pushed across the bed make space for the laptop to take its place there.

I email Lisbeth once the laptop powers up and logs on to the hotel's Wi-Fi. My British songwriter is mostly likely in blissful slumber as it's nearing 4:30 Sunday morning across the Atlantic. A long note is composed to my composer as my song notes are communicated with background information on the context. My goal is to have Lis write eight songs. It's a nod to the era of albums when eight songs was the norm on an album – four songs on each side.

Send button is hit. Laptop and notebook are closed and put away. It's almost 11 and time to turn in. Picking up the remote I turn off the television. Not sure when the last episode of Big Bang played and I have no idea what show came on after it. Oh well.

Best shower ever.

* * *

The next morning finds me at the Smokey Row Coffee Company in Downtown Pella. SUV is packed and ready for the three and a half hour drive home that will come after Lorelei and I finish our coffee date. I'm purposely early to get settled in and get the lay of the land. This is Lorelei's town and she is used to these surroundings. I want to make sure I have a level of comfort before she arrives.

Smokey Row Coffee is a confirmation as to why there is a "no chain" rule when traveling. This coffee shop has personality all over it. The coffee shop is the lower floor of a two-story brick building on the corner of Franklin Street. The corner of the roof is a small dome that reminds me of a bank from the 1800s.

The coffee house inside is a deep rectangle with long brick walls at the sides, a smaller one at the back, glass windows, and door at the front. Julie would love this place.

An antique shelf of bagged coffees, accessories, and store t-shirts invites patrons to purchase them upon entry. Then it's the long counter. Everything in the place is long and narrow out of necessity.

There are traditional small tables – one might call them intimate – with booths along one wall. Calling them booths is being kind. They are extra intimate allowing one person to sit on each side of the table top. The booths have vinyl covering the bench seats and my back has final vote on where to sit and the booths win.

I position my back to the back so Lorelei's entrance cannot be missed. The booth I've selected is close enough to the front to see me but far enough from the counter which runs almost the entire length of the opposite wall so that customer commerce doesn't get in the way of reunion.

The sun shines brightly outside the building. It is a beautiful Sunday in the Midwest. No more so than when the tiny bell on the door announces a new customer is entering. The light of the sun behind her overpowers the indoor light before her, giving Lorelei an almost angelic aura. At least I hope it's her. I'm fairly confident based on the pictures on Facebook.

Standing, I raise a piece of paper lengthways with LORELEI written so large the letters take up the entire page. Since we don't know each other I was trying to think of a way to decrease any uneasiness by playing on the theme of picking up a stranger at the airport. It is my hope Lorelei is amused by it and my playful icebreaker is received well. If not...I'll leave this part out when I tell Julie and the girls about today.

Lorelei sees her name in large letters immediately and it stops her in her tracks a few steps inside the door. She hesitates. A squadron of butterflies takes off in my stomach. She begins giggling. Her head moves around to let her eyes survey the surroundings.

"Is this the coffee shop or the airport?" she asks. Lorelei makes eye contact with me again and says, "That. Is. Hilarious." She makes her way toward me with a smile. The squadron of butterflies returns to the hangar. We're off to an admirable start.

After navigating the velvet ropes separating the traditional tables from the counter - creating a natural corridor for people ordering - she stands before me. We both smile though I'm not sure if it's for the same reason. We freeze for an instant before Lorelei makes the first move and throws her arms open.

"Hey, Eric, bring it in," Lorelei beckons. We embrace long enough for a greeting but not so long as to feel weird.

Lorelei has a friendly, easy-going demeanor instantly putting me at ease. Since I'm the instigator of these coffee meetings I play host and feel an extra burden to make everyone else feel comfortable. Lorelei immediately communicates no burden and no host duties are necessary. Hug ends and we are seated. Lorelei first. Host duties may not be necessary but manners are always in play.

I start to take her in upon taking my seat. She looks fantastic. Her brown hair is as brown as it was way back when. Her blue eyes have lost a little of their sparkle but whose haven't? Life has a way of doing that to us. We all yearn to be free from school and to be full-fledged adults but - in the midst of responsibilities and obligations that are part and parcel of adulthood - we recognize too late we traded simplicity for complexity and that genie is never going back in the bottle.

Lorelei is dressed casually as am I. She has on a pair of blue jeans and a dark blue, long-sleeved shirt that is tucked in. A pair of black flats completes her look. Because I'm a guy and I notice this stuff, she wears no ring.

"Lorelei, you look fabulous," are my next words to her. It's true. Women half her age would be jealous of how flawless her skin is.

"Thanks, Eric," she says, dipping her chin a bit as to convey a bit of self-consciousness. "You're very kind. I mean, look at you. Have you aged at all?"

Now my chin dips and I have this stupid thought wondering if I've dressed too casually in my alma mater's pullover, jeans, and black shoes. Then I realize how ludicrous the notion is and get over myself.

"Oh, come now," I reply as I playfully bat her compliment out of the air, "I've aged at least five years." We both smile. "Thanks for meeting with me."

"I'm happy to," she says. Even when she's not smiling it's like she's smiling. How does she do that? "As you can imagine," she continues, "I don't see a lot of the old gang...any old gang. I don't think I've seen anybody from the old school, like, ever."

"That's why I was afraid you might not come. It's been almost 40 years since we've seen each other." Seemingly I'm now giving Lorelei reasons not to be here.

"Yeah, I know. If you hadn't reached out on Facebook I probably wouldn't have. Social media has a way of bridging gaps. And I'm kinda curious. Wanted to find out what happened to the kids I went to elementary school with."

"I can definitely help you with that." The thought announces itself that we are people in a coffee shop with no coffee. "Hang on. We should be ordering something, shouldn't we?"

Lorelei chuckles. "I suppose we should, yes."

Our attention turns to the large board behind the counter. "What's your pleasure?" I inquire. "It's on me."

"What? No. You drove all this way to see me I should be buying you coffee. Seriously. I insist."

"Okay," I defer. "Thank you. That's very kind." A few seconds pass and then the option appears. "I'll have an Iced Americano, please."

"Aces," Lorelei nods. "I'm going to have the Red Eye."

"The Red Eye? Coffee with shots of espresso? You are hard core."

"This bubbly personality doesn't fuel itself," she replies with a smirk. "I'll be right back." She gets up and takes her place in line. Two people are ahead of her so it shouldn't be a long wait.

Giddiness threatens to overtake me and I fight it. Have to keep my head but it is tough. Nothing of substance has been discussed but we both seem to be at ease out of the gate. No awkwardness. Yet, anyway. *How is it she's not married* I wonder. Lorelei's return snaps me out of my internal musings.

"Here you go, one Iced Americano." She hands me a 20-ounce clear, plastic cup with the magic brown liquid and ice plus the straw that goes with it. The straw is removed from the wrapper and jabbed through the cup lid. The first sip of my iced drink lands strong, the impact of the bitter and the energy of the caffeine hitting instantaneously.

"Ah, my morning cup of giddyup. Thank you, Lorelei."

She chuckles after taking her first sip. "Didn't you write a lot of stories in school?" she wonders aloud. "Yeah. I remember now. Anytime we got a writing assignment in class you were always the one who had the longest and the best story. Guess that way with words never left you, huh?"

Lorelei sees a smile from me. "Excellent memory. Yes, I like to say the English language is my playground. That has *never* left me." If only Lorelei knew the story I'm working on. But that truly is a story for another day.

"I have to admit I was a little suspicious as to why you'd be reaching out after all these years. The Facebook thing was fine but a face-to-face meeting made me nervous," Lorelei confides. Leaning in closer she whispers, "This isn't going to turn into a Criminal Minds episode with my naked body full of stab wounds being found in a ditch, is it?"

She hits that last sentence as I'm taking a sip and it comes back at her. The Iced Americano sails over Lorelei's left shoulder barely missing her. She sits up in triumph. "Probably should have warned you about the wicked sense of humor."

Dabbing my lip buys me time to compose myself to the point I can share in the mirth. "Whew. Did not see that twist coming. You're a live wire, aren't you? Well done." Then I lean in and whisper, "Not sure yet. We'll see how this goes."

Lorelei beams. "Love it when people play along." She takes another sip and we begin catching up in earnest. "Tell me about yourself, Eric. What have I missed the past 40 years?"

The thought that I'm being interviewed walks itself across my mind. "You know, a friend of mine says all my stories begin with the phrase, 'It all started back in second grade'. I guess this one would start, 'It all started after fifth grade'."

"Yes. After I moved away. Well done," Lorelei approves.

"The Readers Digest version of the story is that I didn't move and graduated from the school district. Graduated college with a degree in marketing. My wife Julie and I met in college. Married a few years after graduation. I started my own marketing consulting business. Sole proprietor. She's an Elementary school teacher." Pause to take another sip.

"We have two daughters, Nicole and Ashley. Nicole is putting herself on a path to become a makeup tutorial YouTube sensation while Ashley works as a personal care giver for the elderly who still live at home."

"Whew, that is the Readers Digest version," Lorelei marvels. "Sounds like a very nice life. What do you like to do when you're not working?"

"I like to write still. Need something to express my creativity. I also do some distance running. I've run twenty half marathons and a couple full marathons," I share.

"Whoa! That's extraordinary. Have you always run?"

"Nooo, I hated running for a long time. I'd run as a workout when I was in my 20s but never more than eight miles. I figured anything longer than eight miles, I'm driving..."

"That's funny," Lorelei interjects.

"...but then in my early 40s a dear friend of mine challenged herself to run a half marathon – she wasn't a runner either – and asked me if I'd run it with her. I said yes. Figured if I hated it I just wouldn't do it again. After finishing the first race I realized it was fun so I kept on running."

"Impressive...especially since you started something like that in your 40s. Does your wife run too?"

"Briefly. Julie watched my friend and I finish the first half marathon and she decided to try it. She ran a few races but found her knees couldn't take the pounding. My daughter Ashley is a runner so we have raced a few times. Run races, I mean."

"That's outstanding when you can share something you enjoy with others...especially your kids. What about your other daughter?"

"Nicole isn't into physical exertion, hence, the internet income dreams. We share musical tastes, you know, Disturbed, System of A Down, Slipknot, Five Finger Death Punch..."

Lorelei almost has her Red Eye fire out of her nose. "Are you for real? I would never picture you liking that kind of music."

"No one ever does. That's just an added perk." I grin. "That's my life story. I'm curious to know yours."

Lorelei takes a sip in confidence there is no danger of a nostril exit. "Hmm. Well, my parents moved us to Springfield, Illinois, after fifth grade. Stayed in that school district the rest of the way. Went to college at Southern Illinois, majored in Business and Administration. Met my husband there. He was a Supply Chain Management major. We got married before our senior year. We graduated and he accepted an offer from Pella Windows so we moved here." She pauses to take another sip.

"He was vice-president of Supply Chain Management and I'm in the logistics division. When orders come in I coordinate with the plant to manufacture the windows, schedule the trucks for pickup, shipment, and delivery, and with the client to receive product," Lorelei finishes her thought.

I decide it wouldn't be rude to ask a question. "Your husband no longer works for Pella?"

Lorelei finishes her sip and stares into her coffee cup for a moment. Her hesitation is that of someone searching for the appropriate words. Lori's head comes up and her eyes meet mine. "He died."

My stomach drops and I'm not sure when it will stop. "Oh, Lorelei, I'm so sorry. That's...that's such a shame."

A hint of a smile of acknowledgment shows on her face. "Thanks. I'm okay. It's been a few years. Talking about it is perfectly fine. Took a long time but I can do it now. Cancer. Long, slow, and painful. For all of us."

For someone who is supposed to be so masterful with words I'm at a loss to find any as I look across the table. As has probably happened more times than she cares to count, Lorelei recognizes my struggles and keeps on going to break the quiet.

"Not kidding. It's okay to talk about. I have twin daughters – Hope and Faith – who are 28. It was devastating for us. Dominic was the finest man I ever knew. He was a wonderful husband and terrific father. He loved those girls and they thought he was perfect. The three of us were lost without him for a long time," she stops briefly to take another sip.

"Eventually we came out the other side and we're stronger for it but there has been an additional aspect of adjustment for me. The girls are out and on their own having lost a dad. I'm on my own and this was the time of my life when Dominic and I were supposed to be living the next phase of *our* lives."

Then she says it.

"But what happens when your happily ever after dies?"

A pin is stuck through a mental note in the corner of my mind that reads, "There's a theme for you". That note can stay put till the drive back home.

"I'm still plugging away at Pella. My job and my friends are such a treasure and, since Dominic died, have given my life the stability I need. Things were not normal for years while he fought cancer so it has been nice to have some normal. I'm still active with my friends but...I'm not sure why I'm telling you this...there's still this giant hole in my life."

Another sip. Another question. "Hole in what way?"

"Hole as in I'm not sure the direction my life should take. Dom and I had mapped out our lives but it was a plan for two, not a plan for a widow. I have a satisfying job, phenomenal friends, and two daughters I adore. But that's all outside stuff." She stops to find the word that should come next.

"Purpose," Lorelei blurts out. "I guess what I'm looking for is purpose…purpose as in destiny and intentionality. My life feels like I'm floating on the plank left over from a ship that sank and each day of my life is going through the motions but not being intentional about it."

My fear of meeting with Lorelei is that our conversation would be superficial. This might be the most real of any of my caffeine chats. Words continue to fail me.

"Eric, go ahead and talk. You're not going to hurt or offend me. Trust me. I've heard it all."

"First, I'm sorry you've had to go through this. I can't imagine what I'd do without Julie. I am so in awe of how you've been able to deal with such a tragedy. Without being *one of those people*' are you talking with anyone?" The pace of my words does not hide my hesitancy to speak them even though Lorelei has given me the go ahead.

"Counseling? Yeah. The grief counselors at the hospital plugged me in to a group of women and men who lost spouses. Plus, the funeral home hosts a monthly grief support group. Both have been a tremendous help but it feels like I've been walking this path alone. I've found my way back to emotional and mental health but there still is no answer on the purpose front." Lorelei's candor is striking.

"You're remarkable. I'm so glad you're taking care of yourself."

"I may not run long distance but I work out." Lorelei brings up her right arm, pulling up the long sleeve as far as she can to execute a biceps flex pose. The point of her flexing wasn't to display her physical prowess but to lighten the mood.

"Whoa, whoa, whoa. I came here for coffee. I didn't realize there was going to be a gun show," I return the playfulness.

Has she always been so natural at putting others at ease? The last of my Iced Americano comes up through my straw while Lorelei polishes off her Red Eye. "Refill?" Lorelei asks.

"You bet," I answer enthusiastically. "Next round is on me."

"Fair enough."

I stand and reach for Lorelei's ceramic cup removing it from the table. I walk past the garbage/bussing area using my left hand to toss my plastic container in the trash while my right carefully places the cup amongst the graveyard of tableware. Then I'm up at the counter to order round two. It's all of three minutes until I return to the booth.

"One more Red Eye for the lady..." I announce, handing Lorelei her cup.

"Thank you, kind sir..."

"...and more of the magic java for me." I sit and sip simultaneously.

Lorelei asks me how I like owning my own business; following up on what it is I do exactly.

"Being a solopreneur is fantastic. I work on my own schedule, commute to work is brief...just walk to my office from the kitchen." I give her a wry smile. "What I do is help business owners with their marketing and advertising. I help them put together a customized strategy for their business and assist them in making the media mix choices that put them in the best position to reach the people they're looking to do business with."

"You know," Lorelei observes, "for a guy whose stories all start in second grade today they've been very short." She's being playful. This reunion idea is superb if for no other reason than I would never have sought her out without it.

"Your lucky day," engaging in her roguishness. "People I know are going to ask what your secret is for keeping my stories short and want to bottle it. Maybe something in a refreshing spritz." I suggest amusing myself with my own ridiculousness. Lorelei snickers. Other patrons turn to look at us to see what is so darned amusing.

"What do you do for fun when you're not qualifying for a gun show?" I ask.

"Paint."

"Would I have seen any of the houses in town you've done? Do you have your own ladder?"

Lorelei snorts and spits simultaneously. A tricky double play. Clearly she's been caught off guard. "Jerk!" She sputters for a few more seconds before she can fully collect herself. "No fair!"

Pulling my hands in and putting them over my heart I use the best Victorian-era voice I can muster, "You wound me, madam." My voice reverts to normal, hands go palm down on the table top, and I lean in and say, "Gotcha."

Lorelei stiffens her back straightening up to her full ability. In the best Victorian-era voice she can muster, Lori says "You have won this battle but the war isn't over." She playfully glares. "No, goofball, I go to Pinot and Pallette in Des Moines once a month. Gets me out of the house and socializing. Coincidentally, people I know get paintings as gifts."

"Julie and I have done that. Our version in Rochester is called Canvas and Chardonnay. It's fun."

"It surprises me how well I do," Lorelei admits. "Artsy stuff is important to me. Most times it's me playing my keyboard in the house or singing karaoke at the Cellar Peanut Pub here in town. But neither unites me with people. Or challenges me. That's what I appreciate about painting. It's not just the art, it's the challenge."

"Outstanding," I nod. The outward nod reflects the inner nod that took note of her keyboard and karaoke. Musical bents never came up with Laurel and Todd. This is a tasty little bit of serendipity.

Lorelei's hands fly across the table and urgently grasp mine without warning. Startled, my body spasms in my seat, my eyes open wide. Realizing what she's done is abrupt, Lorelei pulls back and slumps a bit in her seat. "Sorry, sorry," she exhales to calm herself. "Didn't mean to spook you like that. I just caught a glance of the clock and noticed what time it is."

Eyes dart to my cell phone. It's just after 11:30. Not sure of the significance.

"Hope and Faith are home for the weekend and we're doing girl things. They decided to sleep in this morning and then meet me for lunch. They're picking me up here and then we're going to Bubba Q's."

"And you don't want to be late?" Still not understanding her almost panicked action a moment ago.

"No, no," Lorelei shakes me off. "It's just that the girls are not... they're...umm...they get unsettled when they see me with a man. Still strange for them to see me with someone who isn't their dad, even if it's not a date, even if it's totally innocent." Her hands go palms up in front of her and then arms sweep in different directions like she's revealing something. "Like this."

Now Lorelei's action makes sense. "I get it. Listen, the last thing I want to do is cause a problem or trigger your daughters. Do you want me to leave now?"

"What a dope I am," Lorelei admonishes herself. "Should never have reacted like that. Protection mode still kicks in occasionally. You're fine." She turns and looks at out the front window. "Besides, they're here."

Two tall brunette twins get out of a Ford Fusion and proceed to walk across the street to us. They have their mother's looks. "Are they anything like you?" is my question as I return my attention to my coffee companion.

"They have a lot of Dom in them but they've got a healthy streak of me too."

"Must be a handful."

"Oh, you bet they are," she confirms. The ring-a-ling of the bell on the door heralds the twins' arrival. The two move in unison toward us upon seeing their mother.

"There are my girls!" Lorelei lights up. It is a mother's joy as seen on Julie's face when she sees our girls.

"Mom!" The two young women protest. "We're 28!"

"I don't care how old you are you'll always be my girls," Lorelei brushes off the protests. "Come here." She wraps both daughters in a vice grip hug.

"Mom, geez! You just saw us this morning." The protests continue.

"Don't care. Happy to see you no matter how long it's been." She releases her grip. "Come meet my friend." Hope and Faith move toward me flanking their mom, one on each side.

She turns to her right and then left. "Faith, Hope, this is my friend Eric. He's a friend of mine from elementary school who is passing through town. We've been catching up."

"Hi," says Faith. "Hey there," greets Hope. Their tone is neutral but not unfriendly. I extend my hand to each of them and return the greeting. Faith has a small, crescent-shaped scar just to the side of her right eye. It's the only way to tell them apart.

I turn back toward the table and grab my cell phone and say, "Your mom mentioned you're going to lunch so I should be heading out. I don't want to delay your plans."

Lorelei's shoulders droop slightly. "Eric, I don't want to push you out the door. Stay a few more minutes. Please."

The two young ladies echo their mom's sentiment. "Oh, don't run out on our account," Faith pleads. Hope nods in agreement.

"No, no, you're fine. I should go anyway," I hold firm about my departure.

Lorelei doesn't hide her disappointment. "I understand. It was just so much fun hanging out and chatting. Thanks for letting me know you were passing through. This was terrific. Please let me know if you get this way again." Lorelei throws caution to the wind and gives me a quick hug in front of her daughters. If the girls are bothered by a man embracing their mother, they don't show it.

"Oh, I will. Kudos on the choice of the coffee shop," I say taking one last look around Smokey's. "Faith, Hope, very nice meeting you. Thanks for letting me spend some time with your mom during girls' weekend." I smile and shake hands with both of them. They smile and nod at me.

My path to the door takes me between them and the wall of booths. I'm out the door and into the noon day sun in ten steps. Half a block after that I'm in my SUV and on my way back to Minnesota. Using the hands-free device in my vehicle I command my phone to call my boo. She answers three rings later.

"Hey, sweetie, how are you today? Any news for me?"

I guffaw at the last question. "Boo, I am on cloud nine-point-five. You won't believe all that's happened since we talked last night."

"I'm sitting on the couch with a glass of wine and a jazz CD in the background. Talk to me," Julie encourages.

"After we talked last night I jotted some notes to record my impressions and what I learned from Laurel and Todd. Oh! Don't let me forget to do that for Lorelei when I get home. Important to jot down thoughts while they're fresh." I momentarily take myself off track.

"Come back to me, Eric," Julie directs. "You were jotting notes last night."

"Oh, yeah. Thanks." Getting my thought train back on the rails I continue. "Got done making notes and got a flash of inspiration for songs that the band could sing. Five! Five songs! Brain going a million miles an hour. Some of the inspiration came from Laurel's and Todd's experiences and some from experiences we had as kids. Got an idea for at least one more song after talking with Lorelei today."

"What did you do with your ideas? Did you write the songs?"

"No. I sent Lis the outline themes with a few lines for context. She'll take that and write the lyrics. Goal is to have at least eight songs. Well on my way there," I respond.

"What was Lorelei like? Was she nice?"

"Nice?" The word is completely inadequate. "Lorelei is a live wire. The fear of awkward got tossed out the window the moment we said hello. Very friendly. Wicked sense of humor. Can't wait for you to meet her. You're going to hit it off immediately."

"I look forward to it," Julie says. "Sounds like you had fun."

"I did but the conversations did get serious at times," my voice drops. "Long story short, Lorelei's husband died a few years ago. Cancer."

Julie's voice exudes sympathy. "How awful. Does she have kids?"

"Twin girls – Hope and Faith – who are a little older than Nicole. "Had a chance to meet them."

Julie's voice rises in surprise like I was someplace I ought not be. "How?"

"They were in town to spend time with their mom and Lorelei asked them to meet her at the coffee shop we were at before going to lunch. She introduced us in passing as I was leaving and they were entering. Didn't have a chance to say much to them other than 'hello and gotta go'."

"Interesting," she says. It's the ambiguous, non-committal use of the word that makes the hair on the back of my neck stand up.

Springing a Leek | 105

Julie has been very understanding and very supportive of this trip down my personal rabbit hole but sometimes I wonder how far I'm pushing her out of her comfort zone with all my activities to get my childhood friends back together.

"Interesting but not interesting," attempting to cut that train off at the pass. Or train off at the past might be more appropriate. "Nothing to see here, boo. I'm yours now and forever and happily so."

"I trust you but not always other women," she asserts. "If you're going to be a rock and roll star, there's going to be groupies throwing their panties at you."

"I don't even know what to do with that," is my response. "Are you serious?"

Julie says, "About the not trusting other women, yes. About the groupies, maybe." She chuckles. "Anything else from your coffee with Lorelei you'd like to tell me?"

"Hmm...as a matter of fact, yes. She has an artistic side and likes to play her keyboard and sometimes goes out to sing karaoke. How about that?"

"That must be exciting to learn," Julie replies. "What about Laurel and Todd? Do they play or sing?"

"They still play their guitars in their spare time from what I gathered looking on Facebook but beyond that I don't think so. It didn't come up. Hadn't planned on talking about it with Lorelei but when I asked her what she does to cope and socialize with her husband being gone, that was one of the things she mentioned. Talk about the dominos lining up. Oh."

"Oh, what?" Julie follows up.

"It just hit me that her deceased husband's name was Dominic so I shouldn't use clichés that involve derivations of his name."

"I'm sure she doesn't fall to pieces over dominoes or anything else but it's nice that you're concerned for her well-being."

"Yeah, I'm probably being silly. Anyway, one of the positives is that Lorelei might be an easier sell than I thought. Todd will be the toughest. That I'm sure about. Laurel..." my voice trails off, "can't get a read on her. Worry about all that when the day comes."

"When are you going to be home?"

A quick glance allows me to notice that I'm at the Story City exit. "I'm at Story City. Little over two hours from home."

"You should be focusing on your driving. Why don't you fill me in on the rest when you get home? There's a spot on the couch reserved for that fine ass of yours," my wife flirts.

"Better set the cruise so I don't speed," I flirt back. The call ends and I check to make sure my cruise is set on 70 miles per hour on the nose.

What a weekend.

* * *

March 31, 2018

Who knew having so much fun could be so exhausting?

Rolling out of bed at 8 a.m. on a Saturday should be less strenuous. Feel like a truck hit me and then backed over me to see what it hit. Sure, it's easy to chalk up dragging my body out of bed to getting older but it's not aches and pains that make me feel a crane is the proper method to extract me from the mattress. No, this sensation that makes hauling my carcass out of bed so challenging is the impossible schedule I've been keeping.

The pace of life is now warp speed since getting back from the coffee meeting with Lorelei and my ol' bod is putting up a very effective protest. Among life, work, and the band reunion I've left little time for sleeping. The descent from the bedroom to the main floor necessitates a tight grasp on the railing...just in case gravity tries to gain the upper hand and pinwheels me down the staircase. There's more grunting and groaning than I'd care to admit. Finally a successful navigation of the stairs and a deliberate amble brings me to the kitchen where Julie is pulling an egg bake from the oven.

"Morning, sweetie," she greets. "This has to cool but should be ready to eat shortly. Coffee?"

"Please. On an I.V. drip."

Julie pours the morning roast in my Batman mug. "Didn't you sleep well last night?" She asks, handing the mug to me.

"Slept great. That's the problem. Last night was the first restful night's sleep I've had in a week. Too much go and not enough whoa," a slight interruption of the thought to introduce the day's first wave of caffeine to my system. "Hoping my body shakes off the fatigue once the protein and caffeine take hold."

Julie pulls a table knife out of the drawer as the ceramic bakeware holds the egg bake, steam rising ever so slowly from it. A spatula goes in and comes away with a corner piece. Julie places it on a small ceramic plate and delivers it to me.

The corner piece has a perfect char on two sides. Charred enough to be crunchy and maintain the structural integrity of the piece but without the burned taste. I pick up the fork at my place setting and plunge it into the egg bake. The first bite is a warm, savory "howdy do" that is about to announce itself to the rest of me. The one-two combination of coffee and the egg bake course through my being.

"This is my favorite thing you make for breakfast, boo."

"Thanks. I do enjoy the savory side as well." Julie makes sure the oven is turned off and then says, "Is there anything else you need? If not, I'm going to start organizing the basement. We neglected it over the winter. It's a mess."

Shaking my head, finishing the next bite before speaking, I reply, "Nope. I'm fine. While you organize I'm going to get ready to face the day and figure out some logistics for the band."

"Logistics?" Julie poses.

"Trying to figure out when to get the four of us together so I can finally tell them about the reunion. You know, the where, the when...all the little stuff," I say with a quick raise of my left eyebrow.

"What are you thinking?" Julie asks.

"Beyond the business side of things, I think it's time to get everyone together and pitch the idea. I want to check with everyone to see if the second Saturday in April would work to meet for supper. Most efficient path would be to find a place to eat in Ames...close enough to make it easy for them to attend. That's what I have so far. Am I missing anything?"

"Let me see if I'm clear on this...you're planning on just the four of you meeting but you're asking them individually with them not knowing it's a group thing?" Julie clarifies.

"That's it."

"Follow me on this, Eric. Todd and Lorelei aren't married so no problem there but what about Laurel?"

"What about Laurel?" I reply not following my bride's thought.

"First you ask her to coffee and it's you two alone. Now you're going to ask her to meet you for supper? If I were her husband I'd be suspicious to no end. Besides, I'm your wife and I want to meet these people you're so desperate to reunite," Julie closes the loop on her thought.

She raises some fine points. The band took so much focus that the practical, relationship aspect escaped me. Seth and Laurel – individually and as a couple – would and should be suspicious if I handle this the way Julie has pointed out.

"Wouldn't it be more natural to say we'll be in the area and want to get together?" Before I can answer she advances her thought. "Not only that but won't Laurel need to talk with Seth about what you want to do? Shouldn't you have all the decision makers at the table?"

Her words hit me where I work. One of the key fundamentals in marketing and in selling is to make sure all the decision makers are in the room. Always. No exceptions.

"And here I thought I married you for your egg bake." I smile. "Obviously all of that was staring me in the face and I still flat overlooked it. You're absolutely correct. And it makes sense for me to say 'we'll be in town let's get together' than just a solo meet again. Second Saturday in April work for you?"

"Yes it does," Julie agrees.

"Let's hope getting the others on board for supper is as easy as you are."

Julie walks up to me and gives me a little peck on the cheek. As she walks away, Julie looks over her shoulder and says, "Glad I could help...and don't call me easy."

* * *

April 14, 2018

Can't remember the last time I've been this anxious. Being at an Applebee's doesn't normally put me on edge but this isn't a normal circumstance. Julie and I are sitting at Applebee's in Ames, Iowa, and today is the day the band reunites though the two of us are the only ones who know it. It took some doing and some scheduling gymnastics but I was able to finagle my four past and future bandmates to join me. Each person thinks it's a casual supper with Julie and me as we're passing through the area.

Applebee's seemed like a safe choice. This Applebee's smells and looks like any other. It's decorated to fit the interest of the area's sports fans. Every square inch of wall space contains larger-than-life photos of the local high school teams, the hometown college Iowa State Cyclones, and the Iowa Cubs; the Chicago Cubs' Triple-A team in Des Moines.

Five o'clock is the meet time but Julie and I rolled in at 4:30 to make sure we are here first and that all is ready when the others join us. I'd called the manager earlier this week to reserve a table for six which meant rearranging some small tables and chairs to make one long table with a chair on each end and two at the sides.

Julie and I are positioned so we can see the door. My breathing is deep and slow in an attempt to keep myself calm. Pressure on my shoulders threatens to push me through the floor. All the work, the planning, the practice...it's all for nothing if tonight doesn't go well. Marketing is all about selling a story, having people identify with it, and closing the deal. Is a good story going to be enough for them to sign on for this particular rock and roll fantasy?

Fantasy takes a flying leap when the first of my once and future bandmates walks through that door. The pressure on me comes down to one word: Rejection. If the others say no to my reunion tour idea, it's over. My band dream rejected yet again for the last time. This final rejection will leave a wound open that has no hope of healing...just a constant ache, like arthritis of my soul.

"It's going to be okay, Eric. Just relax and stop putting pressure on yourself," Julie says. We've been married long enough for her to recognize what my silence means. A nod is my only response. My eyes are fixed on the entrance. My heart jumps each time the door opens. The room feels warm. A voice in the corner of my head whispers, *Get out of here while you still can.*

Then it's too late to run. The door opens and Lorelei strolls in, her head doing a side to side sweep until she catches sight of my hand in the air signaling that her place is over here. She smiles and alerts the hostess she's with us. We never break eye contact as she makes her way over. I rise to be ready to give her a proper welcome.

"Lorelei's here," I announce to Julie.

Julie looks up. "Wow. She's pretty. Is she the one who lost her husband?"

"Yes."

Lorelei is wearing blue jeans with a pair of black, knee-length boots, with a white, knit top, and jean jacket. Her thin-strap, black purse swings on her left shoulder like a pendulum about to fly off.

"Eric!" Lorelei is a force of nature, throwing her arms wide as she gives me a hello hug. "You must be Julie! Hi!" She throws a hug on Julie who returns the hug in self-defense. "It's wonderful to finally meet you!"

"Eric has told me so much about you," Julie says as each woman steps back from the embrace. "I've looked forward to meeting you."

"So excited to be here," Lorelei replies, hanging her purse on the chair.

She notices we're at a table that's not for three. Her brows furrow with a lack of understanding. "Seems like the party's bigger than I was expecting."

"A few more friends will be joining us," I confirm. "I hope that's okay."

Lorelei smiles. "More than okay. Surprises are fun."

Heart's still racing but the fluttering is calming down. Lorelei's response is promising but three more people have yet to weigh in.

"Please, sit down," I invite; pulling out the chair she hung her purse on. I do the same for Julie with the chair next to the end. I seat myself to Julie's right.

"Eric tells me you have twin daughters," Julie starts the conversation. "We have two daughters also."

"Yeah. They're a handful, those two," Lorelei says, pulling out her phone and locating a picture of her with the twins. "Hope and Faith. They're my whole life."

"Gorgeous," Julie admires. "They look just like their mother. What do they do?"

The conversation between the two moms is off and running. Julie pulls out her phone to show Lorelei pictures of Nicole and Ashley and they start trading proud mom stories. I'm not necessary for the chat at this point and that's fine by me. The conversation calms me and lets me focus on watching the door open and close till the next guests arrive.

Minutes pass before I recognize that my right leg has been pounding like a jackhammer. Guess the heart flutter traveled south. If the ladies to my left notice my nervousness, they don't let on. A flash of light reflecting off the glass door as it opens catches my attention. Laurel and Seth walk in and are greeted by the hostess.

Popping out of my seat, I move to greet them. Julie and Lorelei notice my abrupt movement and turn their heads toward the door. "Laurel and Seth are here. Be right back."

"Do I know them?" Lorelei asks Julie as I dart off.

"I think so," Julie says. "I know them from Eric's class reunions."

Laurel and Seth walk toward me as I approach them. Laurel is wearing a white skirt with a yellow sleeveless blouse. The neckline reveals a little cleavage. Seth is wearing a pair of khaki shorts, an untucked Hawaiian print shirt, and sandals. Seth, who was in the class behind the rest of us, has aged well. His hair shows no hint of gray...still as dark as when we were in high school.

"Laurel, Seth! Great to see you!" I give Laurel a hug and Seth a firm handshake. "Come on, we're over here." Laurel and Seth follow me to the table.

As we get closer Laurel says, "Oh, who's with Julie?"

Julie and Lorelei stand up. I announce each to our two new guests. "Laurel and Seth, you know my wife Julie and this is our friend Lorelei." The four greet one another. Laurel has a look on her face that conveys she should know who Lorelei is but can't place her. And the reverse is true too.

"Laurie!"

"Lori! Oh my gosh!"

There is a gleeful hug once the respective light bulbs go off. My heart is flutter-free for the first time since Julie and I arrived at Applebee's.

"How long has it been?" Laurel asks, backing away but each woman keeping their hands on the other's upper arms.

"I moved away after fifth grade so," Lorelei's eyes go up toward the ceiling when one is trying to mentally grasp information just out of reach,"...too damn long ago."

The five of us start laughing, one because it's funny and two because it's true. Leave it to Lorelei to put everyone at a state of comfort. There are smiles all around.

I guide Laurel and Seth to their side of the table with a sweep of my right hand. Laurel and Julie sit to Lorelei's left and right respectively. Seth and I sit across from one another. Hmm. Apparently it's women at one end, men at the other. The next few minutes are spent catching up. It's what have you been doing, talk of kids, and sharing of photos on phones.

A reflection flash catches me in the eye and causes me to flinch. My attention goes to the door. The flutter comes back.

"Excuse me, one more party to join us." Four more sets of eyes go to the door as I get up.

Laurel turns back toward the table and asks, "Is that Todd Kane?"

Julie nods. "I've never met him but Eric has shown me pictures. That's Todd."

Seth says just before I'm out of earshot, "This is not the evening I thought it would be. What's next?" His tone is not cheery.

Todd scans the room and sees me heading straight for him. He's wearing a pair of blue jeans, short-sleeved plaid casual shirt,

Springing a Leek | 115

and cowboy boots. His hands are on his hips, non-verbally communicating he's spent enough time here already and is fine if he turns around and goes home.

"Todd! Hey, man, great to see you. Thanks for coming." I reach out for his hand and we exchange a hearty handshake.

"I didn't have anything else going on so why not?" Todd stays non-committal to the evening. The hope is the positive vibes currently at the table are greater than the negative one in front of me.

"Table's this way, come on."

Todd is a stride behind me till we get to the table and he sidles up beside me. All eyes look up with a mixture of anticipation and uncertainty about all of this.

"Hey, everyone, it's Todd Kane." All seated at the table rise making me feel I'm the bailiff and Todd is a judge just entering the courtroom. Individual introductions are made starting with Julie, then Lorelei, Laurel, and Seth. The two of us then head to our end of the table.

"While you went to escort Todd here the server came over and we ordered two servings of the sampler platter appetizers," Julie tells me.

"That's fine by me."

"I think the headline is that Eric is Todd's escort," Seth teases. Todd smacks Seth's arm with the back of his right hand. Seth and I beam. Todd actually smiles. Oh, the humanity.

The women shake their heads. "Sometimes I don't get guys," Laurel states.

"What's with the hitting?" Lorelei chimes in.

"And the Three Stooges? What is so flippin' funny about the Three Stooges?" Julie laments.

"Nothing!" the artists formerly known as Laurie and Lori respond in unison.

Seth's joke brings the mood back to upbeat all around. This is what I envisioned. Childhood friends gathered together sharing a meal, memories, merriment, and - God willing - music.

"Has anyone asked what the heck this is all about?" Todd refocuses on the table. "Anyone else think it was going to be just you and these two?" Todd gestures in Julie's and my direction.

Seth is the first to answer Todd's inquiry. "We sure did. Thought it would be just us and them for dinner. Not upset about the extra people but curious why the deception."

Laurel and Lorelei say nothing but their expression and body language concur with Seth and Todd. Julie is in the corner of my eye looking at me waiting to see what the answer is. The word I didn't want to hear – deception – stings me.

I nod in understanding. "I know, I know. Please forgive me. I wasn't sure how to do this without it getting weird." Julie tenses up beside me. She doesn't have a sense of where I'm going with this and it's making her nervous. "Earlier this year it hit home about turning 50 and I got nostalgic, remembering childhood and our times in elementary school."

"And you wanted to get us back together," Lorelei puts the pieces in place.

"Exactly," I confirm. "It would have been tacky as hell to just reach out to everyone and say, 'Hey, remember how we used to be friends as kids? Let's all get together'. Maybe it wasn't the best way to handle it but the only thing I could think of was to reach out individually to re-establish our friendships. I figured everyone here knows me so there are no strangers."

Silence. This is when everything could unravel. They could tell me to take a flying leap and walk. Seconds pass and more seconds. In all, probably five but it feels like an eternity.

"You went to a lot of effort to make this happen," Laurel observes.

"I did."

"Let me guess," Todd says, "the day you stopped for coffee you weren't just passing through, you had coffee meetings with all of us."

"Yes. Although, I did stop by the comic book store I told you about."

"You did all this so the four of us could reunite?" Lorelei says seemingly to herself. "I think it's sweet."

Julie relaxes.

"Thanks for understanding. Nostalgia is a strange motivator," I say, poking fun at myself. "Julie has been very supportive through the sentimental journey." All eyes move from me to my wife and look at her warmly save for Todd who maintains emotional distance.

Lorelei puts her hand on Julie's shoulder, giving it a squeeze. "Thanks for supporting Eric in finding us. Not every wife would do that."

Julie smiles. "Getting to know his childhood friends again and learning about you all through him has been a joy for us both. You all have led such interesting lives. He told me how you were as kids in elementary school and now as adults...it's like I already know you though I haven't met all of you before now. I'm so happy it worked out for all of you to be here. I know how happy this makes Eric." She reaches out and takes my left hand.

Our server slides in with our appetizers, setting them in the middle of the table. Todd and I lean in opposite directions to give the server easier access. I catch a glimpse of her nametag.

"Thanks, Heather," I tell her.

"Are you ready to order?" she asks. "Or do you need some more time?"

"More time," Todd answers for the group.

"Oh," Heather realizes, "I need to get your drink orders. Not all of you were here when I first came up so you all just have water. Can I get anyone anything else?"

"I'd like a glass of unsweetened iced tea, please," I start us off.

"I'd like a McGolden Light with three olives in the bottom of the glass," from Julie.

"Mojito, please," Lorelei asks.

"Strawberry margarita," Laurel requests.

"Glass of Blue Moon," Seth orders.

"I'll have the same," Todd brings the round to a close.

"Sounds good, guys," Heather chirps happily. "I'll be back with those."

The evening goes as I'd hoped it would from then on. Among ordering our food, eating our meal together and the conversation that flavors it, this supper together is only slightly ranked behind the family meals with Julie and the girls in my level of enjoyment. This night feels very much like a family reunion.

There is light conversation mixed with serious moments when talking of life's happenings since we were last together. We have a mutual appreciation of the paths we've taken and the lives we've led that have brought us here.

"Okay, hang on a minute," Laurel brings a halt to the flow of the conversation. "Who's 50...of the four of us?" She raises her hand.

"Next week," Todd answers.

"June," I say.

"September," Lorelei shares.

"Oh, great, I'm it," Laurel laments.

"Sooo, one senior citizen at the table?" I tease looking around at the chance I've missed someone. I chortle having greatly amused myself.

Julie gasps putting her hands over her mouth. Not supposed to joke about a woman's age, I know. But why not live dangerously? Laurel glares at me but there's a hint of a smile in her eyes so I know she's not angry. Lorelei and Seth purse their lips together, holding back a snicker that is a forgone conclusion. Todd smiles. Don't think I'm getting a chuckle out of him but any reaction is a victory.

Laurel turns her attention to her husband. The effort not to snort is taking its toll; his face is now as red as the apple on the menu. "Don't you dare, Seth. Don't you dare."

Lorelei breaks first and all it takes is the first one. The table erupts and joins in even Todd the curmudgeon. It turns into that thing when everyone is almost calmed down and then one person starts guffawing and everyone is back to hysterics. I have to remove my glasses to clear the tears from my eyes.

"Oh, stop, stop," Julie pleads. "My stomach hurts."

"I think I'm going to pee my pants!" Lorelei exclaims.

Our laughter has not gone unnoticed by our fellow patrons. No one seems to mind but no one gets the joke. Soon their attention turns back to their own tables. The six of us manage to regain our composure.

"Inappropriate much?" Laurel fires across the table in mock disgust.

"Oh, like every day of his life," Julie steps in. "You should try being married to this guy."

"You have my sympathies," Laurel deadpans.

"Hey!" I protest briefly. "Okay, I earned that. But it's okay. At your age, you probably won't remember how I offended you."

The period of my sentence barely hit the air when Julie backhands my shoulder. "Eric! Stop that!"

"Ow!"

"That's for Laurel," Julie admonishes me. "Respect your elders."

Laurel's eyes go wide as she is taken off guard by Julie's sly humor. A pause. The table roars again. Laurel perhaps the hardest, appreciating her surprise at Julie's humor.

"Things must be very interesting at your house," Lorelei says.

"Oh, you have no idea," Julie confirms.

"True story," I add. Scanning our group, spirits are high and the mood light. Everyone is enjoying themselves.

Heather returns to clear our plates asking if we'd like refills of our drinks which we all answer yes. We are all quiet for a few moments, reflecting. We've been together for about 90 minutes and, thus far, tonight is exceeding expectations. This seems to be an acceptable time to unveil the grand plan.

"Julie, would you get the picture out of your bag, please?"

Julie nods, leaning toward me, her large bag resting on the floor between our chairs. She pulls out a twice-folded piece of paper in the shape of a square and hands it to me. The four others watch intently with the intensity I'm about to perform a magic trick.

I begin unveiling the idea by first unfolding the paper. "The year was 1977. We were in 4th grade. Four kids had a vision of the future," is how things get underway.

"For crying out loud, get to the point," Todd interrupts. "Spit it out."

Julie stares daggers at him while the other three furrow their brows wondering why he's in such a hurry and what I'm driving at. "Do any of you remember T.E.L.L?"

Todd, Laurel, and Lorelei look at me in a state of non-recollection. T.E.L.L is not ringing a bell. Not sure what I think about that. I hand the now flat piece of paper to Todd since he was so insistent in me getting to the point.

"I...remember now. Oh good God, of course you kept this," Todd snorts like a bull handing the paper to Seth without making eye contact.

Seth examines the paper and shrugs, not knowing what he's looking at, then passes it to his wife.

Laurel takes the paper holding it in both hands. She studies it intently. The table remains silent and I become aware how quiet the entire restaurant is now too. My heart quickens its pace. Julie's hand moves to my left thigh and gently squeezes in support.

"This...this is that band...from 4th grade?" Laurel searches for confirmation of her recollection.

"Correct," I answer.

Lorelei's face shows a quizzical expression, a mix of amusement and curiosity. She leans over to view the picture with Laurel. She grasps the side of the paper with her right hand, turning it slightly to get a better look.

Laurel releases the paper letting it rest on the table top. Seth is resting his chin on his hand deferring any comments until he sees what his wife thinks.

"Oh. My. Goodness! Yes!" Lorelei exclaims. "I remember this. On the playground. You drew this to show us what our band would look like." She lets go of the paper and returns to her previous sitting position satisfied her memory has not failed her.

Laurel reaches across the table to hand the paper back to me. Her face is non-committal. My eye contact is with her but I can sense how tense Todd's body language is. The count thus far is Lorelei, positive, Todd, negative, Laurel...hard to read.

"You did all this to, what, show us a picture?" Todd breaks the silence.

"Yeah...I'm a little confused by all of this." Laurel seems to be leaning toward Todd's side.

Seth leans back in his chair and folds his arms. Everyone is waiting for the other shoe to drop.

Deep breath in, deep breath out. "Let me tell you a story." I share the Cliff Notes version of the tale of when I spoke to Aniko's classes and sharing with them the story of The Band That Never Was. I'm hoping my friends have the same reaction Ani's students had and that my friends will want to do something about it.

Lorelei's face goes from its normal bright to a muted empathy. "Eric, that's horrible. Who would say that to a kid? So you never learned how to play drums?"

"Not until a few months ago, no. One of the students in my sister's class has been giving me drum lessons the past few months. But before that, no."

"That doesn't seem like Trip at all. He was always good to me. Band was one of my highlights all through school," are the first words Laurel utters since viewing the picture.

"Yeah, me too," Todd echoes. "But so what? You went through all this work to get us together to tell us about a 7th grade sob story about something you wanted to do in 4th grade and never did?" One thing hasn't changed. Todd was never one to shy away from saying what he thinks.

"Not exactly," I answer. "The night after I told my story to Aniko's classes, I couldn't sleep. Somewhere in the night it dawned on me that it had been 40 years since the four of us were on that elementary school playground talking about being a band."

I pause to take a sip of iced tea. The sip gives me an opportunity to take stock of the effect my tale is having. Only Todd seems unmoved. Then it's back to my explanation but then not.

"Fine. You couldn't sleep. Why are we here?" Todd presses.

Rip the bandage off it is. "I want us to become the band. I want T.E.L.L to become a reality and for us to do a little reunion tour." There. I said it. Julie grips my thigh a little tighter.

Lorelei and Laurel's eyes go wide and mouths hang open. Seth looks at me like I've lost my marbles. Todd rolls his eyes and sneers. Not exactly surprised by it but not thrilled either.

"I don't even know what to do with that statement," Laurel says.

"A band? At our age?" Lorelei lightly objects. "How would that work?"

That's the question and invitation I've been expecting. "Julie, would you please grab the packets out of your purse?"

Julie releases my thigh so she can reach down to her oversized purse that sits on the floor between our chairs. She sits upright and hands me four comb-bound packets that contain the business plan for the band. I keep one copy and hand each one of my friends their own copy.

"What's this?" Todd asks.

"The answer to Lorelei's question," I begin after handing Lorelei her copy last. "Listen, I'm not expecting us to become a band that constantly tours. But what if we played a few dates for fun, just to fulfill what we talked about as kids?"

"What are we holding exactly?" Laurel asks. She still appears perplexed by what's transpired the last few minutes.

"It's a business plan. I figured there'd be plenty of questions – understandably so – and I want to make sure I have this all laid out so you have a clear understanding about how this all works wrapped up in a nice, neat bow."

"You're insane," Todd says with all the sensitivity of a brick. "You want to have a reunion tour for a band that never was? And you barely play drums? You think you can play concert level in a handful of months?"

"The reunion isn't about performing. The reunion is about us getting back together – the four of us – and fulfilling a lifelong dream. And, yes, I think I can be ready for performing. I'm not claiming I'll be the greatest drummer ever. But I'm not going to embarrass us either." I finish the thought but casually drop another shoe. "That's why I've kept the arrangement of the songs simple."

Laurel leans toward me. "The songs? What songs?"

My focus turns to her but I include the others by turning my head as I respond. "I've been working with a freelancer to write and arrange some original songs for us. They're based on our experiences and experiences with which our contemporaries can identify. The songs are in the back of the business plan packet."

"Are we still going to be called T.E.L.L?" Lorelei wonders. "Doesn't that seem a little, well, childish? No offense."

"No, that's okay. I get it and I agree. The new name of the band is Onions At A Crime Scene."

"Onions at a what now?" Laurel checks to make sure that her hearing hasn't gone haywire.

"Onions At A Crime Scene. Listen, I know it's left field but it's just off the wall enough to catch on. I can explain the origin of the name later. It's secondary to the plan itself."

Lorelei chuckles in genuine amusement. "It is a bit goofy but a neat goofy." She flips through the pages to gauge how many pages are in the packet. "I'll play along."

Laurel comes back in. "What genre is this band…is Onions At A Crime Scene?"

Todd smacks his right palm on the table. We all jump as do the people at the tables around us. "We are not a band! Am I the only one who thinks this – he's – nuts?"

Ignoring the outburst, I answer, "Think of the Mamas and the Papas meet ABBA meet Live."

Laurel says nothing. She is taking in information but not sharing what she thinks of it.

Lorelei makes a face that conveys I may have just said the first rational thing she's heard. "Interesting. Gotta admit, kinda liking it. Not there yet but warming up to the idea."

"Let me get this straight," Todd cuts in without injuring the tabletop. "We have a new name, a genre and, apparently, some songs. Why do people care about seeing us play? We…" Todd stops himself. Lorelei, Julie, and I smile. Todd catches what he said and starts again. "This imaginary band, why would people want to come see a concert of a band they've never heard of that has never performed before that has no hit songs?"

Though he remains skeptical I take heart that he's engaged. From a sales perspective, objections aren't necessarily a *no* but a request for more information. I can give him that. As long as we're all seated here, I'm still in the game.

"It's all about the dream. How many people are out there who are of our generation who gave up a dream for any number of reasons? Not only can we be an inspiration but a motivation for people to realize it's not too late to chase and to accomplish their dreams."

"Even if that's true," Laurel pops in, "it doesn't fully address Todd's question."

"Think of it this way. The Grateful Dead didn't have a Top 40 hit until 1987 and they were cultural icons by then. Even if we don't have a hit single – if we have catchy songs that resonate with people – they will be drawn to our music...even if they've never heard the songs before or if they've been hits."

"That may be true 30 years ago before the internet," Todd remains on the offensive, "but today with the internet people are going to look for us online and they're going to find, what? Nothing?"

My head shakes. "They'll find enough. I have built a website that all searches will point to and people will find out about the history of the band, our album, interviews, tour dates, everything."

Laurel shakes her head trying to clear cobwebs. "What... what? Slow down. This is too much too fast."

Todd picks up her sentiment and runs with it. "We have an album? What interviews and tour dates? What the hell are you talking about?"

My hands come up like I'm pushing against an invisible wall. "Not yet. But I'm thinking we can record the songs at some point and sell them on music streaming services. I'm confident we'll book some tour dates that we can put on the site. Interviews with radio stations too. I have a lot of media contacts which will be helpful."

"Tour dates?" Lorelei queries. "How many tour dates and where?"

"I'm thinking three. Like I said, I'm not suggesting we do this indefinitely. Just a few dates over a few months or so and call it done." Lorelei keeps asking questions I really want to answer so I keep on going. "As far as where the gigs would be...Minneapolis, St. Louis, Chicago. Small clubs but certainly not dive bars. Nothing is set up but I've identified some possibilities. It's all in there."

"No, no. Come back," Todd directs. "Again, how are people going to find out about us in general to determine if they want to come to a performance?" He is like a dog with a bone on this.

"You said 'us'." I can't help but tweak the most skeptical member of our party. Todd gives me a weak glare, more his use of the word, 'us', not so much that I'm teasing him about it.

"Part of my strategy is to use the Evel Knievel method of creating demand in an entertainment act."

"Evel Knievel?" Lorelei brings her eyes off the page. "As in the stunt rider?"

"Correct." Without skipping a beat, I provide the details on how Evel Knievel created demand for his stunt riding act when he was the first of his kind. I add that social media can help create a grassroots demand too.

"But people are going to go on the internet and find almost nothing about a reunion tour for a band that hasn't done anything in 40 years. I mean, ever," Laurel says in case it hadn't occurred to me.

"Yes. How many times do people search for something and the more they can't find the harder they try? It's all curiosity and believing something must be out there...they just haven't found it yet."

Todd comes back in like he's Laurel's tag team partner in this objection match. "Baloney. You know what? This is like...when was that?" Todd looks up to the ceiling searching his memory banks for the correct reference. "6th grade!" He looks at me. "Back in 6th grade we had that Bigfoot club. There were about half a dozen of us who met regularly to try to prove the existence of Bigfoot. We looked for articles in the Des Moines Register, National Geographic, you name it. We found nothing except maybe an article a year on some so-called sighting. Remember?"

"I remember."

"We looked so damn hard and found nothing and we just kept looking. We never found anything and we just...kept...looking. Aw, crap." I grin at my former best friend as he realizes he's just made my point for me.

Lorelei chuckles not missing the irony of Todd's walking into my thesis. She grins at Todd. He shoots her a look of mild annoyance more out of embarrassment than irritation at her. She asks, "Let's say we agree that this so-called reunion should happen.

How do we actually know we can play together or even sound decent together?"

Lorelei's question makes me smile. This type of question goes to logistics not my sanity. Progress. "If, and I stress *if*, we are up for it I thought later we could go do some karaoke and find out. Maybe that's how we make our decision on whether this is a go or no go."

"Band or not, I'd love to do some karaoke," Lorelei lights up. "I'm up for that."

Laurel picks up her phone and checks the time. "Well, we certainly could do that. I'm not saying I'm in for this band thing but karaoke does sound fun."

I emphasize perhaps the most important point I can make here, "Hey, I'm not expecting any decisions tonight. None. Other than we sing karaoke. That's it. I'm sorry to be throwing all this at you at once. I know this is out of the blue. I know this is a lot to take in. This is why I've done what I've done the way I've done it. But I realize you're trying to process in a few moments what I've been working on for months."

Lorelei and Laurel exchange a look and then look toward Todd. They nod. Lorelei's the most animated. Todd the least. An unexpected voice asks a question.

"Hey," Seth starts, "I know I'm not part of this band thing but I have a question because if Laurel's involved then I'm involved." He looks around to see if he can continue and, seeing no resistance, does. "Who's paying for all of this?" Seth asks me. "You've incurred some costs. Probably spent a little bit up to this point but there will be more coming up. We on the hook for that?"

Again this is a logistical question not a *should this even happen* question. I'm a bit surprised it's taken this long for someone to ask about the money. "Thank you, Seth, I appreciate the question. First off, I didn't come up with the idea to spend your money or take on any debt. I'd like us to break even at the very least but maybe make a little money."

Heads are nodding which is a positive sign. "My oldest daughter gave me the idea of getting the tour sponsored by an energy drink company. I mean, doesn't every concert tour have a corporate sponsor? It's..."

"A corporate sponsor? You've officially lost it. A sponsor for a band that doesn't exist..."

"Todd, stop," Lorelei sticks her arm out like she's Diana Ross. "I want to hear this."

"There are two energy drink companies that responded to my initial inquiry, requesting formal proposals. At this moment, both are considering sponsoring the tour. If either comes through for us, all our expenses would be paid. Recording our songs in the studio, travel expenses...all of it."

Everyone at the table except Julie exhales in contemplation. A low murmur of conversation in the restaurant becomes noticeable. I'm not in sell mode anymore so I am only speaking when answering questions. Not sure how to take Julie's silence other than quiet support. I wonder what she thinks about the others' reactions at this point.

"I know I've been skeptical..." Todd starts.

"...borderline jerky..." Lorelei inserts.

"...and I'm not saying you're not crazy – but I'm a little less so. Still not on board but I'm not dismissing it."

That's a start. My gut told me Todd would be the tough sell before I ever set up this meeting. The fact he's still thinking about it is a win in itself. Todd looks across the table at the two women. "What do you ladies think?"

The two look at each other before responding. Lorelei answers Todd first. "The idea seems fun and I'm intrigued but I still have more questions before I'm committing to anything. Eric's got a lot of legitimate answers. Laurel?"

Laurel looks down at a business plan she hasn't read. Laurel is a bottom line person and she is trying to bottom line my idea in her head as much as she can. "I'm with you, Lorelei. Intrigued is the word. But not ready to say yes. Seth, what do you think?"

"All of this is a bit out there for me and I know we went to school together," Seth turns and looks me in the eyes, "but I'm not sure I trust your motives with all the manipulating of circumstances and of people – including Laurel. But," he says, turning his gaze back to his wife, "if you decide to do this, I'll support it."

"I get it. I do. Your consideration is all I'm asking for tonight. No pressure," I assure.

Heather makes a return appearance. "No rush. Here's your bill." I pluck the debit card out of my wallet before anyone can react and place it on the little tray she's holding and then send her on her way. Four surprised faces stare at me.

"Hey, I told you I'm not here to spend your money. Julie and I invited you here, it's our treat," I tell them.

"We're happy to do it. Regardless of what happens, I've enjoyed being a small part of this journey and getting to know you all tonight." Those are the first words Julie's uttered since I dropped the Onions bombshell.

Then the explosion truly happens. "What the hell is this?" Todd's voice is loud enough that the rest of the patrons in Applebee's fall silent. Todd ejects himself from his chair and in one motion, grabs me by my shirt, pulls me from my chair, and nearly lifts me off the floor before anyone knows what's happening.

"You had no right! I ought to beat the shit out of you for this!" Todd isn't speaking so much as growling. His face is red. His carotid artery is throbbing. His knuckles are white as a sheet. His nose is almost touching mine. I can smell what he had for lunch three days ago.

"Hey!" Julie springs from her seat as do the rest of our not-yet band. She tries to separate us. Seth grabs Todd trying to keep him from following up on his threat. He cannot get Todd to break his grip.

"What is wrong with you?" Laurel accuses. "Have you lost your mind?"

"Let him go, Todd!" Lorelei implores.

"Is this all some sort of sick game to you? Screwing with people's lives? Screwing with our lives? My life? Is it?"

Todd's reaction doesn't shock me. His ferocity does. In the meantime, four servers – all men – run to us. People at nearby tables and booths try to distance themselves. Those people who aren't nearby lean toward us. Seconds later, two servers have my shoulders and two – plus Seth - have Todd's. I take note that five grown men are on us and can't budge Todd. I may be in a little trouble here. For my part, I'm not resisting. I get why he's angry with me.

"Sir, sir! Stop! Let go!" says a server whose nametag reads "Dan". Todd can only see me in this moment. All around him doesn't exist, only his rage at me. A woman I haven't seen before approaches and identifies herself as the manager.

"Break it up! Break it up! Hey! I'm talking to you!" She is now almost nose to nose with both of us. "You take this crap out of my restaurant now or I'm calling the cops and you can take it up with them!"

Todd relaxes enough to let go of me in the form of a shove, pushing me away. Anyone with a grip on someone else lets go simultaneously. Julie is about ready to go for Todd's throat. I place my hand on Julie's arm to keep her where she is. Everyone takes a breath. The service staff isn't confident that this is over.

"Get your things and get out now," the manager demands. Heather approaches cautiously and hands me my card and receipt.

The six of us grab our stuff from the table. Todd spins on his heels and is headed toward the door. Seth, Laurel, Lorelei, Julie, and I keep our heads down and exit as quickly and quietly as we can. The greeters usher us out into the Saturday evening. They don't tell us to have a nice night.

Lorelei races toward Todd. "What was that all about? You've been questioning Eric's sanity but you look like the madman here."

Todd doesn't back away from her accusation. "Did you read what's in here?" He holds up the business plan. "Did you? It's all here...our lives for everyone to see in these damn lyrics." Todd looks around Lorelei and points a furious left index finger at me. "You're a bastard!"

"Calm down, Todd," Laurel tells him and then turns to me. "What is he talking about? Why is he so upset?"

"It's the songs!" Todd answers a question he wasn't asked.

"Shut up and let Eric answer the question, you jackass!" Julie yells back at him. She has had enough of him this evening.

I gently take her arm and say softly, "It's okay, boo. I don't blame him. It's okay." I turn my attention to Laurel to answer her question. "I told you all earlier that the songs are based on our lives, our experiences. They're not meant to be biographical but can certainly be taken that way. The songs are personal..."

"Very personal!" Todd punctuates.

"...and I don't blame any of you if you're upset with me. This is a personal journey for me too." I look over at Todd and address him directly. "And if it would make you feel better to beat the crap out of me, here I am. I won't stop you." Julie gives me a look that says anyone who wants to take a shot at me goes through her first.

Laurel raises her right hand that holds the business plan. She places in on her left hand and flips to the back of the packet where the lyrics are. "Well, then maybe we should read them."

Lorelei nods.

Seth looks back toward the door and catches sight of four servers and a manager staring daggers at us. Kicking us out isn't enough for them. They want us off the property. "Uh, I think maybe we should take this elsewhere. I think they're close to calling the cops on us."

"Agreed," I reply. "Any suggestions where we take this? Are we taking this anywhere?"

"There's a park nearby," Laurel announces. "Let's drive over there. You all can follow Seth and me."

"Fair enough," Lorelei agrees. "We'll all go." She turns back to Todd and steps into him. "Won't we?"

A grunt of agreement from Todd.

"Okay, then," I say. "See everyone there."

Five minutes later, safely away from the withering glares of the Applebee's manager and staff, we are gathered at the pavilion of the local park. It's a beautiful Spring evening spoiled by the tension that could be cut with a chainsaw. We have reassembled at the picnic table. Todd and I are at opposite ends. Lorelei and Laurel are on his right and left while Seth and Julie are seated to my right and left. Julie is holding my hand.

"Now, then," Laurel starts off like she's calling a board meeting to order. "I think the way to go is for us to read the lyrics. Let's go song by song and see what we think. Sound like a plan?"

"Yes, I like that idea," Lorelei endorses.

Todd grunts.

Laurel proceeds. "Let's turn to the back of the packet and start with the first song. We'll read it and then exchange thoughts before moving to the next." She takes a deep breath. "Okay. First song, *Take The Day*."

With that the reading begins. Seth reads over his wife's shoulder. Julie has my copy and reads along. I am a statue. Don't need to read the packet. I wrote it.

"Cute song," Lorelei breaks the silence. "I like it. Very hopeful."

Laurel tosses a glance my way. "Get the inspiration and motivation you're going for." She then turns to her right. "Todd?"

He only nods.

"Next song. *1986*."

The next round begins. There is a refreshing breeze. It's a beautiful night but I'm not enjoying it. I knew there might be some blowback but not *we got kicked out of an Applebee's* blowback. What the hell is Todd's problem? Has he changed that much since we were kids? Did I do something I'm unaware that has him carrying so much rage towards me?

"I remember doing that!" Lorelei says. "Totally did that." She turns my way. "This brings back fun memories."

"I was a town kid so I walked to school but I recall seeing the busses come in to school and there being these numerals all over the frosty windows," Laurel adds.

"I did this. So did he. Your eights were always fat on the bottom and skinny at the top," Todd says not taking his eyes off the page.

His comment goes unacknowledged by me. Don't give a damn how he thinks my eights looked.

"Moving on," Lorelei says. "*Happy Ever After* up next."

My stomach knots itself over and over. If Todd was pissed about his song, well, let's see if Lorelei wants to kick my ass. Still silent, I read faces. The lyrics play in my head almost in time with the reading speed of the others. Lorelei's eyes well up. Laurel's eyes widen. Todd's expression softens. Tears run down Julie's cheeks. Seth is as expressionless as I am.

Laurel pulls her eyes off the page and puts them on the woman across from her. "Oh, Lorelei, I am so sorry. How awful."

Tears are in the corner of Lorelei's eyes. "It's okay. As I said at supper when you and I were talking about Dom, I've had my time to mourn." Her eyes come around to mine. "I see what you did, that my story was inspiration, not biography. I'm fine with it."

I nod at her in thanks for understanding.

Julie reaches out and puts her hand atop Lorelei's. "I'm so, so sorry for your loss. I can't even imagine."

Lorelei pats Julie's hand. "Thank you. Actually, what Eric wrote was lovely. Think it captures my feelings accurately whether that was the intent or not. It actually makes me feel less alone."

Todd looks at Lorelei and says the first words since wanting to drop me at Applebee's. "I'm sorry too. But, seriously, don't you feel violated? Doesn't this piss you off?"

Lorelei shakes her head. "In getting to know Eric again, I think I know him well enough to know there's no malice in these lyrics. He wants authentic and, from what I've read thus far, that's what it is. Laurel?"

She nods. "It's very authentic. I can see people identifying with what we've read so far. Shall we continue?"

"I don't have to read the next one. Don't really want to," Todd announces staring at me. I engage the stare down and neither of us blinks. I'm about ready to go after him. I've had enough of his bullshit.

"Let's see what got us kicked out of Applebee's," Laurel says. "*Everything Changed*."

The only sound is that of page flipping as all are examining the song lyrics that caused Todd to lose his shit. Julie has never read the lyrics so she's reading them off my copy. Julie gasps as she reads. Seth puts his hand over his mouth and looks at me out of the corner of his eye. Not sure if he needs to be added to the list of people at this table who want to take a poke at me.

"Wooo," Lorelei says. "I had no idea, Todd. I can understand why you're upset. But it's no more personal than the song about me losing my husband." Laurel's head jerks up off the page to look at the other female member of the *about to be extinct band* if things don't improve.

"You lost something you had," Laurel observes. "Todd lost something he never had. And maybe never will. That's so personal." She turns to look at Todd. "I get it." She pauses, looks over at me, and back at Todd. "But I still think you overreacted."

"Maybe," Todd replies. "See if you think that after you read a song about your pain."

"Fair enough," Laurel tells him. "I'm guessing *No Way Back Today* must be mine." Laurel's eyes meet mine. I slowly blink and tilt my head forward as a confirmation. My breathing is slow and deep. Hope is dwindling with the daylight and it will be dark soon. Tonight has painted a picture that I've wasted my time on a pipe dream.

"Okay, people," Laurel announces, "this is totally taking a situation and using creative license. Supposedly, this is my song but the only similarity is that soon Seth and I will be empty nesters and I'm not the basket case the woman in this song is. BUT I can tell you I know a lot of women personally who are the woman in this song. It is dead on." She shakes her head in wonder. "Dead on." She looks over at me. "This is amazing. You and your collaborator have done some impressive work."

"I know I'm not part of this band thing but I have to say, this stuff is legit," Seth echoes. "Impressive."

Still not in the frame of mind to speak so I nod deliberately in response to the comments.

Lorelei takes in what I noticed moments ago. "We'd better finish this fast or we're going to be reading in the dark." The rest of the group takes the cue and continues reading the remainder of the lyrics as quickly as possible. A few crickets sing to us.

Minutes later Lorelei brings her head up. Her eyes sweep the rest of the group. "I've read all the songs and they're exceptional. If we do this, I could easily sing them. What do the rest of you think?"

"I agree," Laurel says. "I'm not committing to anything but the songs make a strong case." She looks left to her husband. "Seth?"

"I'm not sold on the idea, yet. But if you decide to do this, you sure aren't going to embarrass yourself singing this. I'll support whatever your decision is, whenever you make it."

Todd shrugs. No one asks Julie what she thinks but does anyone have to? Probably not.

The other four look at each other not sure what happens where we go from here. "I'll ask it," Laurel states. "What now? What's next?"

Lorelei purses her lips. She taps her right index finger on them. "Hmm. I think the next step is to see how we sound together. Karaoke anyone?"

"Excuse me?" Todd says clearly taken off guard. "We're supposed to sing together now?"

"No, no, that makes sense," Laurel nods. "Eric has this vision that we can be an actual band. Karaoke was brought up earlier. Maybe we *should* sing together. Any suggestions as to where we can do that?"

"A.J.'s on East Court in Des Moines," are the first words to leave my mouth since arriving at the park. "Apparently they have the best karaoke in the city."

"Done?" Laurel asks Lorelei.

"Done." Lorelei confirms. "Todd?"

"Seems like he's got this all worked out," Todd tosses a thumb in my general direction. "Let's see where it goes."

"Looks like we're in agreement," Seth says as we rise as one, "A.J.'s on East Court it is. We can all find our way there?"

We all assure Seth we can. The group leaves the table behind. My path takes me past Todd and I turn in to him and stand toe to toe. It takes a second for everyone else to realize what I've done and they freeze as they survey the situation.

"This goes beyond a song I wrote," comes out with no set up. "What is your problem with me, really?"

Todd stares at me. The wheels are turning trying to determine if he's going to tell me the truth or sweep the question aside. He takes a long slow breath in and lets it go in the same manner.

"You always thought you were better than me, smarter than me. I was always the sidekick, always in your shadow. It was suffocating. The best thing that ever happened was moving away from you." Todd may as well have punched me in the heart because his words just did. He finally spit out the poison that has been festering in his heart all this time.

"How you felt and what I actually did are two different things. I never said I was better or smarter than you or anyone else. I sure as hell never treated you like a sidekick. You were my best friend." I exhale like a bull that's about to charge.

"It devastated me when you moved away. Even more so when you didn't stay in touch. I felt abandoned. I've never had a best friend since because I couldn't go through that again...to invest so much of myself in a friend only to be ditched."

We engage in a stare down. Neither he nor I make a move. Anger and animosity between two former best friends is palpable. The others have the sense to stay back and let Todd and me resolve this.

"Would it help to knock the crap out of me and be done with it? Would that settle things so we can move on?" I offer.

The women gasp. Seth takes a tentative move forward in case he has to break up a fight. The only things missing are an ominous whistle, a dust cloud, and tumbleweed rolling past us at high noon. His hands and mine are fists at our sides ready to be thrown. Todd's hands finally relax then mine follow suit.

"No. No need for fighting," Todd answers. "You and I have some issues to work out but they can wait for another day. I guess I just needed to say what I said. The song you wrote hit me sideways and with all the other stuff between us, I...well, it didn't get expressed the way it should have. Karaoke?"

"Karaoke it is," I confirm with no emotion whatsoever.

With that, we're off to A.J.'s on East Court.

* * *

Four cars pull into the parking lot of A.J.'s on East Court inside of 35 minutes. The ride over in our car was quiet as Julie left me to sort through my thoughts and feelings. I'm perplexed and disheartened. Todd's buried resentment of me is inexplicable. Our friendship played over and over in my head on the drive over and I can't for the life of me figure out how he can feel the way he does.

Lorelei and Laurel are giving this idea a fair hearing despite the disastrous nature of the night. Even if the ladies sign on for this reunion tour, how much fun is it going to be if Todd hates me the entire time? Why bother to doing the tour if we're not going to enjoy it?

The six of us step out of our respective vehicles silently acknowledging one another. The travel time and separation seems to have given all of us time to process and breathe a bit. Reading the body language of the others gives me a vibe that much of the tension has dissipated. Let's see how long that lasts.

"Shall we?" Laurel asks. She extends an arm to usher us toward the entrance of A.J.'s on East Court. We make our way to the door and closer to our singing debut. Tonight may be the closest the band comes to being a reality. Excitement and dread form a nauseating cocktail in my gut as we step through the doorway. We are greeted by a place packed with party people. It is rowdy in all the right ways.

A.J.'s on East Court is a big enough bar with a neighborhood bar feel. The drop ceilings are ten feet high so it makes for an intimate, at-home atmosphere. Wainscoting on the lower part of the walls feature wood slats with a light walnut stain lined up vertically around the establishment. The walls are painted a deep red above the wainscoting.

We manage to squeeze ourselves past the masses to get further inside the room and a fuller view of our surroundings. Lorelei spots a sign above the bar and reads it aloud, "Be your inner rock star tonight."

All eyes except Todd's put themselves on me.

"What?" I reply defensively.

"You just can't help yourself, can you?" Todd mutters under his breath not taking his eyes off the sign.

"I see a table for us over there," Julie alerts us. "I'll go grab it." She darts for a high top table that will fit six people comfortably.

We follow Julie, pulling up to the table that has a black top and six metal barstools with black cushioned seats. We're fortunate to have found this table. Not much space to be found whether it's a high top table or the traditional ones. Our seating arrangement is the same as it was at the park keeping Todd and I apart.

"I'm going to go snag the song book so we can see what our options are," Lorelei says springing from our table.

Karaoke started about an hour ago and the show is in full bloom. A group of people are on stage and singing their lungs out. The crowd is singing along with them. Calling it a stage is being generous. It's a carpeted area with a large flat screen television behind the singers with monitors in front so performers can read the lyrics. Not fancy but it works.

Lorelei is back nearly as quickly as she departed. "What's our pleasure?" she asks flipping through the song book.

"Eric," Laurel says to me, "you're the mastermind that put this together...do you have any specific songs in mind?"

"I do," is my reply as if Laurel has to ask. "We have two men and two women and we want to see how we sound together so how about 'California Dreamin' from the Mamas and the Papas?"

The three look at me and then each other. Three heads nod. "That's our song," Laurel says.

"How are we doing this?" Todd wonders. "Who is singing what?"

"Harmony is my speed, melody is not," I offer. "Todd, if you can stay somewhere in the neighborhood of baritone I can hang with you."

"Works for me," he nods. "Ladies?"

Laurel looks at Lorelei. "I sing melody, you harmony?"

"That's what I was thinking. Let's get signed up for a slot and see if we have time for a little practicing before doing this before a live crowd," Lorelei puts forth.

"Go for it," Todd says. "If we're doing this, let's do it right."

Lorelei practically bounces to the side of the stage to sign us up. "Looking at who is signed up ahead of us, I think we have about 15 minutes until we're up," she informs us upon her return.

Julie and Seth had gone up to the bar and ordered themselves drinks while we had been deciding what to sing. Julie has a tall glass of Bud Light Lime with three big green olives at the bottom.

Seth has a glass Blue Moon. Julie loves being out and she's enjoying the bar vibe. Not sure what Seth is feeling.

"I do like this pick, Eric," Laurel says. "Our voices will be the stars, no doubt."

"Whoa, whoa, whoa," Todd puts a halt to the proceedings. This song is men singing melody and women harmony. What about that?"

Lorelei balks. "What about it? We can do it any way we want. This is our group, baby!"

The emphatic reply takes us by surprise and we all chuckle. I'm thinking a bond is forming and crossing my mental fingers it's not wishful thinking.

Laurel and Todd do the countdown and then they hit the opening phrase, "All the leaves are brown..."

Lorelei and I come in, ""All the leaves are brown..."

Laurel and Todd, "and the sky is gray..."

Lorelei and me, "and the sky is gray..."

Our eyes widen as we exchange a look of mutual surprise and delight. We blend well together. Damn, we sound terrific and it's not just me that is thinking it. I can see it on their faces.

Julie and Seth are swaying in time to our acapella cadence. Seth holds up his lighted cell phone. We catch sight of it and smile. We finish the last note and let it hang for an instant. We applaud for ourselves and then high five each other.

"Holy crap, we sound amazeballs!" Lorelei exclaims. She sends her hands in the air like she's signaling a touchdown.

"I know I've been resisting this," Todd follows, "but I gotta admit, we did sound decent."

Laurel's next in offering her assessment. "For us never having sung together, our voices complement nicely. We might – *might* – have something here."

The three look at me. I think they were expecting me to be the first to say something and be all "see, we should definitely do this" and they're a bit surprised when I don't. A key principle in sales and marketing is to know when to stop selling and close the deal. The whole reason we're here is to close the deal. Is what happens on stage tonight enough to tip them to a yes? We'll see.

"This is why I wanted to get us together," I reply. "This."

We practice the song one more time and then sit tight until our turn comes. A loud round of applause diverts us from our conversation and alerts us to the end of the latest karaoke performance. The couple on stage was a hit and the crowd lets them know it.

Lorelei urgently bounces on her stool. "Guys, guys!" But before she can complete the thought the announcer on stage takes the microphone to bring on the next act.

"Up next on the A.J.'s on East Court stage, singing the classic song, *'California Dreamin'*, here are…Onions At A Crime Scene!"

Three heads snap to Lorelei. "You didn't!" Laurel says.

"Is everyone insane?" Todd is incredulous.

"What?" Lorelei mildly pushes back. "I wanted to see how it sounded. Kinda digging it."

"History will show this is where the Onions were born!" I over-dramatize.

A confused clapping commences that turns into determined applause as we jump to the stage, grab mics, and glance over at the board operator to make sure he's ready for us to begin. The lyrics are displayed on the screens in front of us. This is it.

The introductory notes play leading up to Laurel and Todd hitting their cue. Then Lorelei and me. We are officially singing together in public.

Thirty seconds in I close my eyes and just feel. Feel the energy of the crowd. Feel the flow of the music. Feel the blend of our voices. It is fantastic. I open my eyes as we're bringing the song into the home stretch. The crowd is egging us on. We are a hit. Julie is beaming and could not look more proud. Seth is smiling and whistling. What the others are thinking is known only to them.

The song trails off and ends. We don't move. The room explodes in applause so loud it becomes a physical force. We look at each other genuinely taken aback by the response but also feeling a tremendous amount of gratitude. We're not sure what to do until the announcer leaps on the stage and re-announces us.

"That was superb!" He belts out. "Onions At A Crime Scene!" He looks at us and says, "You'll be back later with another song, yes?"

We all nod emphatically without even checking with each other. Lorelei signs us up for another slot on the spot. We exit the stage and return to Julie and Seth. There are high fives all around. Julie comes up and wraps me in a hug and smacks me with a big kiss. Laurel gets a similar greeting from Seth.

"What a blast!" Lorelei blurts out. "We were *sick!*"

"Oh, come on, Lorelei," I say, turning away from Julie slightly and tease, "you're just saying that because you love to hear yourself sing."

Lorelei sticks her tongue out at me in response but follows it up with a high five.

"That was fun," Todd concurs. "Slick pick on the song, Eric."

I nod slowly at my former best friend. "Thanks."

Laurel looks around the bar. "We certainly are a crowd pleaser. I'm not trying to embellish but they honestly seemed to enjoy what we did. What's our next song?"

All eyes are on me as I pick up the song book and flip through pages of candidates for the Onions' next performance. I look at my three friends with a mischievous squint mixed with smirk and pause for effect before turning the three-ring binder toward them to reveal my selection.

"Talk Dirty To Me" – Poison.

Three sets of eyes go wide when they register my recommendation. Lorelei – of course – thrusts her fists in the air and screams, "Yeah! Yeah! Yeah! What a frickin' beautiful choice! I love that song!"

"Guess that settles it," Todd confirms. "A.J.'s on East Court is getting a big dose of Poison tonight."

"I don't think I've heard that song in years but I can sing every word," Laurel says. "It's unanimous."

We have some quick practicing to do until we give these folks a performance they'll never forget. They'll remember where they were when the Onions were born.

Damn right they will.

* * *

April 28, 2018

A late April breeze blows through the back yard. The leaves on the enormous silver maple wave to me as the wind moves them. This Saturday morning finds me sitting in my favorite chair on the deck sipping a medium roast coffee. The air is still cool enough for the steam rising off the liquid to be visible as it does. The patio door slides open behind. It is the only thing that separates the kitchen from the deck and the great outdoors.

"How ya doin', hon?" my wife inquires bringing a pot of coffee with her. She raises the pot offering another round of my morning brew. I extend my cup and Julie refills it.

My arm retracts once the mug is full. A shoulder shrug begins my response to Julie's query. A verbal reply completes it. "I'm okay, I guess. I don't know maybe there's a little emotional letdown after meeting with the others. It's been two weeks since our get together and...nothing. Not a word from anyone." My eyes fall to the coffee as if there is something new and interesting to be found there. But there isn't.

"Don't lose hope, Eric," Julie encourages. "No one has said 'no' yet. This idea may not be at the top of their priority lists like it is yours."

Another shrug.

"Anyway, remember that Aniko and Jared are coming over to barbeque with us today. They'll be here about 5. Please make sure the grill is ready to go," she requests.

"Will do." Doing the mental math I realize we're short a few people. "What about the kids? Theirs," I add quickly knowing Nicole and Ashley have out of town plans this weekend.

"Aniko said the kids are all at friends for the weekend so it's just us adults." Julie ducks back inside the house sliding the door shut behind her.

Julie's not fooling me. She knew today was the day the others said they'd let me know by whether they are in or out. The barbeque is a diversion.

The past couple weeks have seen me especially prickly to be around. The hope was that my friends wouldn't go up to deadline before letting me know of their decision. It's been challenging to not contact them, to get a sense of which way they're leaning.

I look down at my phone. No texts, no missed calls. A hard breath out. I look out across the back yard. A cardinal rests atop the chain link fence. A rabbit hops his way across the neighbor's yard until out of sight. Moments like this are why I start my Saturdays on the deck with my coffee. Normally it helps me relax but not this Saturday.

Two Saturdays ago Todd, Laurel, Lorelei and me had the first face-to-face meeting we'd had in decades. Sure, the evening had its bumpy moments but, all in all, it was a good night for us. The saving grace was karaoke. Singing the songs we did brought us together more than just in physical proximity. We came together as a group. We rocked that damn bar with *California Dreamin'* and *Talk Dirty to Me*. I thought the place was going to shake itself apart after we finished that second song.

The first song helped us to mesh, to blend. It also eased any nervousness we had. When *Talk Dirty to Me* began, we were fired up and didn't hold anything back. It was unadulterated joy. The crowd was belting out the tune with us. It felt like a concert performance and my inner nine-year-old jumped up and down with the crowd.

And then it was over. We all had a fantastic time. High fives and hugs were exchanged. Believers were made, I think. But it was also a fantasy in a bubble, a step out of our reality. The problem is reality always re-asserts itself without hesitation or mercy.

Singing together on a bar's karaoke stage is one thing but dedicating ourselves to a reunion tour is quite another. It's a life change, a reality change. And perhaps a change the others simply are unwilling to make.

Here I sip and survey and ponder what should have been. And second guess. Oh, yes, there is plenty of second-guessing myself and what I could have done differently that night to get the three closer to a yes than where they are; if they're even in the neighborhood of a yes. Maybe they've already decided no and are just reluctant to tell me because they don't want to hurt my feelings.

The patio door slides open again and Julie walks out holding a priority envelope, the kind that needs to be signed for. It doesn't occur to me immediately that it's for me. "Here you go. Delivery guy just stopped by and left this for you." Julie slides back inside and slides the door closed behind her.

Fancy dressing for a rejection letter. Yes, I'm ready to embrace pessimism. Rockstar said no thanks. Liquid Ice said no thanks. All the energy drink companies have passed on sponsoring us. I've been in sales and marketing long enough to be prepared for rejection. Even the best ideas can get brushed aside. No matter how hard you work or how creative you are, no matter how much you believe it will be a benefit for the client, 'no' is the answer you get.

This is officially the moment that will signal the end of the Onions, the tour, the whole thing. I pull the tab at the edge of the envelope and open it. I tip the envelope and dump out two loose pieces of paper. My eyes scan the message after tossing the cardboard envelope aside.

"Dear Eric. Thank you for submitting you sponsorship proposal to us. This is not the type of activity our brand normally sponsors. However, your proposal captured our imagination and our brand is very interested in sponsoring your band's upcoming reunion tour.

You'll find enclosed a comprehensive sponsorship form. This form allows you to provide more detail on how the sponsorship money will be utilized so we can make an informed, final decision. To confirm, our brand would be the exclusive sponsor of your reunion tour should we decide to sponsor it. Please complete and return the form via email at your earliest convenience."

Sonofabitch.

My surprise comes out under my breath. They didn't say no. They may actually say yes. My mind races. There is potentially a national sponsor for a concert tour, for a reunion tour, that may never happen. *Don't count your chickens yet*, a voice that sounds eerily like my mother's whispers in the corner of my brain. Not a done deal yet but hope remains.

When I was a kid I played this game with Mom when we went grocery shopping. As we made our way up and down the aisles, I would find a toy or a box of cereal I wanted and would sneak it into the cart. The point of the game was for the item to successfully make it to checkout without Mom noticing until she pulled it out of the cart and put it on the conveyor belt. Nine times out of 10 she'd look at the item, look at me smiling mischievously at her, and tell me to put it back. The cashiers thought Mom was mean but I didn't care if I got the item or not. It was considered a win if I got the item to the cashier. Mom knew I was going to do it and she still couldn't catch me sneaking stuff in the cart.

Just before I would depart to go put the item back I would shrug my shoulders and say, "Can't blame a guy for trying." Then off I'd go and when I returned the last of the groceries would be going into the bags. Mom would smile at me and shake her head. Every time we went grocery shopping we'd play the game and I'd see how far I could get. "Can't blame a guy for trying" just got me a step closer to a freaking tour sponsorship for a band that doesn't exist and a tour that doesn't have any dates on the calendar! I begin rejoicing again.

The door slides open behind me. "What's going on? I heard a commotion," Julie says, poking her head out the door. "What was in the envelope?"

I stick the letter in Julie's face to read for herself. Her eyes get as wide as dinner plates, almost cartoonish. "Holy crap!"

"I know!"

"What is this? Are they in?" Julie inquires.

"It's a letter of interest to be the exclusive sponsor of the reunion tour of Onions At A Crime Scene! Potentially an exclusive sponsor! Exclusive...sponsor."

Julie asks the obvious question. "What are you going to do if the others don't agree to be part of the band?"

"Oh, don't go throwing reality in my face," I say, brushing aside her seeming negativity. "Let's just enjoy the moment, the irony of it all. It's beautiful."

"That's all well and good but the fact remains you have a potential sponsor who is expecting a tour," Julie states with the impact of a large, soaked blanket.

"Don't spoil my irony with your inconvenient facts," I reply. "I know. I do. But this is the first hopeful thing that's happened since karaoke. I've felt like a lone wolf and, largely, I have been because I've kept the whole idea under wraps for so long."

"Yes, I know that. But that doesn't change the fact you would be expected to fulfill a contract," Julie persists.

"Fine. I'll tell them they are now contractually expected to fulfill a tour. They should immediately fall in line." My tone is sarcastic in a playful way.

"Okay then, smarty pants drummer of a band that doesn't exist," Julie fires a sarcasm salvo back at me, "what are you going to do about this letter?"

"For the moment, nothing. I'm just going to enjoy this. If the others are in, I'll need to write the long-form proposal the brand is requesting. On the bright side, I have the website ready to go live; I just have to add the brand's logo. The rest is adding them to our promotional materials as I get tour dates and such." I pause as a squirrel runs across the yard and up our silver maple. "Until I know that their brand is officially in, I'm going to keep this letter to myself."

"Why do you keep saying 'the brand this and the brand that'? Why don't you say their name?" Julie says.

"Simple," I reply in between sips of coffee. "I don't want to jinx it. No names until it's a done deal. The Rock and Roll gods may get angry if I get cocky."

Julie shakes her head as she retreats back into the house. "You and your superstitions."

* * *

"Hang on...you're doing what with who?" Aniko is confused and not afraid to show it.

It's just after six. Jared and Ani are with Julie and me on the deck. It's been months since we've been able to spend time together. The grill has worked its usual magic and the four of us are enjoying steak, corn on the cob, and zucchini. It's a perfect evening to be dining out. Outside, that is.

I'd spent the time between my morning coffee and firing up the grill making notes and plans to be able to submit the requested official proposal to our potential sponsor. Scenario planning will be key if I'm to pull this off. But, coming back to Aniko, it is clear I have not shared what I've been up to since talking to her class. First, another bite of the steak I've grilled. Mmm.

I take another run at getting Ani to comprehend what I've trying to get across. "Remember when I spoke to your class about my rock and roll dream going down the tubes? Well, I decided to track down Todd, Laurel, and Lorelei to find out if they wanted to kick start the rock and roll dream." Another bite of steak then I continue.

"Hired a freelancer to write some songs, did research on possible venues, hired Nick to teach me how to play drums, and now we'll see what happens."

Aniko waves her hands in a motion suggesting she's trying to shoo flies. "Stop. Hold it." She brings her hands down and takes a deep breath. "You're actually doing this? You're going to tour as a band? A band. This is happening? How did I not know about this?"

A quick swallow so I don't talk with my mouth full and then, "Maybe. I got everyone together a couple weeks ago to share the idea and, well, let's say the reactions were mixed.

"We got kicked out of an Applebee's in Ames because the other guy in the group took offense to one of the songs that was inspired by his life," Julie interrupts.

Aniko looks at me, "This is crazy! Are you going through a mid-life crisis or something?"

I frown. "No, dear sister, I am not having a mid-life crisis. I just have some unfinished business and hopefully the other three feel they do as well." I let all that sink in by taking another bite and waiting till I've swallowed it before continuing. "As to why you didn't know about it, I asked Julie, Nicole, Ashley, and Nick to keep it under the radar."

"Kind of like an item on a bucket list," Jared offers, inserting himself into this conversation for the first time. Jared, ironically, is a band teacher in the same school district as Ani. He stands slightly taller than me. He's slender in build, helped by being an avid biker. The pedal kind.

"Exactly, except you know how I feel about bucket lists," I answer.

"We are all well aware how you feel about bucket lists," Julie says with an eye roll.

"Yes, bucket lists are focused on things to do before you die... why not be focused on what to do while you're alive," Aniko repeats my feelings on the subject she's heard many times. "Yes, we know."

"Are the songs up to snuff?" Jared asks, trying to get the conversation back on track. "Do you think you can actually pull a band together this fast and start a tour so soon?"

"They're superb. I gave my freelancer the subject of the song and a sentence or two and she worked her magic." Another bite. "I'm hoping we get to play them."

"When will you know if the others are going to join you in this band thing?" Aniko asks.

"Keep your fingers crossed..." before I can finish my thought my cell phone dings, alerting that a text has come in. Our rule is no phones at the table but I'd kept mine in my pocket just in case one or all three friends try to get in touch tonight. "Excuse me," I say to the fam, "gotta check this."

Laurel: Skype @ 7 tonight? 3 of us r here. Need 2 talk.

My reply is in the affirmative. Two seconds after I hit send on my text back I get a thumbs up emoji from Laurel to confirm we're a go. I look up from my phone and announce, "I'm going have to step away for a few minutes at seven. The three are apparently in one place and want to Skype so I'll find out what the next move is then."

"If there is a next move," Jared says. "This is such a remote possibility."

"If there is a next move," I repeat.

"Oh stop it, Jared," Ani scolds seeming to have a change of heart. "I know I've been skeptical tonight but Eric has made it this far with his idea so you never know what could happen."

"I'm just being real," Jared responds. "A band doesn't happen out of nowhere. These people have lives. Maybe they don't have the emotional investment in this that Eric has. I'm not trying to rain on the parade but it's true. These things aren't just done on a whim."

"I was there the night Eric told them," Julie declares. "They were shocked by it at first but by the end of the evening they seemed to be considering it. Eric did a great job of putting together a business plan that showed them how serious he is."

"You do realize how preposterous all of this sounds, don't you?" Jared presses. "For someone like Eric who conceived the idea and has been putting together all the details over time, sure, it makes sense. But to anyone else, it's...out there." Jared is nothing if not practical and rooted in logic. He's not one to throw caution to the wind. That would be me.

"You do realize," comes from me dripping with venom, "you sound like you're channeling Mr. Tripolino."

Everything stops as Julie, Ani, and Jared catch the meaning, the tone, and my death stare. I understand very well how nonsensical this quest seems but all I'm hearing is another music teacher telling me I'm not good enough. And I have had enough of that. Seconds of silence tick away as no one knows how to respond to my conversation stopper.

The tumbler of iced tea on the small table next to my chair comes with me upon my departure from the deck. I'll apologize to Jared later. I shouldn't have taken my disappointment and frustration out on him. Nerves are still a bit raw.

The glass door slides behind me and closes me off from my family. Fifteen steps later I am in my office and plop in the office chair. The PC is brought out of sleep mode and Skype is activated. The computer clock reads "6:58" as I log in and sit tight till I'm hailed. Butterflies swarm my stomach. I'm about to learn if my bandmates are up for a reunion or if all this time and effort have been a colossal waste of my life.

The Skype medley alerts me to an incoming a video call. Call accepted then a momentary pause before Laurel, Todd, and Lorelei appear on screen. It looks like they are gathered around Laurel's kitchen table. Laurel is at the end with Todd sitting to her right and Lorelei to her left.

"Hey, Eric," Laurel greets. Her hello is followed by salutations from Lorelei and Todd. "How are things?"

"Good," I reply. "Sister and her husband are over for a grill out. You guys?"

All three respond with positive comments. The small talk is not what we're here for. Can we just rip off the bandage and move on with our lives? I become aware that I'm swiveling back and forth in my office chair, a sign of my anxiousness.

"Okay," Laurel says, "let's get down to business, shall we?" Three affirmatives follow from the rest of us.

Here we go, I think.

"Lorelei, Todd, and I have spent the afternoon discussing your idea – your proposal. Admittedly, there's a lot to discuss and to consider."

A rising wave of discontent and impatience originates at my feet and begins its ascent. Snark remains dominant within me following the exchange on the deck. *Just tell me if we're doing this or not, whatever the decision.* This preamble is unnecessary. Laurel abruptly halts her exposition seemingly reading my mind or perhaps just my expression.

"Yeah, anyway," Laurel picks up. "We're in. The Onions At A Crime Scene reunion is on."

No response from me as I have an inner body experience. Images flutter through my mind like a deck of cards being scattered by a game of 52 pickup. The four of us on a playground. KISS. Sheila E. Junior high disappointments. Regrets. Talking with Ani's class. Drum lessons. Research. Planning. Friending. Coffee meetings. Getting thrown out of Applebee's. Karaoke.

"Hey, doofus," Todd leans toward the camera barking at me. "Did you hear Laurel? We are doing this. We. Are. Doing. This."

"Yeah, isn't it exciting? I'm pumped!" Lorelei adds bouncing in her seat.

"We're doing this," I say dumbfounded.

"YES!" that sounds suspiciously like a "duh", comes from the others in unison.

"Holy crap! We're doing this!" I yell, propelling my fists to the sky and spinning in my chair. "Onions At A Crime Scene!"

The four of us cheer. It's a shared moment of joy, a joy that comes from knocking logic on its rumpus. We are going to embark on a reunion tour for a band that never existed. Till right now.

My feet hit the floor to break my spin so I'm facing my bandmates once more. "This is fantastic. I wasn't sure you three would say yes but I'm so happy you did. Not to look the proverbial gift horse in the mouth but why?"

"I guess for me it was part nostalgia, remembering the dreams we had as kids. Plus, you aren't asking us to commit to anything long term. Three gigs fairly close to home and we're done. Touring, at least. We better stay in contact and hang out after the tour's done though," Lorelei says moving in toward the camera.

"I was leaning against it," Todd reveals. "Forty years is a hell of a long time and the whole band thing never made it out of 4th grade. But then I re-read your proposal and then went on YouTube and watched the KISS performance you and I saw way back. It was then I figured this would be fun to do."

"Yes, it would be fun," Laurel echoes. "Plus, your numbers make sense. In reviewing them they didn't seem out of line. If we can secure a sponsorship, it's a no-brainer. But..."

Dammit. There's always a "but".

"...this can't be just you doing all this and the rest of us just show up to play and sing. Onions At A Crime Scene needs to be a team, not just a band."

I like the sound of that.

"We need to divide up responsibilities so we are all contributing to the band's success," Laurel finishes.

"What do you have in mind?"

Lorelei jumps in. "I'm in charge of scheduling and running practices. By the way, the first one is next Saturday here at Laurel's at 1. That work for you?"

"Yes, ma'am." I respond without hesitation.

"I got logistics and transportation," Todd announces. "Someone has to haul all the equipment." Any excuse for him to drive something big.

"I'll handle financials," Laurel says, picking up the responsibility baton. "I'll host all of our practices too."

"And I'm doing, what?"

"You get the hard stuff," Laurel answers. "You get securing gigs and marketing. No one tells our story better than you do and that's going to be huge in getting venues to bring us in and for people to show up to see us."

The use of "us" and "our" and "we" in all of this may be the most exciting thing to me.

"That makes total sense," I agree. "Can I say this is how I envisioned this? Not necessarily the division of responsibilities but the four of us working together, the four of us being equal partners in this. It means more than I can express. Not only because you are part of this journey but that you took the time you did this afternoon to decide whether or not you wanted to do this, as well as how we will proceed from this moment on."

"Eric, thanks for all the work you've done to get us here," Lorelei says softly. "It means a lot to me that you did all that you have to bring us back together. Since Dominic died I haven't looked forward to a lot and in some ways I shut down emotionally. I'm soooo looking forward to this."

Springing a Leek | 161

"I owe you an apology for that thing at Applebee's," Todd offers. "I was a jerk and shouldn't have reacted the way that I did. The song was too real for me and, I guess, the wound is still closer to the surface than I let myself believe."

"Apology accepted and, for what it's worth, I'm sorry that I blindsided you. Sometimes I get so zealous about an idea that other people's feelings don't always get considered and things like that happen. I promise, no more blindsiding...for any of us."

A quick glance at the clock alerts me to the fact that we may want to wrap this up because we all have lives to get back to...and I'm sure the fam on the deck would like to know what's what. "Not that I want this conversation to end but I think you all have spent enough time today on this and there's still some Saturday night to enjoy," I say. "Shall we adjourn till Saturday's practice?"

It's then that the other three look at the clock and realize ending the call would be the prudent thing to do. "All right then," Laurel starts to bring the curtain down on the call. "We'll do that."

"Everybody stop!" Lorelei exclaims. "We just can't say goodbye! Boooring! We're a band darn it and we're going to end this call as a band!"

Todd looks at Laurel and Lorelei then asks, "What did you have in mind?"

"Onions At A Crime Scene on three," she fires back. "1, 2, 3..."

"Onions At A Crime Scene!" we shout in unison flinging our hands in the air. Then Laurel ends the call.

I'll be damned. We're actually doing this.

CHAPTER FOUR

BACON AND ONIONS

May 5, 2018

"OW!" A sharp, instant pain radiates from my left triceps. "What the heck?" I look to my left at Lorelei. She's standing next to me with that devilish grin of which I have grown fond.

"Well, you said pinch you," she shrugs and giggles. "Just thought I'd oblige."

Gathered here in Laurel's garage in Ames ready for our first practice as Onions At A Crime Scene, I had asked aloud to be pinched to make sure I wasn't dreaming.

"I was speaking rhetorically," I fire back at Lori with an over the top reaction acting like her pinch nearly severed my arm. To amp that up a few notches I call out, "Laurel, Lori's being mean to me!"

"No, no, no," Laurel shakes her head and wags her right index finger at me. "I am not the mother of this group. Do NOT go there."

"I sure as hell ain't the dad of this combo," Todd throws in. "Rhetorically, metaphorically, or any other way."

We revel in the silliness. The endorphins are pumping and probably the adrenaline too. Laurel did the band a solid allowing us to hold practices here. She and Seth just finished adding on what amounts to a third stall to their already massive garage. Seth is going to use it as a workshop but Laurel convinced him to delay moving in until after the Onions finish our concert tour. Finish *our* concert tour. Has such a righteous ring to it.

This new addition is a stall unto itself with a garage door facing the driveway and a regular door as the entry/exit to the Escalade and CTS parked on the other side of the wall behind Lori. The space itself is 16 feet wide by 20 feet long. More than enough space for my drum kit, Lori's keyboard, a couple of guitars, plus the wires, amps, and accessories we need to make our brand of magic.

"Troublemaker," Lori says with a parting shot as she backhands the spot on my arm she just pinched then returning to her place behind the keyboard.

"OUCH! Geez, woman, don't make me tug your pigtails!" I protest rubbing my arm once more.

"Oh, like you did on the playground in 4th grade?" Lorelei says sticking out her tongue at me to punctuate her point.

"Settle down, you two," Laurel softly scolds, "let's get focused on why we're here. We wanted to start at one and it's a little bit after." Todd nods while putting the finishing adjustments on his guitar.

"You're right," I say. "But hang on one second. There's a quick finishing touch that needs to be made." Reaching down into my briefcase I pull out a piece of paper, a drawing I sketched 40 years ago. Before I left home I put a piece of Blue Tack on it so I could stick it to my drum kit. It is positioned strategically so the fans that Seth has set up in our practice space don't blow it away.

Todd shakes his head at me. "You're ridiculous. Always so sentimental."

"Says the man in the KISS concert t-shirt," I send back at him with a sardonic snark in my voice.

"Yeah, yeah," Todd accepts the teasing. "I've gone to at least one KISS concert every year since 1989...so I think I'm entitled to wear one of their shirts to my band practice."

"Aw, you called it 'your band'," Laurel tags herself in to the teasing. "That's adorable."

Todd blushes and responds with, "Well, who are you supposed to be with those leather wristbands...Leather Tuscedero?" He fails to hide his fluster at getting called out on taking emotional ownership of our group.

"I'm supposed to be me," Laurel asserts. "I rock." Her tone confirms her ownership in our merry band of music makers.

"Hey," Lorelei chimes in, "if we're supposed to be a band, we need to look the part." She has a treble clef tattoo behind her right ear that is visible when she pushes her hair back. Resting on the front left hand corner of her keyboard is a California Raisins figure that has one gloved hand pointing at her keyboard and the other pointed to the garage ceiling.

"There's looking the part and there's going overboard," Todd turns his teasing to our keyboardist. "I mean, are you trying to bring back the 80s?" He looks at Laurel and me, extends his arms in Lori's direction, palms facing up and says, "For cryin' out loud, look at that, she actually has a Trapper Keeper with her! Why?"

Bacon and Onions | 165

Laurel's and my heads turn to Lorelei. Lori swiftly bends snatching up her Trapper Keeper then waves it defiantly in our faces. "Look, it keeps my notes organized and they don't fall out. '80s or no '80s, still the best!" At first we don't know what to do with that then all of us start roaring amused by the ridiculousness of the argument and delight in gathering here, taking the first step in this improbable quest.

"Okay, okay," Laurel inserts putting her hands up in a double stop position. "We actually have business to attend to...namely, the three songs we want to practice today. First song, *Take The Day*. Everyone has the sheet music on their iPads?"

Todd, Lorelei, and I respond with a simultaneous yes. Todd and I exchange sideway glances to put a finishing touch on our bickering. Looking left, I make eye contact with Lorelei and then narrow my eyes telling her she's still on thin ice. Lori, in turn, sticks her tongue out at me again.

"I will pull this car over right now!" Todd yells feigning we're on his last nerve.

"Yes, Dad," the two of us reply with a heavy lilt.

"Dammit!" Todd barks. "I walked myself into that trap!"

Laurel shakes her head once more but ignores our foolishness. "Everyone have their instruments tuned?" she asks.

Three answers in the affirmative.

"Let's get our vocal instruments tuned."

Laurel leads us through some humming and lip trills that seem suspiciously similar to making bubbles in my milk when I was a kid. Then it's the traditional Do-Re-Mi drill. We finish the warmup to Laurel's satisfaction.

"Sounds like we're a go," Laurel moves us forward. "Ready, Julie?" In the midst of us is our official video biographer pointing a Canon video camera at us. My wife gives Laurel an okay sign with her left hand.

"Let's do this," Laurel says. *"Take The Day.* Eric?"

I jump in, "One, two...one, two, three, four!"

Lorelei converted the sheet music and lyrics my freelancer had written to an iPad-friendly format and digitally shared them to our devices. Each one of us has an iPad on a stand so we can read the song off the device rather than off paper on a traditional music stand. Each of us practiced our parts individually before today's session so we're familiar with how our part of the song sounds but this moment is the first moment the four of us have heard all parts together.

Laurel starts with the first line on her own, "How could we forget?" Then the rest of us join her. "Those sweet childhood days. Naivety and carefree fun. In the schoolyard, as we played. We go back to yesterday."

It's absolutely the most beautiful sound I've ever heard. The hair on the back of my neck starts doing the mambo and butterflies on steroids zoom about my stomach. We've positioned our instruments in a way so we not only hear each other but we see each other. This is not how we'll appear on stage when we perform but we need to bond with the music and with each other.

Part of me feels like it's disassociating from my body and is floating above me, observing. My "ghost eyes" see past and present as one. It sees four 50-year-olds and four nine-year-olds singing and playing at the same time.

"Old friends, we can't let this dream end. God only knows what's around the bend. Seize the moment, take the day. Sing and laugh and dance and play," we sing.

Images of a sixth grader being told he couldn't sing and a seventh grader he wasn't good enough to play drums flash in my head.

"You know we had this rock dream. That we'd become a band. We'd rock out all night. Our name up there in lights. Microphones in our hands. Moms and Dads didn't understand," goes the next part.

Listening to *Take The Day* being played and sung is freaking magic. If this is how the first song sounds, I cannot wait for the songs that come next. The goal of the songs is to be a biography of our lives but also for our contemporaries who, like us, are in a nostalgic stage of younger, simpler times before marriages, mortgages, kids, and obligations.

It's a first practice, sure, but we sound like we've been playing awhile. Our individual efforts have clearly paid off. Our instruments blend well but what is more gratifying is so do our voices. I shouldn't be surprised since I knew we sounded terrific together after our karaoke night at A.J.'s on East Court. But that was to songs we were familiar with. How would we sound with new material?

Damn good. That's how.

Ghost form descends back into my body and I'm fully in the moment when I realize Laurel, Lorelei, and Todd are looking at me with huge smiles. I'm not sure what their ghost selves are showing them but it must be at least as splendid as what I saw.

Laurel's head bobs as she sings. Todd is grimacing the way all serious rock guitarists do. Lorelei's fingers flash with fanatical flair as she strikes the keys.

I catch a look at Julie as she records. She has a huge grin on her face. Laurel and I catch sight of Seth walking up next to Julie. He is smiling as well, his fists raised in the air in triumph. Onions At A Crime Scene has a hit on its hands. We let last notes hang in the air giving us the opportunity to enjoy every last moment of the song.

Lorelei lets out a "Wooo!" that reverberates through the garage. Then all six of us erupt in applause.

"That was out of sight!" Julie exclaims looking up from her camera. "I can't believe this is the first time you've played together. You sound terrific."

Seth claps. "Great sound. Nailed it right out of the box. Tour ready now."

"Oh stop," Laurel brushes off her husband's exaggeration. "But we do sound legit."

"Legit?" Lorelei repeats. "We sound like a band. A *real* band."

I hold back comment waiting for Todd's assessment before adding my two cents. "Safe to say I was the least excited by all this. Had a lot of doubts. A lot." He shakes his head. "Gotta say this isn't the bad idea I thought it was."

Five sets of eyes come my way. My smile is damn near ear to ear. "Song two, anyone?"

Nods abound. "Moving to song two," Laurel says. "*Happy Ever After*".

Digital devices are set to display song two. Different butterflies populate my gastric region. *Happy Ever After* is the song inspired by Lorelei's loss of her husband. Lorelei's read the lyrics and has practiced the song on her own so the tune isn't a surprise but it's tough not to be nervous for her and how this song feels as we perform it as a group.

When you enter life as an adult now constrained by employers and bills you take for granted how much time you have. At 30 you're no longer a young adult but a full-fledged responsible adult. But there is time. There's so much time to live and to make plans and to achieve and to accomplish. Time to raise kids. Time to be empty nesters. Then there's the time that is taken away from you. The loss. The loss of freedom that comes with jobs and kids. The loss of friendships due to growing apart or moving apart. The loss of parents or spouses through death.

The next thing you know you're 50 years old and time is no longer your friend. More time behind you than ahead of you and that time seems hollow when you must spend the rest of yours without the person who was supposed to be with you till death do you part but was taken from you three decades too soon.

As much as we have joyful and hopeful songs filled with feel-good nostalgia, we also need songs of loss, of transition, of looking back. We are not exclusive in our sense of loss, our acceptance that — though our best days aren't necessarily behind us - they are numbered.

The days ahead of us will find us wiser but also slowing down and with a slow decline in our physical capabilities. I've often asked myself how old I am, if I didn't know how old I was. Many times I've answered "35" because I honestly feel as strong as I did then. Gray hairs coming in at my temples with more frequency tell me to re-do my age math.

Our playing of the song is solid but a bit tentative, musically walking on eggshells in our empathy and regard for Lorelei. We're playing and singing the song but three of us aren't fully engaged with the song because of our vocally tip-toeing around the subject matter. Granted, we're playing well; our individual practice is showing. But, Lorelei notwithstanding, Laurel, Todd, and I have some things to let go of if this song is going to have the emotional impact we want it to have on our audiences.

Once more the final notes fade on a song. Everyone is holding our collective breath as we wait for Lorelei's reaction. This is the first time we're all hearing this song but so too for Lorelei. A small "whew" rather than a big "woo" comes slowly from Lorelei. She dabs a small trail of tears from her right cheek. No one says a word. No one breathes. Lori picks up on the silence.

"What?" sounds almost like a challenge as it comes out. "Oh, come on, I'm not a fragile little flower," Lorelei asserts. "The big blow was losing my husband not this song. I think the song is lovely and so damned real it makes me cry for others who know this loss but I'm okay. OH-KAY," she emphasizes.

The rest of us exhale. Our lips form a smile knowing that we've come through one emotional minefield just fine. One more rogue tear makes a break for it down Lorelei's cheek. We look away for a moment out of respect.

"Can I make a comment?" Julie asks. We three nod yes. "You guys sound good but it just seemed like you were holding back. Everything was technically correct but it didn't have the impact it should have. I don't want to offend you but that's how I heard it."

"That's because we were holding back, weren't we?" Todd confirms.

"Yeah, we were," Laurel agrees.

"Well, stop it," Lorelei says. "This is just one of a library of our songs that packs a punch and we'd better be able to deliver the punch. And take the punch."

"I agree with this," I chime in, "but it is our first time through and we played and sang well. Hitting the musical notes to me is the most important the first time through. Hitting the emotional notes will come with more practice and recognizing to dive in and not be tentative." Placing my right hand over my heart I finish with, "And that's coming from someone who was holding back for the same reason we all were."

"Do you have any gut-wrenching, rip-your-heart-out-experience songs about your life?" Todd drops in my lap.

"Yeah, the song is called 'Waiting A Lifetime To Put My Dream Band Together After Being Told How Worthless I Am'. How's that?" An eyebrow raise is my final punctuation that lets Todd and the others know I'm teasing but also reminding them I am not without a lingering soul wound.

Todd grunts and nods in acknowledgment of my response. "Should we do this song again now or after we run through the third song?"

Laurel is the first to answer. "Let's move ahead to *No Way Back Today*. My turn for the gut wrencher." I shoot Laurel a look of apology that she shakes off. "Sorry. I didn't mean that to come out like a shot at you or the song. Just a little nervous at hearing something based on my life for the first time. I'm fine with the song but, well, we'll see how it goes. Then we can go back and run through the songs again making adjustments where we need to. Yes?"

"Yeah, I like that idea," Lorelei says. "Shall we?"

Laurel nods and I start the count. And we're off.

No Way Back Today is an apt song for our generation, for any generation actually. In the literal version of the song it's about a mom who will be an empty nester whose final child will be off to college and, for the first time since giving birth to the first child, will have a house with only two spouses living in it. But it's about more than that. It's about a loss of identity. An identity crisis born of what you do rather than who you are.

We all do it. Our identities – our self-worth – become intertwined with what happens outside of us. Men, for example, typically define our worth by our jobs, our careers. Two decades ago a mentor had seen me on such a course and brought it to my attention. He cautioned me to emotionally step back from my career. Not because it was a bad career but because he could see that I was defining myself based upon how well my career was going.

He told me, "If you are what you do then when you don't, you aren't. That's why men have such difficulty when they lose a job whether being laid off, fired, or retired. If you're not a policeman, a firefighter, a teacher, a salesman...then what are you? A serious identity crisis results from the loss of self and, in many cases, profound depression. It's okay to identify with your career but don't let your career become your identity."

Those words had hit me where I live. Upon reflection it was clear my mentor knew exactly what he was talking about. My career was definitely my identity even more than being a husband and a father, because my career was also wrapped in with my role and identity as provider for Julie and the girls.

I heard my mentor's voice in the back of my head when Laurel shared with me her struggle at the coming reality of being a mom with no kids in the house. It's what inspired the song but my hope is that Laurel and others take the song to heart and it will help process the loss in a healthy way that is freeing.

Our performance of *No Way Back Today* is much stronger than *Happy Ever After*. Having that processing moment between the two emotionally-heavy songs helped us purge some of our tentativeness. We still have five songs to get through in our next practice but this first practice has exceeded my expectations. Maybe it's our age, our experience, or our comfort with this endeavor but this session has been free of the clumsiness I had expected of people who had never played together before.

We are far from flawless and there are some things we need to work through and we haven't even started on how we engage with the audience as we perform but this is a solid effort.

Final notes of the song hang in the air before disappearing completely. Seth walks up to his wife and puts his arms around her. "I'm fine," Laurel says. "I just think of an empty house and how quiet it's going to be and it gets to me. It's okay." Seth gives Laurel a hug and then goes back to his observation position by the garage door.

"Laurel, trust me," Lorelei offers, "it's not going to be as bad as you think it may be. There's going to be an adjustment, definitely. There will be days when you cry for no reason. You may miss yelling at them for not putting dishes away or picking their dirty socks off the floor or forgetting to take out the trash for the hundredth time. But, you'll see your boys more often than you expect. Isn't that the case, Eric?"

"Absolutely," I pop in. "Julie and I found we were happily surprised how much more time we had for each other and opportunity to recommit to each other in ways we hadn't had the chance to in years because the girls had to be the priority. We were always putting ourselves and our marriage behind Nicole and Ashley. Plus, now I get to chase Julie around the kitchen table naked and not worry about anyone walking in on us." I shoot a smile at Julie.

My wife covers her face with her palms mostly from embarrassment but also from my inappropriate comment. Seth, on the other hand, claps in anticipation. "I can't wait to be an empty nester!"

Laurel rolls her eyes at her husband and me over the typical male behavior not to mention the one-track mind. "How are you ever going to chase me around the table when I'm on tour?"

"Oh!" Todd exclaims at Laurel's quick comeback.

"Snap!" Lorelei adds.

More laughter. This is a genuine joy with these three childhood friends I share so many experiences with and now get the chance to come alongside on this quest. I'm not sure how all of this ends but I do know I'm enjoying the hell out of the beginning.

* * *

A couple hours later we call it a wrap on our maiden voyage practice agreeing to keep it to four hours. It's important we keep this a fun experience and not descend into serious tediousness. Practice now behind us, it's time to gather and socialize. Laurel and Seth are gracious hosts for our first post-practice supper.

The six of us are on the deck seated in a semi-circle, the grill ready to accept burgers and brats we've all brought. Seth is filling the role of grill master expertly. The deck runs the entire back of the house with a patio door allowing easy access to the kitchen. Laurel has seated herself after bringing the last of the condiments out and placing them on the table.

Each of us is enjoying our beverage of choice while we pass time till our food is ready. Laurel and Lorelei both have a glass of pinot grigio, Julie has a bottle of Leiny's Summer Shandy, Todd has a bottle of Bud, and I'm working on a bottle of Mike's Hard Lemonade.

We're in a jubilant mood after running through the songs and making some adjustments. Perhaps it was because we had the bar of expectations set low or maybe we are genuinely surprised at how we exceeded our expectations. Whatever the case, our reunion tour is legit. We still have five songs to master but we have time to worry about those later. For now, it's enjoying being together. It is a beautiful evening to do so.

May in Iowa is a bit of a crap shoot. Sometimes it can be the best of Spring and sometimes it can be the hottest of Summer. This May evening is the best of both worlds...the warmth of a summer evening with the low humidity of a Spring night. Laurel and Seth's place is at the rounded end of the cul-de-sac with woods and a small stream running behind it. The trees are large enough that they shield us from being beaten by the sun without hindering our view of a magnificently blue sky. As we chill on the deck a soft breeze excuses itself as it brushes by us. It is glorious.

"This is the best," Lorelei announces closing her eyes and lifting her face to the sky.

"Yeah," Laurel agrees, "Seth and I spend a lot of time out here. We eat as many meals as we can on the deck. It's our backyard escape."

"Get any deer back here?" Todd asks.

"Quite a few," Seth answers. "They've gotten used to us so they come closer than they used to. It's great."

"I don't think I'd ever move from this spot the whole summer," Julie says, looking at me. I nod knowing she is correct.

"Summers as a kid were so wicked," Lorelei continues her thought path. "Anywhere I could hike, swim, or bike I would go and wouldn't come back till sundown."

"And our parents didn't think anything of it," Todd finishes.

"I loved floating down the river at Halverson Park," Laurel adds. "Since it was only a few miles from home, Mom and Dad would let me camp with my girlfriends. So many summers, so many memories."

"As kids you couldn't keep us inside in the summer," I toss in. "It was a punishment to make us come inside. Kids today think making them go outside is punishment."

"Careful, grandpa," Julie teases, "you're about to yell at those kids to get off our lawn."

My eyes narrow at her. She chuckles.

"You know one phrase you don't hear anymore," Todd opens, pausing for a second to take a swig of his beer, 'summer reruns'."

"Oh man," I begin my reply, "kids today have no idea what it's like to have only two opportunities to see a television episode – when it originally airs and summer rerun."

"Yeah, or waiting to hear a song on the radio and running to your cassette recorder to tape it so you could make a cassette of your favorite songs," Lori opines. "Today you just download your favorite songs to your phone or listen to the channel of your choice on Spotify or Pandora. I like doing that but you know what it is? You never have to wait for anything. Nothing is special. If you want it, you just go get it. A lot of things just get taken for granted." She sighs.

"Yeah," I start with a knowing nod, "delayed gratification is now found only in the Smithsonian Institution." There is a moment of reflection before I add, "But, man, I love Amazon Prime."

"Truth!" Todd validates as do four others. "None of that 'allow four to six weeks for shipping' crap we had to endure as kids. Two days. Bam! Done."

"And the internet!" Lori exclaims adding another perk of modern society. "Best shopping mall ever!" She accentuates with a fist pump.

"Okay, okay," Laurel pumps the brakes to insert a topic change. "As long as we're being nostalgic, since we're now a band, my question is; what is your best concert memory?" Before any of us can respond she continues, "I'll go first. Corey Hart, Austin, Minnesota, August 30th, 1984."

"Corey Hart played in Austin?" Julie asks to make sure she heard correctly. I nod as Laurel fills in the details.

"Oh yeah. He was so cute. Remember *Sunglasses At Night*? Great live song. Riverside Arena was going nuts. Sixteen years-old with a bunch of friends rockin' out on a summer night. God, that was extraordinary." Looking over at Todd, Laurel asks, "Todd, how 'bout you?"

Todd responds without hesitation, "December 18, 1984. KISS. Cedar Rapids, Iowa. Same as with you, Laurel, 16-years-old, head bangin' with my buds. We managed to score tickets about 20 feet from the stage...Gene Simmons up close spitting fire..." Todd leans back, looks to the sky, and basks in the memory. "Seen them in concert almost every year since. Even with the replacement members."

Eyes turn to me. "That's easy. Joan Jett and The Blackhearts, February 8, 1989, Mayo Civic Center, Rochester, Minnesota. I was not yet 21. First time I got to see her live. I was ten feet from the stage. It was phenomenal," I answer with a wistful tone. "You know how you can go to concerts and it sounds nothing like the album because the band can't recreate the sound live that they did in the studio?"

"Oh yeah," comes back at me in unison even from Seth who pauses to flip a burger so he can answer with the rest of our group.

"Not Joan Jett. Nope. I spent moments listening with my eyes closed and it sounded exactly like I was in my room listening to her albums growing up. Loved it. I saw her again a few years ago up at Treasure Island Casino. Same thing. In fact, I told Julie and the friends we went with that they should close their eyes and listen."

"We did," Julie inserts. "Sounds exactly the same. Great performer."

"Hang on a sec," Laurel jumps in. "Why didn't you go see Joan Jett when she played the Surf Ballroom back in 1983? That's like 35 minutes from where we lived."

A sigh starts my reply. "Mom and Dad wouldn't let me. I was 15 and there were no adults I knew who would take me – they certainly weren't going to. Lawrence Welk was their jam. They were afraid of the drug culture back then and that something bad would happen to me."

"Oh, that sucks," Lorelei sympathizes. "Your favorite artist is half an hour from you at the height of her popularity and you're not allowed to go. You must have been devastated."

I nod. "Sure was. I understood. I wasn't mad or anything but, man, I was so disappointed. I managed to get my hands on the concert poster. I have it framed at home."

"True story," my wife confirms.

"What about you?" I ask Lorelei, "What's your favorite concert memory?"

"June 7, 2008. Sex Pistols in Vegas. Eight shades of hellacious."

Seth's metal spatula hits the deck with a thud-clang. Todd nearly chokes on his swig of Bud. All of our eyes widen as we look at Lorelei in shock. Of all the things she could have said, I'm not sure any would have been more surprising than this.

"What?" She looks back at us surprised by our surprise. "This girl's got a whole lot of rebel inside her and sometimes that rebel just needs to cut loose. A few girlfriends and I went to Vegas for some fun and we thought 'what the heck, Sex Pistols'. Let's just say there was a lot of rebellion that night...that trip."

"Girlfriend, I want to party with you," Julie admires reaching over to high five Lori. A loud smack emanates from the two women's hands as they meet in mid-air.

Seth changes our course before the nostalgia train can get further down the tracks. "Burgers and brats are up," Seth announces. Laurel hangs back while the rest of us can get up, grab our paper plates, and head over to the grill. Lorelei, Julie, and Laurel take brats from Seth while Todd and I get burgers.

We then each go through the line at the table to adorn our meats with our choice of condiments and veggies. I load my burger with red onions, pickles, and mustard. Seth puts the remaining burgers and brats on a ceramic plate and puts it on the table in case anyone wants seconds. He takes a burger, loads it accordingly, and takes his place near his wife.

Julie prays before we eat. It is a prayer of gratitude. We indeed have much to be grateful for. After a group "Amen" there is a small space where Lorelei inserts, "Ladies, remember, brat to mouth."

What follows is a domino-effect wave of shock. Seth almost drops his plate, catching it in the proverbial nick; Todd chokes on his last gulp of air; I almost brain myself on the siding of the house, lurching backward in what is about to become one big-ass belly laugh; Julie's left hand covers her mouth as she gasps while Laurel's eyes bulge and she exclaims, "Lori, oh my goodness!"

Lorelei shrugs admiring her mischievousness. We all explode in side-splitting howls.

"You are my kinda gal," Todd says raising his bottle of Budweiser in salute.

It's times like this that remind me why I started down this path in the first place. All the work, all the effort, all the struggle, all the years. Worth. Every. Moment. We haven't even hit the stage yet and I feel like this has been a success for no other reason than I got my childhood friends back and for feeling part of something bigger than myself.

Once the laughing fit has subsided and we begin our meal, Laurel starts the evening's conversation. "We're set on the first three songs. Practice next Saturday we run through *1986, Everything Changed, All Those Ones and Zeroes,* Innovation Generation, and *It's Our Time Now.*" The rest of us have food in our mouths so there is a mumble of agreement.

"Eric, I think we need a warm up gig," Laurel adds. "Jumping in to three performances isn't in our best interest. Having a performance before a friendly crowd would be a safe place not to be perfect."

Chewing on my burger allows me to mentally chew on Laurel's suggestion. It has merit, no doubt. Once I've swallowed the latest bite I reply, "I don't disagree with you but that's one more venue, one more city to figure out. More logistics. You've given this some thought. What are you thinking?"

"A family and friends show," Laurel responds. "We invite a friendly audience and put on a free show for them. It allows us a real-world environment experience, allows us to gauge the impact of our songs, and allows us to get feedback from people who will be honest but not brutal."

"That," Lorelei says nodding, "is a fabulous idea."

"Seconded," Todd ratifies with a countenance that would imply we're using some parliamentary procedure. "But that is a lot to pull together in a short amount of time if we want to book one performance a month July, August, September. We haven't even played all the songs as a group yet and now we're talking another show..." Todd's voice trails off and we're left to consider the words he left hanging in the air.

Out of the blue, Seth blurts, "Bacon! Crap! I meant to wrap the burgers in bacon!"

"Bacon," comes out under my breath. "That's it."

Julie furrows her brow at me. "You're concerned about your burger not having bacon?"

"No, no," I wave Julie off. "That's the answer."

Five brows furrow in my direction. "Not following," Lorelei says speaking for the group.

"Six degrees of separation. Kevin Bacon. Don't you see it?" I ask in desperation.

"Lay it out, Eric, so we can follow," Laurel directs.

My mind is open wide and it sees the puzzle pieces that were there all the time but I didn't recognize them for what they were. This whole thing has been about my ability to bring things together but it doesn't have to be. Images, names, possibilities come into focus.

"Here's the deal. It's about our relationships," I begin. "Our family and friends show *should* be at the Surf Ballroom in Clear Lake. Historic. Iconic. It's the perfect place to kick off a reunion tour. I know people who can make that happen."

"I like where you're headed," Todd says. "Keep going."

"Beyond inviting those we know we can speed up the process by contacting our old classmate Sara..."

"...and she organizes an impromptu class reunion," Laurel finishes my sentence. "Genius."

"It is a great idea but who is Sara?" Lorelei asks.

"Sara came to our school not long after you moved," I bring Lori up to speed.

"Is she that redhead who was always into stats?" Todd asks.

I nod quickly. "Yes. Sara is also adept at organizing anything including all of our class reunions to date."

I go on to explain that Sara holds all the contact information for our class and she is friends with everyone on Facebook. She'd be able to pull this impromptu class get together fast. Not all of our classmates still live within 100 miles but some are close enough to give us a decent crowd when combined with those friends and family we invite.

"Relationships are how we book the venues we need and get promotional support necessary in each city. We leverage relationships to help us get an 'in' to the decision makers and media folks. The friends and family show can be used as a springboard to create buzz and help get us booked. Julie can video the show and the girls can upload parts of the concert on YouTube and other social media," I conclude.

"That's not a horrible idea," Todd complements me with his left hand. "Makes sense."

"It does, doesn't it?" Lorelei agrees.

"My friends," Laurel makes it unanimous, "we have ourselves a plan. Let's wrap the Onions in bacon."

The six of us grab our drinks, raise them in the air, and exclaim as one, "Bacon!"

CHAPTER FIVE

COME ON, GET ONIONS

June 30, 2018

"ONIONS...ONIONS...ONIONS!"

The Surf Ballroom is jumping as the crowd chants for us moments before our first performance. I'm able to see a sliver of the crowd through the tiny space from where the stage curtain falls short of reaching the stage wall. A horde of butterflies does supersonic laps around my stomach. It feels like the rollercoaster is riding me and I'm about to send my lunch back the way it came. I can't remember the last time I was this nervous. This is the dream, man. Forty years since the four of us gathered on an elementary playground; a child's dream has become an adult reality.

We're just minutes from hitting the stage and making our official debut here at the legendary Surf Ballroom in Clear Lake, Iowa. For most bands their debut is in some third-rate, hole-in-the-wall dive bar where the patrons are too drunk to know their ass from a hole in the ground. But not Onions At A Crime Scene. No, we're making our first appearance at the Place Where the Music Died. The place that featured the last performances of Buddy Holly, J.P. "The Big Bopper" Richardson, and Richie Valens before their ill-fated flight on February 3rd, 1959. Laurel, Lorelei, Todd, and me are about to play on the same stage they did.

My buddy Mark Skaar was instrumental in getting the Onions booked here as he and the booking agent for the Surf Ballroom are good friends. Mark and I go way back to my on-air personality days when we worked together at the same radio station. My radio career began during high school at a small-town radio station about 45 miles from the Surf Ballroom.

Mark's love of music kept him happily behind the microphone while my path in the radio industry took a turn to sales and marketing. Mark is the morning personality at a local classic rock station about 10 miles from Clear Lake. Mark's been able to meet many of the famous bands who have played here in the past 20 years – including KISS – and has been emcee for many of those shows.

I'd reached out to Mark and gave him the Reader's Digest version of the Onions story and he needed zero arm twisting to help us get booked at the Surf. Mark was kind enough to interview me on his morning radio show to give us a little love over the airwaves. Our YouTube views and website traffic spiked immediately after the interview. Gotta love the power of radio. Let's face it, radio was the first social media.

Laurel worked on filling the Surf Ballroom while I worked on securing the venue. Laurel through Sara made this event one part class reunion, one part family reunion, one part kick-ass celebration through our *six degrees of separation* strategy and execution.

Laurel, Lorelei, Todd, and I – plus Seth and Julie – went on a full-court press to invite friends and family through personal invites via email and social media direct messages. We were purposeful in our invites to family and friends we believed would come out to support and celebrate.

"Some crowd, huh?" Lorelei asks me. The sudden question while I was firmly in my head nearly sends me into the rafters.

"Jumpy much?" Lori teases amused by the fact her simple question gave me such a start. "Little preoccupied?"

"Yeah, just a little," I tell her. "The goal has always been to get us here but it's been all objectives and tasks and connecting dots... all logistics and execution. This? This is pure emotion, pure performance...so outside my comfort zone." My thumb gestures toward the curtain and the crowd on the other side of it. "You're telling me you're not anxious?"

A smile of unadulterated joy lights up her face. "Are you kidding? I'm riding a wave of adrenaline and endorphins, baby. No nerves. Just excitement."

"I'm not an envious person by nature, L, but I am a little jealous." No smile lights my face only a fleeting look of melancholy.

"You put so much pressure on yourself, Eric. This band has been resting on your shoulders this entire time and look at where we are. We're about to take the stage. It's happening! Relax and embrace the good." She throws a hug on me and gives me an extra squeeze before releasing the embrace. Her words and hug have the intended of effect of calming my nerves.

"Have you seen how many people are here?" Todd asks abruptly ending the moment Lori and I are having. "This place is packed. The fire marshal is here and says we're at capacity. One more person and we'll exceed code. How sweet is that?" Todd is as jubilant as Lori. The butterflies in my stomach throttle up once more.

Packing this place is done on two levels. Level one is filling the booths that form a horseshoe along the sides and back of the ballroom. The booths are as they were in the 1950s with a maximum of four people to a booth. Level two is filling the dance floor and is a standing-room only proposition. It's not unusual for the Surf to be packed but it's not something I had anticipated to be the case for us.

"I have," Lorelei answers, "but Eric hasn't," she says. "Too nervous to look."

"Hey, did anybody get the license plate of the bus Lori just threw me under?" I mock my keyboardist. "No, I haven't taken a look. I want to hang back till that curtain parts to take in the crowd."

"Wuss," Todd sends a shot over my bow. "What are you afraid of...the people might disappear if you look at them?"

"Not at all. Trying not to psych myself out before we debut." Deep breath as I realize that if I keep time by my heartbeat our performance will be over in about 15 minutes.

"Why are the people disappearing?" Laurel asks entering the conversation midway.

"Eric thinks if he takes a look at all the people here before we start playing they'll evaporate," Todd brings Laurel up to speed.

"Hey," I protest, "you said that, not me. I'm just over here trying not to lose my shit, okay? Is it okay with you that I'm nervous?"

Laurel smiles enjoying the playful bickering among bandmates. "It's fine. Nerves are no big deal. We should all be a little nervous or something's wrong." Then, turning to Todd, "The crowd is phenomenal. Only ten minutes till show time."

Deep breath. And another. And another. The energy level ramping up makes it appear the assembled heard Laurel and are suddenly getting louder with their chanting and whooping. I take a quick glance to the stage hidden by the curtain. The equipment hasn't moved. Our instruments, monitors, cables, and microphones are exactly where they need to be and haven't moved since we finished sound check 90 minutes ago.

"We should probably take our places," Lorelei says.

We nod and move toward our instruments as one. The crowd gets quieter as I get closer to my drum kit. It's not that their sound level has decreased it's the pounding of my heart has increased to the point I am only able to hear it.

I fidget in my seat till I'm comfortable. Physically comfortable anyway. I look over at the stand for my cymbal. Taped to the stand is the set list for tonight. We're kicking off with *Take The Day* then *It's Our Time Now*. We want to keep the crowd's energy up so we're starting off with two of our most anthem-like, upbeat songs.

```
Surf Ballroom Set list:
Take The Day
It's Our Time Now
California Dreamin'
Everything Changed
No Way Back Today
1986
Happy Ever After
All Those Ones and Zeroes
Innovation Generation
Encore: Talk Dirty to Me
```

Deep breath. Then another. Heart doesn't slow down for an instant. Over to my right is a now-laminated, hand-drawn picture of our band taped to my snare drum. The picture where the dream started. The picture that led us here. Hard exhale. Cannot get my nerves to settle down. This is a friendly show and I feel like I'm about to step off a high dive blindfolded. I'm so grateful that Laurel suggested we kick off our tour with this show. I'd hate to feel this nervous at our first official tour show.

A flash in my head. The Partridge Family. The episode where they play their first gig has a scene where Mrs. Partridge is nervous but the kids aren't. When the curtains part, Mrs. Partridge is fine but all the kids have stage fright and are unable to move. They're statues as Mrs. Partridge frantically runs from child to child attempting to awake them from their fright and relax enough to do what they've practiced – being a band. I'm praying the Onions are not in for a similar start to our playing career.

"Help us, Shirley Partridge," I whisper under my breath.

"Hey, Eric, you ready?" Lorelei inquires, snapping me back to reality with the question three people are seeking an answer to. I nod hesitantly. "Are you still nervous?" Lori follows up.

"Depends," I respond.

"Depends on what?" Lorelei asks.

"No, I think I need Depends. Very nervous," I clarify.

The four of us crack up at my poking fun at myself. This last little moment between us before the show starts has a calming effect on me.

"I know the energy drink companies turned us down but I'd hate like hell to get a Depends sponsorship," Todd adds.

"Come soak up the Onions with Depends!" I announce in a dramatic voice.

"No!" three voices protest. "Not happening," Laurel adds.

My buddy Mark strides up, his shoulder length brown hair rustles with the breeze his speed creates. All six-feet, five inches of my friend approaches us to confirm we're all set to go before he introduces us for the first time on tour. Mark gets four thumbs up.

"Onions At A Crime Scene," he says, "let's make some history." He slips between the curtain and the stage wall I'd been peering through a few minutes ago. One last time we look at one another. No words are exchanged just looks of anticipation and joy.

"Ladies and Gentlemen," Mark's voice sounds from in front of the curtain, "welcome to the legendary Surf Ballroom in Clear Lake, Iowa! Tonight we are here to kick off the reunion tour for four very special people with a unique dream. It is my pleasure to be able to introduce them to you tonight. Please put your hands together for... Onions At A Crime Scene!!!" Mark exits stage right clapping along with the audience that is roaring even louder. My countdown can only be heard by us. Mark isn't halfway off the stage when Laurel starts off the intro line to *Take The Day*.

"How could we forget?" Then our instruments come to life and the four of us sing as one:

"Those sweet childhood days. Naivety and carefree fun. In the schoolyard, as we played. We go back to yesterday. Reminisce of good times. So glad, that this day came..."

There is again a surreal disassociation as my body plays the drums and my mouth makes the sounds that match everyone else but my mind wanders to take in the scene in front of me. We purposely instructed the guy in charge of the house lights that they be kept at a level so we can at least see the crowd on the dance floor. Julie, Nicole, Ashley, Seth along with the boys, Lori's twin daughters, Aniko, Jared, and the kids are front and center.

Further scanning reveals our schoolmates from the class of '86 and Ani's high school English students. The sight of the teens is such a shock that I almost drop a beat. It's the group of students with whom I shared my crushed rock and roll fantasy back in January. They are jumping up and down as one yelling. Some are holding up hand-made signs with slogans on them.

"Onions Rock!"

"The Dream Lives!"

"Eric = Awesome!"

"Our Favorite Onions!"

My drum instructor Nick has a sign that matches the gift certificate he had made me – Batman behind a drum kit. Tears well up and a few manage to escape and make a run for it down my cheeks. This journey was bound to be emotional and I knew it.

The expected emotions were supposed to be from the joy of being here with my friends and realizing a dream. The emotion from experiencing the support and the reception we would get was never given much thought. I'd hoped people would like our music and be entertained. Okay, maybe even a little inspired. Never was this outpouring expected. Heck of a way to launch the reunion tour.

Take The Day winds up and we go into *It's Our Time Now*. This is the first time these people have heard our songs unless they were able to check out our videos on YouTube. This allows us to get a sense of how people respond to our songs, especially our generation who – hopefully – can identify with our message and our feelings.

The energy coming at us never lets up even for an instant. My focus comes back to the four of us. Lorelei looks like she's having a Sex Pistols good time. Her fingers fly across the keys while she and I are in perfect vocal harmony to Laurel and Todd's melody. A killer smile is her default expression.

Todd is shredding his guitar for all he's worth. His singing and playing is spot on and with gusto. Every once in a while he cuts loose with a tongue stick out that would make Gene Simmons proud. Todd was the reluctant one, the one that took the most convincing, and now he looks like he's having the time of his life.

Laurel's smile is almost as big as Lorelei's. She's all over the stage, stopping next to Todd to sing together with a shared mic, and then sprinting back to Lori's keyboard, giving them a moment together to show off their musical talent. They exaggerate their motions and the crowd loves all of it.

Laurel pulls up in front of my drums and we go note for note. Then, with a pre-planned signal, the Surf goes dark with only the footlights providing illumination and I unleash my secret weapon – LED light up drumsticks. The crowd comes unglued. It is an eruption of astonishment and delight. It is freaking fantastic. The only thing that could make it perfect is if Sheila E were here to see my homage to her.

Once we hit the next verse, the lights come back to their previous level and my drumsticks are powered down, for now. We wrap the second song. More cheers and clapping as the final note fades over the crowd.

"Thank you!" Laurel exclaims. "What a tremendous welcome! You guys are awesome! Wow!" She slides her pick under one of the strings. "Whenever I'm not playing guitar I like to keep a pick in my G-string."

Laurel didn't warn me of her impending one-liner but my reflexes are quick enough to fire off a perfectly-executed rim shot. Cheers, shouts, and laughs rise up from a large segment of the audience...the large segment that is not any of Generation X's children or teenagers or her sons.

"Gotta keep you on your toes, people!" Laurel warns. "We're as unconventional as it gets, right?" The question isn't for them, it's for us. And, yes.

"What brought us here is a terrific story and we wouldn't be here if not for Eric," Laurel continues as the three of us move in next to her. She and Todd bookend Lorelei and me. I don't know if anyone else notices but from the ballroom perspective, the four of us are spelling out T.E.L.L. Circle of life, folks.

"When Eric pitched the idea to us, we decided to go out and sing karaoke to hear if we had what it takes to be the band he envisioned. At a bar in Des Moines, Onions At A Crime Scene was born," Laurel pauses giving the crowd a chance to applaud. "This is not a song we wrote but this is the song that launched our band and what led us here. We'd like to sing that song for you now."

Laurel pulls out a harmonica from her pocket and sounds the note to get us in key. As at AJ's, Laurel and Todd lead while Lori and I echo. The under 40 crowd doesn't know the song but they are clapping as loud as their elders simply because we make the song ours. The hair on my arms is standing and dancing on its own. *California Dreamin'* is a song I've always liked but it wasn't necessarily my favorite. Can't say that anymore. This is a special song for all of us and always will be.

Being at the front of the stage now gives me a perspective I don't get behind my drum kit. Cell phones are held high everywhere. Oh, baby. We're going to be all over social media. Guess we'll know by the end of the night how those in cyberspace react to tonight's launch.

Final notes hang in the air and the audience gives us vigorous applause. We bow and re-take our previous positions. Laurel segues into our next selection. "Our reunion tour is meant to share pieces of us with you as well as celebrate and acknowledge our shared experiences." Laurel pauses to brush a stray hair away from her face. "We've all had amazing experiences in the last 30 years or so and also had some experiences that were heart breaking. This is one of those songs." A brief pause to let us play the first few notes. "This is Everything Changed."

My stomach knots up as Todd sings the song that got us kicked out of an Applebee's; the first song where we're not all singing together. Todd's going solo on this one with him and me singing the chorus. The energy level of the crowd has changed as they not only hear Todd's song, they feel Todd's song. The tale being told doesn't just resonate with people who loved and lost but those who regret a chance not taken, a road not traveled.

When we get to a certain age, we realize time is not the friend it once was. You get to a point where there are some things you cannot go back and undo. We all can identify with that. It doesn't take much effort for Todd to convey his angst, his regret. Part of me wonders if he still wants to throttle me for the song. He hasn't said anything about it since the night he almost separated my head from the rest of my body but still I wonder.

The song ends and we let the air hang silent for a few beats longer than most. We want the impact to be fully felt and fully processed. Todd's head hangs, his eyes rest on the floor. If you didn't know better it would seem that his forever love just now broke up with him.

An appreciative, determined applause rises from the concert goers to let Todd know they respect what he went through and for having the guts to stand in front of them and be willing to share such a personal wound. Todd brings his eyes back up to look at the audience, nods at them, and simply raises his right hand as you would to wave at another driver. He says nothing. He doesn't have to.

Four songs, four home runs. This is a friendly crowd filled with people who know us but, if we stink, they would be polite not vibrant. This is an exhilarated crowd that doesn't take a song nor a note for granted. This gathering of friends and family maintains its energy, not letting up for a moment even during our serious offerings. It's not unusual to see couples of all ages dancing to our slower tunes.

The booths are full but where there might be conversation with music as a soundtrack for their chats, tonight there is full attention on the band with toes tapping, picture taking, and posting. I survey the room where Surf Ballroom staff is working concessions, providing security, and offering support. We get a lot of thumbs up.

We press forward never catching our breath. The four of us trade looks showing our amazement to one another. At one point, Laurel turns to me and mouths, "Oh my God." I smile and nod.

At another point, Lorelei darts away from her keyboard, comes up behind me, and musses up my hair as we sing. I'm pretending to be bothered by her intrusion but it's so over the top it's easy to determine I'm goofing around as much as she is. A quick glance Julie's way finds her smiling and clapping, not minding another woman is hamming it up with her husband. Lori's twins are shaking their heads with that "Oh, Mom, you're embarrassing us again" expression.

Too soon, we get to our last song *Innovation Generation*. *Innovation Generation* is a terrific tune. It's not just about nostalgia and recalling the glories of our youth. It's a song of redemption, a song of validation, a song of how Generation X is largely a maligned generation that doesn't get the credit it deserves for how it has influenced today's society and paved the way for what Millennials are known for today.

So, Millennials, you're gamers, huh? We were first.

Atari, anyone?

Oh, you want television on demand? We had it first.

It's called the VCR.

Your cell phones go everywhere with you?

Mobile phones started with us.

Cable news networks? We were raised on them.

This is CNN.

You want your MTV?

We're the MTV generation.

Social media and connecting online?

Look up Hypertext and Friendster then get back to us.

Feel like you're on your own growing up?

We were the first latchkey kids.

You have anxiety that the world is going to end?

We grew up in a Cold War era wondering if we would die in a rain of nuclear fire courtesy of the Soviet Union.

As it turns out Generation X and Millennials should be best friends. We have more in common than most people might think.

We're the OG versions of who you are now. We're you with more experience. You want to change the world, to make it a better place? Us too. We lived in an analog world that transitioned to digital where your entire life has been in a digital world and analog has no meaning, no context. We can help you translate, trust us.

The thought brings a warm feeling looking out into the audience and seeing a significant number of Millennials in attendance. Generation X paved the way for much of what the generations behind us take for granted today or thinks they invented. Our song is also a celebration of generations in a way that provides a bridge between both.

Sooner than any of us would like the song winds down and, with it, our concert. Truthfully, only the concert is over after the last song. There will be the after-party that will allow us to mix with our fans and greet our adoring public. We hear the loudest ovation of the evening following the last song's end.

The four of us gather again at the front of the stage, line up, grasp hands, take a bow in unison, and then bow one more time because it seems fitting. We release our grips on each other's hands and wave to what seems like every single person, one by one.

The curtain closes in front of us separating us from the ballroom. We turn to each other and start high-fiving. Then a quick run off to the side of the stage where we waited to begin our concert a little over an hour ago. The crowd hasn't stopped cheering and clapping.

"Whoa! This is phenomenal!" Todd exclaims with delight and shock. "I never thought this was anything but a cheesy idea. Not anymore! This band is the real thing!"

"We were magnificent!" Lorelei follows up. "This was supposed to be a fun distraction for me, a chance to do something fun with friends but we are totally bad ass!"

"I admit," Laurel continues the thought flow, "I hadn't totally bought in until we started practicing. I mean, how capable could we be in a handful of weeks when we'd never played together before?" Her eyes narrow as she nods with determination and endorsement. "We are *goooood*."

The three turn to me expecting comments of self-congratulation but that's not what they get. I am so choked up no words will come out. This night has meant everything to me. This night was 40 years in the making. What we did tonight was beyond my greatest hopes. Tears start and won't stop.

"Oh, Eric," Lorelei comforts wrapping me in a hug. "You've put so much of yourself into this and made such a great effort to pull this off. Look at how great this is. You had the vision, you found us, brought us together, and we are totally rocking it. And, you know what, we're not done yet."

Lorelei releases me so I can wipe the tears off my face. "Whew. Didn't expect to be that emotional but it's been…a long, hard road. Thanks, guys, for embracing the vision," are my first words able to make it out.

The crowd does not let up. Now they're chanting. "Onions encore!" Clap, clap, clap-clap-clap. "Onions encore!" Clap, clap, clap-clap-clap. "Onions encore!" Clap, clap, clap-clap-clap.

Onions At A Crime Scene doesn't have a deep song library so what does one do for an encore? We had a feeling something like this might happen so we were prepared, just in case. The chanting is allowed to continue just because we want the drama to build.

"Ready?" Laurel looks around to make eye contact with us, extending her right arm, palm facing the floor. The rest of us do the same so our palms are stacked. "Onions on three," she says. "One, two, three..."

"Onions!" the four of us shout in unison bringing our hands up over our heads.

The curtain draws back once more, the chanting stops, to be replaced by insane cheers. "Let's do it," Todd states, leading us in a jog back on stage. The clamoring gets louder at the sight of us.

"You got it," Laurel announces to the audience. "One more song." She throws the guitar strap over her head which lands on her left shoulder. "Earlier we sang the first song ever sung by this band." Laurel stops to look around to make sure we can proceed. "Now we're going to play the second. Think a lot of you will recognize this one."

The first trail of notes land in the ballroom and, I swear, the roof is going to blow off the joint. It is a sound of absolute euphoria. What's stunning to me is that it's not just our peers who recognize *Talk Dirty To Me* but our kids as well. Getting such a reception for this song is tremendously gratifying.

It's the final song of the night for us too so we let it all hang out turning the dial to 11 and a half. The encore is truly our song of thanks to our family and friends for helping make tonight such a stunning success.

Not sure who is jumping up and down more – our peers or their kids. They're singing along with us which is just crazy fun. It's difficult to pay attention to the music while trying to take in the moment and watching Todd, Laurel, and Lorelei absolutely tearing it up. In that instant I am not the drummer of the band but simply a fan as well. I allow myself to marvel at their talent and their passion. Sweat running down my forearms rollercoasters up, over, and down the goosebumps popping up.

Then we bring it home. "...ooh, yeah!" the final lyrics are sung and my ending downbeat brings the song and the show to its finale. "Thank you, Surf Ballroom, goodnight!" Laurel shouts her right arm flying up to a wave. The curtains fly shut, the house lights come up, and house music begins playing, although hearing it over the clapping and whooping is almost impossible. It doesn't stop for another ten minutes.

The four of us leave our positions and head to the men's and women's dressing rooms. We are all soaked with the hard-earned sweat of a job well done. A quick wardrobe change is in order before mixing with the people who came to see and support us.

The next couple of hours are spent schmoozing and catching up with everyone. Every person in the place is greeted and commiserated with. Other than the day I married Julie, I have never hugged or been hugged as much. The concert may have ended but the energy level hasn't dropped one bit. The band, our songs, and our reason for being have all been accepted without question, without hesitation. As we talk with folks, we're shown videos they've taken, social media posts...it's a little overwhelming that people have cemented a relationship with us and our music this quickly.

Then there's the media itself who have joined us – reporters from the local television station and the newspaper spending time interviewing each of us for a human interest story with a decidedly local twist. Any media attention we can get is welcome. Buzz has to start somewhere.

This impromptu class/family/friend reunion is a hit. Simple, laid back, and totally bitchin'. What more could the Class of 1986 ask for? It's a nice touch that our kids can be here to experience this. That's not the normal class reunion for sure. Furthering the enjoyment is reuniting our class with Todd and Lori which is a happy bonus for them. Our classmates had been informed of the composition of the group but hadn't seen half the band in decades. Stories go back and forth in the catching up of Todd and Lori to what's happened since they moved away.

Our friend and classmate Randee makes sure she talks to us when she can catch the four of us together. Randee stands about five-four with sandy blonde hair with curls that won't stop and brown eyes with a twinkle of excitement. She must have an aging portrait in her attic because she looks 29, not 49.

She's clad in a pair of tan capris, a brown blouse with the top two buttons unbuttoned, a tan stud in her right ear, a brown stud in her left ear, and a pair of brown sandals. She hasn't changed that way either. Back in high school she coordinated her outfits the same way. Now she's before us with something we apparently must hear without any further delay.

"Hey, guys, wonderful show!" Randee starts. "I love this!" She opens her arms and sweeps them around. "The band, the music, the tour, all of it. But you're missing something," Randee informs us putting her left hand on her hip and pointing her right index finger toward our faces. "Merchandise!" Her index finger moves to Laurel's left wrist. "Love, love, love the wristband. I can custom design leather wristbands for Onions At A Crime Scene. You could sell them at your merchandise booth at your shows."

"We thought we'd just make some t-shirts," I admit. "Hadn't considered much else. Is this something we should do?"

Laurel, Lori, and Todd agree it is an intriguing idea and we give Randee the go-ahead to design a leather wristband for our group. "How much do you charge?" I ask. No one does anything for free. But Randee shakes her head.

"I don't want anything. Tonight you've shown us something special and I want to support you. I'll email you the design in a week or so and we can go from there." We thank Randee and then she moves on to socialize with classmates she's not seen in years. Once Randee's out of earshot Todd asks, "Merchandise? Aren't we getting a little ahead of ourselves?"

"Wouldn't a KISS fan be all about the merchandise studying the master of merchandising, Gene Simmons?" I tweak my friend.

Todd shakes his head at my teasing and shrugs his shoulders. "I guess you have a point there."

"Just because Randee is going to design something doesn't mean we have to move forward with it," Lorelei answers Todd.

"It's fantastic that we played our first gig and someone has an idea to help us. Why not take a look?" She finishes then turns to Laurel and comments, "You trendsetter, you. You wear the rock chick leather wristbands and now everybody wants one," she chuckles.

Laurel chuckles with her. "Yeah, tell my boys their mom is a trendsetter and see what they say."

With that, we go back to socializing and bask in what has been a dazzling and dizzying evening.

* * *

A shade before midnight the last of the non-family members are gone leaving us to ourselves for the first time since walking into the Surf Ballroom this afternoon. A mutual exhaustion comes upon us but it's a fantastic exhaustion. I may go to bed tonight and wake up Monday. Glad we decided to book hotel rooms and don't have to travel a long distance tonight.

The last official piece of business before departing is to pack up our instruments, equipment, and cables into Todd's trailer for transport. The best we can do for a road crew is our children. It's free labor and makes quick work of packing, hauling, and storing.

My girls, Lori's girls, and Laurel's boys decide to loiter in the parking lot while the rest of us head back into the building one more time before calling it a night. One final visual sweep satisfies us all is well, we haven't forgotten to pack anything, and we can officially bring this first gig to its official end.

Julie puts her hand on my arm just as I am about to suggest we disappear into the evening which has turned to morning. "Hang on a second, guys." The four of us plus Seth look at her wondering what could possibly be left to do tonight.

Julie pulls out a cardboard priority envelope from her large handbag. "This came in the mail today and it looked important. With the concert being tonight I didn't want to distract you with anything so I held on to it till now when the event is over."

Julie hands me the envelope since it has my name on it. If it were a paper envelope, it might be just regular mail or even some sort of rejection notice. But there's something different, something suspenseful yet hopeful about this type of mailer. I grab the cardboard tab and pull, unzipping the envelope, removing a letter, and scanning the words quickly.

"Oh shit," I say feeling my knees buckle a bit. Julie puts her hand on my right shoulder to steady me, just in case.

"What is it?" Lorelei asks. "Is it good news?" Laurel, Seth, and Todd give me looks that ask the same question.

Making eye contact with them, almost in a daze, I reply, "We got a sponsor. We got a tour sponsor."

What ensues is an echo effect of stunned whispers one right after the other. "We got a sponsor...we got a sponsor...we got a sponsor...we got a sponsor."

"WE GOT A SPONSOR!!!!" we shout as if we already hadn't figured that out. I think the entire city of Clear Lake heard us. Hell, Buddy Holly may have heard us. We're jumping up and down, high-fiving, fist pumping, and dancing on the ballroom floor. It takes us two minutes before we're calm enough for Laurel to ask the question: "Who is sponsoring us?" Everyone stops celebrating; realizing that knowing who our benefactor is would be helpful information.

"Yeah, who are we going to be rocking with?" Lorelei follows up with anticipation.

A semi-sheepish expression on my face is what they see as I reveal the identity of our benefactor. "Centrum Silver," I announce with as much fanfare as I can muster. This is the brand I didn't want to tell Julie about for fear of jinxing it.

Crickets. Serious crickets.

Todd scowls. "Are you joking? Centrum? Vitamins for senior citizens? We're not going to be sponsored by an energy drink, a beer, a soda, or a battery but by vitamins for old people?" Todd sweeps his hands, pushing the news aside, rejecting the information.

"I know, I know, it's not sexy," I acknowledge. "But we have a sponsor. No out of pocket costs for us. At all." My words are not making a dent in turning the mood around. Julie gives me two thumbs up and a toothy grin. She knows it's a big deal even though it might not be from our "dream" category.

"Well, it would certainly speak to our generation," Lorelei says in a half-hearted attempt to be excited about our sponsor.

"Hold on," Laurel interjects. "Before we get all bent out of shape, how much is the sponsorship worth and what do we have to do for it?"

I answer the second question first. "The sponsorship means their brand goes where we go and on our promotional items...banners at our concerts, at our personal appearances, on our website, mentions in our media interviews, anywhere the Onions go, Centrum Silver will be there."

"How much?" Todd insists I answer Laurel's first question.

My eyes never leave Todd's as I reach into the envelope, remove the check, and hand it to Laurel to reveal. The dawning reality moves across her face that instantly goes white, her eyes almost popping out of her head. It's a bit unnerving.

"One hundred thousand dollars," Laurel responds apparently hypnotized. Or traumatized. Take your pick.

Todd's head jerks so violently sideways in Laurel's direction that a vertebrae cracks in his neck. "Did you just say one hundred thousand dollars?" wondering if his ears malfunctioned.

"One hundred thousand dollars," Laurel repeats still dazed and somewhat confused. Lorelei and Seth pounce to each side of her to see with their own eyes how many zeroes are on that check. Lori looks up at Todd and confirms with amazement, "One hundred thousand dollars."

Still not believing what everyone is saying, Todd comes over to see for himself only to find what everyone has said is true. He puts both hands on his head like Publishers Clearinghouse just showed up at his door with the balloons and the big check. "I love Centrum Silver!" he yells at the top of his lungs thrusting his hands in the air. "I'll take Centrum Silver every damn day for the rest of my life! It's the best vitamin for old people ever!"

We make such a commotion our kids come flying in from the parking lot to see what happened. They reach us just at the moment we all yell, "We love Centrum Silver!"

What a magnificent moment. What a grand night. What a wonderful way to kick off the tour.

Thank you, Shirley Partridge.

CHAPTER SIX

LIGHTS, CAMERA, ONIONS

July 27, 2018

"This is crazy. You know that, right?" is how our interview begins.

It's 10:30 on a Friday morning and Onions At A Crime Scene is on-set at a regionally syndicated Minneapolis-based television show called The Jason Show. The host is – wait for it – Jason. It is he who sits directly across from Laurel with Lorelei, Todd, and yours truly in a line off Laurel's left shoulder. We're in front of a live studio audience in Minneapolis promoting our Saturday night gig at First Avenue.

Thanks to an introduction assist from my long-time radio buddy Jay Philpott – an on-air personality for one of the local radio stations – we have booked the legendary First Avenue for our performance tomorrow night. Jay also put us in touch with The Jason Show's producer to get us some publicity before tomorrow night's show and help sell more tickets.

Our interviewer continues his thought, "I know we live in an internet-sensation era but a reunion tour for a band that didn't exist six months ago? That's wacky." Jason looks to the audience. "Am I right?" The audience responds with spirited applause accompanied by a few hoots and hollers.

The pace of life has picked up significantly since the Surf Ballroom performance. The reaction to our songs by comments from the show's attendees and by comments on our YouTube channel made it clear we needed to get our songs released before our first tour stop. The Centrum Silver sponsorship money gave us the means to get in the recording studio and produce our first album *No Way Back Today*.

Going from practicing in Laurel and Seth's garage to performing in a studio under the watchful ear of a producer and an engineer surrounded by recording equipment and sound-proofed walls was totally tubular.

The four of us wanted to minimize nerves as much as possible so they wouldn't hinder our process and consume precious time. The solution was to make the studio our own.

I brought the MTV beach blanket received as a high school graduation gift hanging it behind me. Lorelei brought her entire collection of California Raisins placing them all over her keyboard. Laurel brought her Alf figurine perching it on the four-legged stool next to her, and Todd has KISS' *Destroyer* album propping it on top of a speaker.

The best touch is that we all brought our old concert t-shirts out of moth balls. I have my Joan Jett t-shirt from '89, Laurel her Corey Heart t-shirt from '84, Todd his KISS t-shirt from '84 and, yes, Lori has her Sex Pistols t-shirt from '08. All shirts are on hangars and are suspended from coat hooks next to the door. The personal touches have the desired effect of putting us in a zone of crisp execution.

The recording and producing of *No Way Back Today* took less time than one would expect from a burgeoning band. It gets done in a weekend. The final product brings about an album which any band would be proud.

Our digital media gurus got our album uploaded and ready for people to buy and download. Onions At A Crime Scene's *No Way Back Today* is another step down our offbeat path as is today's appearance on a television talk show.

"Talk about a wonderful story," Jason continues. "I...love you guys!"

The four of us smile and turn to the audience waving in acknowledgment and thanks. From the TV viewer's perspective we're waving to a packed studio full of hundreds of people. In reality, it's a crowd of about 100 people sardined into a confined space to give the illusion of a large studio audience. Regardless, we are delighted to see such strong reactions from a group of people we've never met nor seen before.

The studio vibe radiates warmth. The set is bright, vibrant, alive. The set we're on is not the set that was here before our interview. During the commercial break the stage crew wheeled away Jason's trademark white, oval desk and replaced it with a couch for us. The couch is on the right hand side of the stage as the audience faces it with a matching, upholstered arm chair across from us where Jason is sitting.

The backdrop for the interview set is comprised of three large squares suspended from the rafters that have space between them to walk through. The middle tile has Jason spelled out large as life.

Each letter starts with a different color that blends as the letters overlap. Behind the letters is a water-blue background with bubbles cascading like carbonation in a glass of soda.

Jason wears his trademark black, horn-rimmed glasses which complement his medium blue suit with white shirt and baby blue tie with white polka dots. His brown eyes have a gleam that communicates, *I can't believe they pay me to have this much fun!*

It can be hard to know what to expect when doing a show like this. Nobodies can be treated as such, just random people filling air time because no better guests were available. That's not Jason. We're getting star treatment as much as guests like Harry Connick Junior, Sally Field, or Justin Timberlake.

"I've read about you online and have seen your website and YouTube videos, which are great by the way, but why do this at all? Is it vanity? Midlife crisis?" Jason finishes with a chuckle. For the seemingly hostile questions, they are far from it.

The crowd chuckles with us at the uttering of "midlife crisis" because it does seem to be the logical conclusion. Jason's questions are reasonable for someone who isn't us, who hasn't been part of this improbable journey from the beginning, who looks at us from faraway and wonders what on earth would possess four apparently sane individuals to do something so inexplicable.

"Let me state for the record," Laurel answers emphatically, "I am not having a midlife crisis. I have no idea about these people." Jason and the assembled audience erupt at Laurel's metaphorical throwing the rest of her bandmates under a large bus. We feign injury at Laurel's remark and shake our heads vigorously.

"Seriously, Jason," Laurel continues, "this started out as a reunion of friends and living out something we talked about doing as nine-year-olds." She looks at us and then sweeps her hand to include the audience in what she's about to say. "It's become much more than that." The three of us nod with her.

"How so?" Jason follows up.

"At first we questioned Eric's sanity and wondered what the hell he was getting us into," Todd chimes in. "Honestly, I was the one who was the biggest holdout. This seemed like the dumbest idea ever. When you consider everything involved, this idea should not have gotten off the ground. But it did. Here we are."

"That begs the question why," Jason folds Todd's answer into his next question. "Why does it work?"

"It works because we work," Lorelei answers. "It's not about fame or notoriety or proving anything or vanity. For us, it's about enjoying our renewed friendship through our music and linking us and our message with others."

"Let's talk about the music," Jason looks down at the blue index card in his hand. "I've obviously not heard all of your songs but, from the videos I have seen, these songs – these lyrics – seem truly personal. Eric," Jason fixes his eyes on me, "where did the inspiration for these songs come from?"

Jason keeps mentioning our videos on YouTube. We're pleased we had Julie video practices and the Surf Ballroom show. Having those videos online has allowed us to get the Onions out there when we've barely gotten out of the gate as a band.

A deep breath in and then back out before I respond. Even though the four of us have embraced the lyrics, I still get a tummy tickle thinking of *Everything Changed* and Todd's first reaction to that song.

"Lorelei said it perfectly in that we're looking to associate with people through our music. Even though many of our songs come from our personal experiences, our songs are the experiences of our generation, with people of all ages. It's about crafting songs that aren't Onions At A Crime Scene songs; it's about singing songs that our audiences have lived. Our songs are authentic, are heartfelt..."

"And heartbreaking, yes?" Jason tweaks the anxious nerve of mine. "Let's talk about *Everything Changed*."

Let's not, the voice in my head answers.

"Zowie!" Jason continues apparently unable to hear the voice in my head. "An emotionally-charged song. Rips your heart out," he finishes putting his right hand over his heart as though his is in danger of being taken out of his body. "Who belongs to that situation?"

"Me," Todd says without hesitation, raising his hand so there is no mistaking who claims ownership of the heartache.

"Can you talk about it?" Jason queries. "Is it still painful?"

"Yeah," Todd nods. "It took a long time and," he looks over at me, "the song re-opened a wound I thought was closed. And – can I say this on TV – it pissed me off. Big time." I nod to confirm Todd's statement. "It's something that will always sting because she was 'the one'."

Jason shakes his head. "Superb. Great stuff." He looks over at Laurel once more. "Let's talk money." Lori snorts in surprise at the non-sequitur introduced to her bandmate. "Your management team tells me you're donating proceeds from your concerts and merchandise sales. Is that true?"

The four of us exchange quizzical looks. "Management team?" Laurel asks Jason for clarification.

Lights, Camera, Onions | 213

"Yes. Seth and Julie. Aren't they your management team?" he follows up.

A simultaneous 'ah-ha' from us. Got it. Management team. Laurel chuckles. "Yes, of course, they are. We just call them spouses. Same thing." Crowd laughs once more.

I'm pleased by our acceptance from those assembled. It's not just polite, it's almost affectionate. I'm also enjoying the lighter side of Laurel and don't mind that she has become the point person for interviews and on stage. This was never about ego stroking or needing this to be all about me. It's always been about the four of us, about the band. Laurel's fronting our group reminds me how she has embraced our merry band of 50-somethings.

"This reunion tour was never meant to be a money grab. The *No Way Back Today* tour is sponsored by Centrum Silver," she pauses for a moment allowing us to turn to the camera and put our palms under the Centrum Silver logo on the left sleeve of our tour's medium blue polo shirts. That ought to make our benefactor happy. We turn back to Jason who is doubled over laughing.

Jason composes himself and says, "About as adroit of a sponsor plug as I've ever seen. Very smooth. Go on. Please."

"We're not doing this to get rich," Laurel states. "With Centrum Silver's generosity and belief in us, we can donate the proceeds from our ticket and merchandise sales to fight human trafficking. It's a scourge that is ruining countless lives. We wanted to make this reunion tour mean even more to us and help others. This is how we are accomplishing that."

"Come to our concert and buy our stuff!" Lorelei blurts out to the audience; here and in front of their TV sets. "Embrace the good. Do good." Cheering fills the studio.

Bring those cheers to First Avenue tomorrow night and bring friends. Lots of friends, the voice in my head implores.

"What's the biggest surprise to this point?" Jason moves on to the next question.

Todd jumps in for this one, "For me, it's the response from others outside our generation. We're all Xers and that's what our songs are about. But the kids of the Xers are embracing us too."

"Acceptance, definitely," Lorelei attests. "We're four ordinary people in a band no one ever knew or had heard of. How were we to ever expect this response?"

"Let's pick up on acceptance, Eric," Jason brings his attention my way. "The reason this band didn't come together decades ago was because a band teacher didn't believe you could be a drummer, isn't that right?"

Todd and I have a quick exchange with our eyes. *Now things get personal for you*, his eyes seem to tell mine. I take the answer to Jason's interrogative in a different direction.

"If Onions At A Crime Scene is built upon a junior high band teacher's rejection, then our foundation is not great enough to sustain this journey. If there's anything we've learned personally and from those who have sent emails or posted on social media, it's that we all have had others doubt us, dash a dream, squash an ambition. What has been so gratifying for us is how others have been inspired by our story and reminded by us that it is never too late to run toward your dreams, no matter how old a person is. If there is anything the Onions should be remembered for, we hope it is that."

"This ain't no pity party, it's an aspiration celebration!" Lorelei sends forth throwing her hands in the air in victory.

"What, are you Dr. Phil now?" Todd asks Lori incredulously. The studio is filled with laughter at the playful bickering that comes from a place of affection not antagonism. "You got any other cliché's of wisdom?"

"Don't block, rock!" Lori quips looking Todd squarely in the eyes.

Todd face palms at being one-upped so quickly. The audience eats it up. It's so funny how I'm the serious one now and the others are the jokesters. I am so okay with that. This is why I wanted to reunite us. The friendship. The camaraderie. The silliness.

Jason throws his arms wide open as a crescendo to the interview, "Let's hear it for Laurel, Lorelei, Todd, and Eric...Onions At A Crime Scene! It's the No Way Back Today reunion tour brought to you by Centrum Silver. Go see them tomorrow night at First Avenue in Minneapolis. Tickets still available. We'll be back after this."

The floor manager gives Jason the signal that we're off air and the commercial break has begun. The audience is still buzzing. All in all, this was a bodacious interview.

"That was terrific!" Jason's excitement over how well the segment went is evident. "You folks have tremendous chemistry. If I didn't know it weren't so, I'd swear you'd been doing this for a long time. This is about the best first time interview I've ever had." Jason leans in and ends with, "No kidding, my audience gets excited about my guests but other than having a national celebrity on my show, they don't get as excited as they were for you today. Thanks for coming on."

Jason stands and shakes hands with all of us. "Good luck tomorrow night." We thank and shake and then it's off quickly so the next segment can be readied before the commercial break ends.

"Don't block, rock?" Todd says to Lori under his breath as we step off the set. "Seriously?"

"Dr. Phil is totally going to steal that," I observe.

* * *

"ONIONS! ONIONS! ONIONS!" the chants continue to climb.

First Avenue is shaking from its foundation on up. Something Resembling Responsible, our warmup act, did a marvelous job getting the audience pumped up for the main attraction. We're on in ten minutes and this crowd is ready.

"Oh crap, oh crap, oh crap," Lori machine guns after doing a fast 180 to face the three of us. Her face is white; not the Lorelei I've come to know. The rest of us give her a collective expression of "What is it?" needing no words.

Lori's eyes are as wide as Frisbees. "Guys! The place is packed. Packed! We don't know those people! This is unreal! They're here to see us!" Lori puts her hands on top of her head in a mixed expression of panic and astonishment.

A look of disdain appears on Todd's face. "Is that what's bothering you...people are here?" He shakes his head as he walks past Lori and moves the curtain slightly. He too does a lightning-fast 180. "Shit! People are here. Lots of people. My god, it s wall-to-wall out there!"

Great. Two band members having a panic attack. Laurel extends her arms at a 45-degree angle away from her body, palms facing the floor. "Okay, no one go near the curtain. Bring it in, Onions." We gather in small circle. Laurel turns her palms to face the ceiling indicating we're all to hold hands. Todd positions himself between the two women so he doesn't have to hold my hand. I look over and nod at him silently communicating, *I get it, old friend. No offense taken.*

We've all been on edge today. After our segment on The Jason Show we decided to have lunch and kill some time at the Mall of America. We thought we were just four friends, two spouses plus four adult women children hanging out at a mall. We failed to realize we're a thing now. One person – one – recognized us from The Jason Show or the internet or something and suddenly the "Onions sighting" brought forth the friendliest mob of people who made us the nucleus of an extremely giddy bubble.

Our social media team was on top of things from the get-go. Nicole posted on Instagram, Ashley went live on YouTube, while Faith and Hope hosted a Facebook live video giving a play-by-play of the action. They absolutely played it up when MOA security rushed to our "defense". The dozens of women surrounding us were thrilled and of no threat to our safety but the speed and exuberance with which the swarm descended – how can I put this? We weren't ready for it.

As Todd would say, "This is when shit got real." Really real.

The Onions did not disappoint our fans. Autographs, selfies, hello videos to be texted to friends or loved ones...whatever the request was, we honored it. The experience was positive and gratifying but it is the first time our "adoring public" interacts with us and we're a little freaked out by our sudden celebrity. We spend more time at the Mall than intended. MOA security gives us a personal escort all the way back to our rental van. It's a quiet, determined drive back to our hotel.

A day later we're still unnerved and now we're holding hands behind the curtain at First Avenue. "Guys, guys," Laurel implores.

"Relax. Enjoy. Embrace. There's a wave of energy on the other side of that curtain. Don't fight it. Ride it. We've already played a gig so we can do it. This is just a gig where we don't know as many people. But they know us. They came here to support us. They're rooting for us. They're on our side."

"Something bigger than us is at work here," I add hoping to encourage not freak us out further. "Whatever it is, people want to be part of our journey. It's now their journey too."

I take a big breath and blow it out hard. "We didn't want to play to an empty room, well, damn straight we're not. Let's go give them an experience they'll tell their great-grandchildren about."

The four of us stand motionless and listen. Not sure about anyone else but I start getting chills. Our eyes dart from one to the other checking to see how the rest of us are handling this. The gaze of fear turns to an expression of delight. We begin fist pumping in rhythm to the chants. We start chanting with the crowd. It is only then we notice Lorelei's twins have been live streaming the entire thing since their mom peeked through the curtain. We're shocked at first and then we get over it. Laurel said ride the wave and so we do.

Laurel exhorts, "Onions on three...one, two, three..."

"ONIONS!"

We take our places on stage. Hope and Faith disappear to find a space in the audience to shoot video. Nicole and Ashley are handling the merchandise table while Seth and Julie hang close by just in case something pops up during the show needing their attention. We have our t-shirts which are teal blue shirts and have Lorelei's signature slogan "Embrace the Good" on the front. On the back is the band's logo across the shoulder blades, with No Way Back Today below it, tour cities and dates listed below it, with the Centrum Silver logo acting as a vertical bookend to the Onions' logo.

We have the leather wristbands Randee designed, Onions approved, and manufactured by a local company. Randee outdid herself. They're magnificent. There is room for both the Onions and Centrum Silver logos on them. Laurel started the trend by wearing a leather wristband at the friends and family show. The Onions make it a signature and we all wear bands on both wrists. The promotional products company that made them gave us a deal on magnets if we wanted them too. We took them up on their offer.

My bandmates are ready to go. Laurel has on the outfit she wore at our coffee meeting; Turquoise dress over leggings with high boots. No sweater this time out. Todd has on a short-sleeved red and black cotton shirt with jeans and cowboy boots. Lorelei is wearing a black tank top tucked in to her blue jeans, a black choker around her neck. Her belt buckle spells ROCK. I'm in jeans, an untucked, short-sleeved official Onions shirt, and sneakers. We look like a suburban rock band.

I glance down once more to make sure my set list and my 4th grade drawing of the band are where I left them. We've mixed up the song order tonight and are starting with *It's Our Time Now*.

```
          Minneapolis Set List:
             It's Our Time Now
           Innovation Generation
            California Dreamin'
             Happy Ever After
               Take The Day
             Everything Changed
```

No Way Back Today
1986
All Those Ones and Zeroes
Encore: Talk Dirty to Me

My buddy Jay Philpott jogs from stage left and gives us a goofy grin and a wink before he disappears to the crowd side of the curtain. Jay is the definition of a character and is one of the industry's good guys. He was more than happy to help us get booked at First Avenue when I told him about the Onions.

Jay and I go way back in the radio industry. My radio career kept me close to my roots while Jay's kept him traveling up and down the dial across the country. These days Jay has settled in behind the microphone doing afternoons on the most popular radio station in Minneapolis.

"Laaaaaadies and gentlemen, iiiiiit's SHOW-time!" he screams barely able to be heard above the din, even with the microphone. "I'm Jay Philpott and tonight is the first show in the Onions At A Crime Scene No Way Back Today reunion tour presented by Centrum Silver!" The crowd cheers for all its worth.

"Please give a Minneapolis welcome to...Onions At A Crime Scene!" The curtains part at the same speed at which Jay exits. He's barely off the stage when we go full throttle. As with the Surf Ballroom show, we're careful to not let our excitement throw us off beat. Nerves before have become unadulterated adrenaline now.

Not even 30 seconds into the song I see it. The house lights are set so we can't see everyone in attendance clearly but we can see a sea of humanity wearing "Embrace the Good" official Onions t-shirts. I was hoping we might sell a respectable number of shirts after the show but for these folks to buy them on the way in and wear them for our first performance is astounding. About half of those wearing shirts also sport Onions wristbands as their fists punch the air over their heads. The other three have to be seeing this too. Wonder what they think about all of this.

"Together we'll make the change we need...have faith you'll be, who you wanna be. Step up and narrate your own future...Life won't be handed to you on a plate." We sing.

When I was a kid I remember looking at men and women who were 25 and thinking they were gods. Think about it...you're out of school, have a job, money, your own place, a car. You can do whatever you want – within the confines of the law – whether it's what time you go to bed, what TV shows you can watch, what food and clothes to buy. If that's not godhood, what is? When I turned 25 I found out how spot on I was. It was like being a god.

"It's our time now."

The last notes are on their way out when suddenly a yell overcomes the assembled crowd – "Embrace the good!" My head jerks left to look at where the yell originated and it, appropriately enough, came from Lorelei. Guess she noticed the shirts too.

"Thank you, Minneapolis! You guys are amazing!" Laurel picks up. "Just wondering if you like our new shirts?" She's playing with them and they respond with a gigantic, "WOO!"

"How about a little *Innovation Generation*?" Laurel asks. Doesn't matter what the response is they're getting it anyway. Clapping and hooting is the collective reply. I count us down and we launch into song two.

"Generation X, would never miss a show, with VHS recorders, they were in the know," we sing.

Before VCRs we had only two chances to see any episode of our favorite shows, when it aired originally and summer rerun. If we didn't see it either of those times, we would never see it. There was no Nick At Nite or any of those other channels or platforms airing reruns of popular shows from the past. The best we could hope for is that our local, over-the-air television station would air the old shows in syndication long after they'd gone off the air.

When I was a kid I'd been able to see reruns of Gilligan's Island, The Beverly Hillbillies, The Little Rascals, Batman, and The Partridge Family after I got home from school. But those were shows from someone else's childhood. My childhood shows were lost. Maybe they'd be in syndication years later but the TV shows of my youth were out of my reach until then.

I was 15 years-old when I bought my first VCR. It was a General Electric and cost $383. It took me five months of saving my money from my allowance, from doing odd jobs, and from bailing hay in the summer. Whatever I could do to make money I did to be able to buy that VCR. Life changed when I got that VCR. I didn't just use it to record shows I wouldn't be around to watch, I'd use it to record episodes or special one-time broadcasts that I could play again anytime I wanted. It was mind-blowing.

We lived in a rural area and didn't have cable so on Saturday mornings I'd record segments of American Bandstand to preserve performances by artists Pat Benatar, Bananarama. Adam Ant, Culture Club, The Fixx, The J. Geils Band, Billy Idol, Naked Eyes, and The Thompson Twins. Every Sunday night a couple over-the-air television stations aired weekly video countdown shows so I'd record those too. This was the closest I'd get to MTV.

How could we have ever conceived that one day we would have almost every show we'd want to watch at our fingertips or that we'd be able to watch an entire season of a television show in a weekend? Let's not even get started on movies. And to think, the seeds of the *on demand* viewing we enjoy today were planted by my generation. We can go into any store – brick and mortar or online – and purchase television shows and movies and play them whenever we want. I have seasons of The Six Million Dollar Man, The Incredible Hulk, and WKRP in Cincinnati on DVD allowing me to relive the best TV of my childhood whenever I want. It's a beautiful thing.

"With your help, we grew and we thrive," we conclude.

Fade out. Applause in large volume. Two songs in to our reunion tour and we're off to a terrific start. The butterflies are still flying amok in my stomach but they're more from adrenaline than nervousness. I don't want to take a victory lap so early in the show but thus far it seems like the audience is identifying with our songs, just as I had hoped.

The four of us move away from our instruments and gather at the front of the stage. "Any Iowa fans here tonight?" Todd asks knowing what's about to happen. The crowd doesn't disappoint. The applause quickly turns to lusty boos. The University of Iowa and The University of Minnesota are long-time Big Ten rivals and any mention of Iowa sparks strong reactions.

Todd puts his hands up at the crowd in a defensive position. "Hey, the Hawkeyes suck! You got two Iowa State grads up here!" He tosses a thumb in Laurel's direction. The crowd comes back to our side with loud cheers to find a common hater of the Hawks. I shake my head. Now Todd's playing with the crowd. Outrageous.

"Can an Illinois girl get a little love?" Lorelei asks rhetorically. The cheers turnaround again to lusty boos. In order of hateability, Illinois comes in third after Iowa and Wisconsin on the Big Ten hierarchy. Lorelei puts her hands on her hips and cocks her head to the right as if to ask, "Really?"

It's my moment to jump in to save the day. "Hey, I don't know about these posers but is there any love in the house for a native Minnesotan and Concordia University alum?" The crowd reverses course once and cheers the lone Minnesotan among our band.

"Now just a minute, mister," Laurel protests, "you grew up in Iowa like we did. What are you trying to pull?" The crowd is starting to get whiplash being emotionally jerked one way then the other repeatedly. They begin to turn on me.

"I was born in Minnesota but grew up in Iowa. As soon as I graduated high school I got the heck out of there and moved back to Minnesota," I assert. The crowd claps with amusement that I was able to successfully escape. "Hey did you hear that Iowa's starting quarterback bought a hide-a-bed? Now he can't find it." The audience hoots when I hit the punchline and now I'm back in their good graces.

"Nice save," Laurel acknowledges. "One thing we have to acknowledge is that without Iowa we would never have met and would have never launched this reunion tour. It was at a bar in Des Moines where we sang together in public for the first time. If you've ever wondered what the first song we ever sang as a group was, it's this one. Laurel then hits the note on her harmonica to get us in tune and then we perform *California Dreamin'*.

It's weird to think a group that has been together for such a short time has a sentimental favorite but we do and this is it. I take a mental step back listening to us while not losing track of what I should be singing. Our voices blend better and better the more time we spend with each other and with every practice.

The audience is almost spookily silent as we sing. There is no singing along, no applause, no sound. They're allowing themselves to take in our voices, what the song means to us, and how we are all here tonight because this song showed us what we could be.

We complete the song and just stand there. The crowd applauds us as we applaud them for appreciating the significance of the song and how it changed our lives. Life changing is something we are here to attest.

The four of us retake our places behind our instruments while the crowd continues to clap. Lorelei speaks after the sound level has come down to the point where she can be heard. "Anyone have plans for your life and something happens that ends those plans forever?" Lorelei looks around as more than a quarter of those standing on the floor earnestly put their hands together in response to the question.

"Me too," she says her head dipping toward her keyboard. "This is *Happy Ever After*."

"Sitting in your chair, the old one that reclines. Your coffee mug warms my cold hands, hands that once held so tight. This sweater holds the scent of you. I think of the time gone by. I cry no tears, the river's dry," Lorelei begins.

Note by note, we share a story inspired by Lori who bares her heart in a room full of strangers who not only sympathize with her but some can empathize. She is certainly not the only one in the room to have suffered loss. There is a sincere recognition that comes with the quiet that has come over the room taking in Lori's every word.

"Somehow I'm supposed to move on with my life. Everybody leaves you but you have to survive."

When a person or family suffers a loss there is an outpouring of support from those they know. Visitation, funeral, maybe their friends and neighbors swarm them with meals, perhaps run some errands or take care of some menial chores. A couple of weeks later all that stops. People move on with their lives. The grieving face a deafening silence as they now confront a life that looks and acts much differently as a large empty space exists where a loved one's presence once was and never will be again.

In the aftermath of loss, other people give you a couple weeks to come to terms with the new normal and then wonder why the grieving don't snap out of it, get over it, and get on with life. Oh, if it were only so simple.

What do you do when the one you said, "Till death do us part" dies before your golden years? The deal is that you get married, have kids, raise them, see them go off to college, graduate, start their own lives. Then you and your spouse enjoy being empty nesters until your kids get married and give you grandbabies you can happily spoil.

Lorelei – and many who share a similar situation – faces a much different reality. Lori had so many future memories to make with Dominic that will now be unrealized. How does that not re-open the wound every time one of those moments becomes a reality? How do you pick up your life and start over when you didn't want an end to the old one?

The five rows of people I can see standing in front of the stage have more wet eyes than dry. It is important that our songs are relatable but Lori's singing makes this song more than relatable; *Happy Ever After* penetrates the soul.

We three sing backup with a subtle delivery to allow Lori's voice to take center stage. Everyone focuses on our keyboardist. Four songs in and this crowd belongs to us. They are all in on this group and what we have to offer. We have to take them through the whole journey because, now, it's their journey too.

The song reaches its conclusion, the final notes floating in the air like so many wisps of smoke. All of us in this venue breathe as one...contemplating, wondering, feeling. I pull my drumsticks back toward my body not wanting to not break the quiet with any accidental noise. Todd and Laurel drop their right arms to their sides. Lorelei picks up her left hand, taking a moment to wipe a tear away. She's not alone. The men and women before us who have shared something so real, so devastating, wipe tears from their eyes as well. Seconds pass and then a respectful yet spine-tingling applause rises, the crowd thanking Lori for allowing them to be part of her experience.

It is a beautiful moment. "Thank you," Lorelei says softly at the response she's received. Just off stage, Faith and Hope are streaming via Facebook Live with Faith's smartphone. Both have tears streaming down their cheeks while giving their mom a thumbs up. She looks their way and blows them a kiss. The rest of us freeze until Lori's gaze to come back our way. When it does she exclaims, "*Take The Day!!!*"

The crowd roars, I count us down, and we are back to blowing the roof off the joint. This is the best amusement park ride ever and every single person in the place is strapped in with us. If there is any residual sadness from the last song, the crowd doesn't show it.

The audience is jumping up and down. They pick up the chorus and sing with us. Goosebumps up and down my arms push the hair to a standing position. A cold wave washes over my body. It is unexpected and surreal to hear our song - even if it's just the chorus - sung back to us.

Laurel turns her back on the crowd to look at me, her eyes wide with amazement, and all I need to do is nod at her to confirm I'm thinking the same thing.

Todd is shredding his guitar. Sweat has soaked the back of his hair. He is going to town. It's clear he's in the middle of a first-rate time. Lorelei is rock and roll grimacing. She's feeling it. We all are. This moment...THIS is why I put myself out there to get the band together. This is when my inner nine-year-old is freaking out, jumping up and down, screaming at the top of his lungs.

The rest of the first show is a non-stop adrenaline high for everyone. By the time we end our show at 10:30 everyone in the house is manic in a *"if there was a better way to spend a Saturday night, I don't know what it would be"* manic. The last note of the encore floats above the audience on its way into the night. The applause and cheers won't stop seemingly trying to call the notes back so the party will continue. We know we should leave the stage but can't.

The four of us line up at the front of the stage clapping for the audience to thank them for what they've given us tonight. They will never know just how much they've done for us this evening.

As we clap and wave and express our gratitude in as many ways as possible, I grab the mic from Laurel's stand and announce to the crowd that if they'd like to meet us and get selfies that they can do so in 10 minutes at the Centrum Silver selfie station next to the merchandise table. I encourage our fans - our fans, how weird is that? - to take pictures and post them on their social media.

The four of us take leave of the stage with one final wave heading down the stairs and to the dressing rooms for a quick change before meeting our fans.

"Damn," Todd says as we descend from the stage. "That's the craziest thing I've ever been part of. Did that just happen?"

"Happen? We rocked their worlds!" Lorelei exclaims. "What a rush!"

Laurel shakes her head, "Never did I ever think people would react this way. I expected polite. I never expected this."

"Best freaking reunion tour ever!" I shout throwing my fists in the air.

The Onions stop moving when we are all back on equal footing. We're all breathing hard and it's not from coming down the stairs. We haven't come down from the adrenaline high but instinctively we all realize we need a moment just for us. Faith and Hope are making a beeline toward us. Their mother waves them off. Hope says, "Meet you at the selfie station," and both young women turn on their heels and depart.

My arms extend, my hands palms up. Laurel grabs my right hand, Lorelei my left. They, in turn, reach for Todd's hands and he completes the circuit. Taking a deep breath I say, "I have no words to adequately express how much your belief in me and in the dream means to me. Other than marrying Julie and the birth of my daughters, there's not a moment in my life that tops tonight. You guys are the best."

"Are you going to start crying?" Todd asks almost annoyed. "Do you have to be dramatic for everything? It was a fantastic night. Can we just say that?"

"Ignore him," Laurel says. "This was so much more than I thought it would be. I'm looking forward to St. Louis."

"St. Louis?" Lorelei blurts out. "We're not done with Minneapolis yet. We have our adoring public to meet."

"It's not fair to keep them waiting," I agree. "Onicns on three... one, two, three..."

"Onions!" we yell in unison. Our hands go skyward in a confetti-throwing motion. A few more for high fives and we're off to our dressing rooms for a quick change before appearing for our meet and greet session.

* * *

We are stunned by what we see coming through the doorway into the meet and greet area where our merchandise tables and selfie station are located. People. Everywhere. Every. Where. Quick, astonished glances are exchanged among my bandmates. We were expecting *some* people. Just not this many somebodies. Cheers and claps rise as we're spotted.

Julie and Seth knife through the crowd to get to us and help us get to where we need to go. Compliments and back slaps come from all directions almost on top of one another. If I could get my arms up, I'd pinch myself but free space is currently hard to come by.

Ashley and Nicole are up to their eyeballs at the table, taking cash and swiping cards from a never-ending sea of humanity. I make brief eye contact with Ash and she widens her eyes at me in a *what the heck have you done* way. I widen mine back at her without knowing exactly what my expression is communicating other than utter shock.

Faith and Hope are there when we navigate our way to the selfie station. A big backdrop stands in front of the wall. Our reunion tour artwork with the Centrum Silver "presented by" showing everywhere. The Onions are positioned smack in the middle of the area. Fans can come up individually or as a group of family and friends. Using the fans' cameras, scores of pictures are taken for almost two hours. Hope reminds each person to hashtag "Onions Reunion" when they post on their social media so we can see all their pictures from the concert and the selfie station.

It's a constant coming and going of people with compliments and encouraging words that spray about like a drive by. One thing that is consistent is the level of enthusiasm people have for our music and our group. We have tapped into something very deep in ways we could have never imagined. Call it nostalgia, call it inspiration, or call it community. Whatever "it" is, it's very real and powerful. It runs through this crowd like a current.

If we had charged for the photos, we could have made a fortune but it's not about the money. The Centrum Silver sponsorship has more than paid for everything so we're happy to put more smiles on people's faces. Who knows, maybe this will help sell more tickets for the St. Louis and Chicago shows.

Julie and Seth are doing a great job of keeping the crowd moving at a steady pace so any bottleneck doesn't last long. The people in line don't seem to mind, taking the opportunity to talk amongst each other about the concert but mostly reminiscing about what the songs reminded them of growing up; about life, about where they are now. Or, for some, what might have been.

Next show we need to have someone tasked with going through the crowd with a recorder interviewing people about their show experience and tap into the conversations.

It's a little more than 90 minutes before one last person gets a selfie with us, shakes our hands, and thanks us for coming out to play. A woman who paid hard-earned money to come hear us play thanks us for coming. I pinch myself. No harm in checking. That woman, who looks to be our age, with a few streaks of gray in her brown hair walks out into the night throws her hands in the air, and screams, "Onions At A Crime Scene!" Those are her last words as she disappears from sight.

Silence. Then more silence. None of us say a word. For the first time in hours there is no sound. Not a word, not a note, not a nothing. We just breathe. Instead of embracing the good, we're embracing the calm.

"What did you guys do? Holy crap! There's nothing left!" cuts through the air like a samurai sword. Every remaining head in the room snaps in Nicole's direction. She is standing in the souvenir booth next to her sister; eyes wide with bewilderment.

"What do you mean there's nothing left?" Julie asks.

"She means there is nothing left, Mom," Ashley echoes. "All of the merchandise is gone. Gone. *All of it*."

Ashley had been in charge of taking card payments using her tablet to swipe transactions with the card reader plugged into the device. Nicole handled cash transactions. We see that the only merchandise remaining are the t-shirts pinned up to the backdrop of the booth. All the shirts, magnets, wristbands – everything – is gone as reported. The girls' wide-eyed astonishment is contagious as now we all wear the expression.

"We're definitely gonna have to re-order before the next show," Seth says nodding his head with a sardonic tone in his voice.

"Are you kidding me?" Laurel responds, exasperated. "That's the reaction?"

"Ho-lee crap," Todd says putting both hands on top of his head, flabbergasted. "They bought all of it? All of it?"

Only Lorelei seems unfazed. "Woo! Embrace the good!" She is jubilantly dancing in place.

"Is that your 'Gitr Done' catchphrase now? Is that where we are?" I tease. Lorelei sticks her tongue out at me in response, not missing a beat of her happy dance.

Faith picks up the question our minds hadn't gotten to yet. "So, question, where does all this money go? I mean, that's thousands of dollars you made tonight. That's before we've settled up on ticket sales."

Glances are exchanged. Our entire mindset was to be able to pay for the tour without coming out of pocket. The Centrum Silver sponsorship made sure the tour was paid for including paying for promotional materials. It's a real possibility – even with having to re-order merch – money will be left over once the tour concludes. Julie and Seth have been accounting for every penny to make sure we're spending responsibly.

Laurel looks directly at me in a way it appears we're the only two in the room. "We decided to donate proceeds to fight human trafficking but we haven't decided exactly who gets the money and when. Shouldn't we get that figured out?"

Butterflies pinball in my gut with an intensity that makes me feel I got caught breaking a prized vase. All eyes are on me now.

My left hand rubs my chin, signifying a ready-made response is not forthcoming. More seconds pass until I'm ready to answer.

"I'm thinking we have Julie and Seth look into organizations that fight human trafficking and provide services to the rescued where we could donate funds. Once the tour is over, all funds after expenses are paid – including sponsor money – will be donated to the selected human trafficking advocacy organizations."

"I can embrace that good," Laurel concurs winking at Lorelei. She purses her lips, shaking her head slowly side to side, feigning dismay that our lead singer hijacked her catchphrase. A room full of nods makes the decision final.

"Excellent," I say. "Can we pack up and go to the hotel now?"

* * *

Morning comes too damn soon especially when bedtime the night before was three in the morning. I roll out of the king-sized bed about six hours after calling it a night. A quick glance at Julie finds her in blissful slumber. The last thing I do before departing the bedroom is to take a moment for a long stretch. A little tired and sore from last night's show but it's a welcome kind of fatigue.

The French doors open quietly as I head for the living room on the other side. They shut quietly as well maintaining Julie's sleep.

The hotel we're staying in offers suites and, with the size of our group, a nice value and experience. Our suite has two master bedrooms on either side of the room with living space in between that includes a full kitchen so we can make our own meals if we want. The coffee maker is my destination. A full pot of hot coffee beckons. Julie had the presence of mind to set the timer before we turned in this morning.

Three cabinet doors are opened before locating the mugs. Moments later I park it on the cream-colored couch with my morning cup of giddy-up, my body ready for the coming caffeine infusion. A large yawn is my audible greeting to the morning. If it weren't for the fact this Sunday morning begins in a hotel in Minneapolis, it would be tough to accept last night wasn't a bizarre dream. But it was not. Not by a damn sight. Makes me wonder if the reception in St. Louis and Chicago will be like last night.

A click from my left draws my attention, French doors opening once more. Julie enters the room. "Morning, love," Julie utters with a yawn following it up with, "Need coffee." She sits next to me on the couch on the spot being patted by my right hand. Julie's wearing her blue, sleeveless shirt with a wine glass on it with the words "wine some" below it and a pair of gray pajama pants.

"Here, take mine," I tell her extending my cup. "I just poured it and haven't taken a sip yet. I'll go pour myself another one." Julie thanks me, accepting the offer. I rise, get myself another cup, and then return to her.

"Did you sleep well?" she asks.

"I made a few mistakes," I retort borrowing an old Steven Wright joke.

"Ha, ha, wise guy. Seriously, how are you today?"

"Tired, as you might imagine. A lot of it is coming off a day-long adrenaline ride. Still trying to come to grips last night actually happened." My first sip of coffee brings a warm rush of *get ready to greet the day* as it makes its way through my system. "Last night was beyond my wildest dreams."

"I know the sex was great but what about the concert?" Julie deadpans taking a page out of my playbook.

The second sip of coffee nearly comes out my nose causing me to sputter. Julie laughs, proud of herself. "I got you! I finally got you! After all the times you got me, I finally got you." Her chest puffs out which is great because she's got a nice chest.

"I have tasted my own medicine and it is bitter!" I acknowledge, doing my best Phoebe Buffet impression from the TV Show *Friends*.

"Would you two keep it down?" a questioning voice of protest comes from the opening French doors on the other side of the room. Ashley and Nicole step in. Ashley's curly blonde hair has a mind of its own, going any which way it pleases. She's wearing a salmon-colored tank top with grey cotton shorts. Nicole's straight, red hair seems undisturbed in comparison. She's wearing a red t-shirt so long it's almost a dress. Both yawn in unison. "Too early," she adds.

"Coffee's on," I inform them, hoping the caffeine rush will help their brains log on a little faster. Nicole tells Ashley to sit down and she'll get coffee for them both. Ashley curls up in the chair that flanks me while Nicole parks herself in the chair that flanks her mother after she hands her sister the promised coffee.

"Is this our coffee or the hotel's?" Ash asks. "It's unquestionably top-notch."

"Hotel's," Julies answers. "I'll see if it's a brand we can buy if you guys like it."

Before any of us can say anything a frantic, machine gun-like knocking assaults our room's door. We all jump, Nicole spilling coffee on herself with a curse as the hot liquid lands in her lap. The knocking doesn't stop.

Setting my cup on the coffee table in front of me, I launch myself off the couch and run for the door. Probably should look through the peep hole first but I throw caution to the wind before throwing open the door. Seven people are poised on the other side. It's the rest of the Onions family, band plus kids. Lorelei's daughters have a look of alerting everyone to the coming apocalypse while her mom and the rest of the crew have a mixed expression of lethargy and confusion as to what all the fuss is about.

Hope and Faith dart past me making a beeline for my daughters. I pivot and extend my right arm to welcome the rest of the confused crew to our humble temporary abode. Not sure there's enough coffee for all of us. The adults line up behind the couch all wondering what has the girls so out of sorts.

"Did you see this? Did you?" Hope and Faith urgently question Ashley and Nicole.

"See what?" Nicole wonders.

"This!" the twins reply in unison. "This!" Lori's girls hold up their phones, one before each of my daughters. "The Onions are trending! The Onions are trending!" they call out like a digital version of Paul Revere.

Ash and Nicole squint at the respective screens in front of their faces leaning in as they survey the digital landscape. Brows furrow. They leap out of their chairs and run for their bedroom. Nicole and Ashley emerge a few minutes later with a tablet and a Mac, respectively. They are logging on while still in motion.

"Shut the front door!" Ashley exclaims. Her eyes come off her screen to look at the rest of us. Her eyes are cartoon wide again. "The Onions are trending."

"You don't say? I hadn't heard," comes from me dripping with sarcasm. "But what does that mean?" Four young women look at me like I'm the dumbest human being on the planet, not even trying to hide how annoyed they are by the question.

"It means a ton of people are posting about you at the same time in a short amount of time. The Onions are all over social media and, when you're trending, it alerts other people on social media that this is a topic they should be aware of. People from last night are posting the crap out of their pictures and selfies from the First Avenue show."

If any of us weren't awake before, we are now. Each of us locates the closest millennial to peer over her shoulder to see what she's seeing. We get immediate confirmation – the Onions are all over social media. Ashley logs on to Instagram and it's a sea of Onions selfies from last night. I actually recognize faces. Hashtags and Insta-stories all over the place. I pinch myself as inconspicuously as is possible. Nope, not dreaming.

"Uh, guys," Todd inquires, "have you seen this?"

Lost in the commotion, Todd broke away from the group and picked up the complimentary copy of the Star Tribune newspaper in front of the room's door. He discarded everything from the Sunday edition except for the Entertainment section. He holds up the front page of the section. The headline reads: "First Avenue Finds Onions Appealing". Under it is a giant photo of the four of us on stage last night.

Todd turns to the page the review is featured and reads it aloud. "An unlikely grouping leads to an uncommon performance of uncompromising fun. Last night four childhood friends embarked on a reunion tour for a band that never existed until a few months ago. Onions At A Crime Scene is a combination of nostalgia, wonder, joy, and authenticity that gives voice to their generation's life experiences. It is not a voice of resentment or regret but one of celebration." Todd takes a big breath and then continues.

"The chemistry of these former grade school buddies belies the fact most of them hadn't seen each other in decades and only practiced their songs a handful of times before last night's performance. If you didn't see this musical triumph, you'd better plan on making the road trip to their upcoming shows in St. Louis and Chicago."

Todd lowers the paper. "What the hell is happening? What the hell?" He stumbles backward to one of the chairs at the room's kitchen table. "They like us. They genuinely like us." He mumbles in shock.

"Can I see it?" Laurel asks extending her hand. Todd hands it over still shell-shocked.

"Ohhh!" Faith exclaims. "The Onion's account shows 35,000 downloads of your guys' songs. You're zooming up the sales chart."

A loud gasp explodes from Ashley as she propels herself away from the desk before we can react to the download news. Hope and Nicole dart over to her and peer over each shoulder. Ashley points to the screen at what has alarmed her. "Eep," is the only thing that will come out.

"What is it?" Lori asks. "What?"

The three stammer until Nicole finally gets verbal traction and understandable words come out. "Ashley opened up the Onions email account. The booking agent for Ellen wants you to appear on the show."

"Ellen who?" Todd asks. Now all eyes are on him as we wonder what cave he's been living in.

"Are you serious?" Hope replies. "Hello? Ellen DeGeneres. Like the most popular daytime talk show since Oprah. That Ellen. This is big time television. This is national exposure. National. This is huge."

"Oh, yeah, well, sure. That Ellen," Todd says.

The room becomes more humid and my legs get rubbery. "You okay, babe?" Julie asks taking my right arm and helping to lower me to the couch.

"Ellen," I mutter.

"Hold up," Seth stops us. "The honest to goodness Ellen show wants the Onions to be her guests?"

Ashley, finally able to compose herself, says, "No, the honest to goodness Ellen show wants the Onions to *perform* on her show."

A collective gasp fills the room. My body becomes the world's largest goose bump.

"Let me see that," Laurel requests. Ashley hands the Mac over to her. The rest of us just look at Laurel as she scans the screen. Turning to Hope she requests, "Google her. Google the sender of that email. Please." Hope taps on the screen a couple times and turns the screen to Laurel. "Whoa. It's legit," Laurel says. "We're going to be on Ellen."

"We are NOT going to be on Ellen," I state emphatically.

Every head in the room spins in my direction; mouths are hanging open in shock. "We're not going to be on Ellen?" Lorelei challenges. "Are you kidding me?" her voice rising and punching each word.

My face is without expression for as long as I can hold it, which isn't long. A giant smile takes over my face. "Of course I'm kidding. We're going to be on Ellen!"

Jubilation fills the space. Who would have ever seen this coming? Not anyone in this room. It's wild to think what the Internet can do to take four individuals like us and instantaneously share our story all over the country.

"I take it I'm ordering room service for us?" Julie asks.

* * *

Ellen's booking agent is legit. I know this because it's Thursday and we're off stage waiting for Ellen DeGeneres to announce us and welcome us on set. Thankfully we all were able to take some vacation days from our jobs to make this appearance happen.

Life is a blur with interview requests from every type of media, local or national. The web is all about the Onions. Downloads, social media posts, emails flooding our inbox...you name it, everyone is riding the bandwagon and we're happy to have them. We were just hoping to have people show up at our concerts; this is beyond anything we could have thought possible.

Our sponsorship rep at Centrum Silver called me Monday afternoon to inform me how happy they are with their sponsorship. It is money well spent. She's even happier to hear that we're donating profits to fight human trafficking.

"Ow!" I yelp at the sharp pain in my forearm that pulls me from my thoughts. Looking over to see what bit me, I see Lori with a devilish grin on her face. The *what was that for* look is unmistakable.

"Oh, you don't think anyone notices you pinching yourself all the time," Lorelei says in response to my expression. "I just saved you the trouble. This is clearly happening. You're welcome."

A deep breath in precedes a response which never comes to pass because we hear Ellen shout, "Please welcome Onions At A

Crime Scene!" Exuberant clapping follows Ellen's introduction. The four of us make our way from behind the curtain and onto the set. Julie and Seth are watching from the green room.

The four of us are dressed in our blue polo shirts and black jeans. The ladies are wearing black ankle boots, Todd has a black pair of cowboy boots, and I'm wearing a pair of black dress shoes. Ellen comes out around the furniture to greet each of us, hugging us all starting with the ladies. She guides us to the white couch opposite her white arm chair.

Ellen is wearing a cream-colored collared shirt with a white jacket and blue jeans plus her trademark high top sneakers. On TV she looks like a pixie. Ellen looks no less the part in person. What I didn't imagine is that she is an unrelenting force of positivity that is almost tangible.

We sit down in the order of Laurel, Lorelei, Todd, and me. Laurel is closest to the giant television that is the backdrop while I am closest to the audience. We recognize the crowd is still clapping. We scan the audience and wave. The difference between a national talk show like this and a local talk show is quickly apparent. No need for tight camera shots or other trickery to make the crowd seem bigger than it is. Easily 400 people are in the gallery and they are excited to be here and see us.

"Wow! Wow!" Ellen exclaims. "That's what I call a welcome!"

Our attention turns back to the host. She is beaming, not just because she's that friendly – she is – but because of the audience's reaction. Ellen is in the entertainment business, yes, but she is also in the interesting business. If the audience isn't interested – if we're not interesting – it could be a short segment. Their welcome has gotten the interview off to a terrific start before the first question can be asked.

"Onions At A Crime Scene, welcome. Great to have you here," Ellen begins. "Have you gotten used to this yet?"

The four of us vigorously shake our heads. "No way," Laurel says. "We have to pinch ourselves to make sure this isn't some shared hallucination."

"It's true," I confirm. "Lorelei pinched me just before we came out here." I extend my left arm to show the red spot. It's proof my story is true.

Chuckles from the crowd.

"That's great," Ellen adds turning to address the crowd. "How many of you have downloaded an Onions song?" Half the crowd claps in response.

"Unreal," Lorelei speaks for all of us. "Thank you!" she exclaims. "You are totally rad."

"I have to say," Ellen continues, "when my talent booker and producer tried to tell me about the Onions, I thought they were talking about that parody newspaper." We chuckle and nod our heads. "But when they showed me the video from your Minneapolis show, the social media posts, the reviews, I was like 'whoa, we need them on the show'. That's when they told me they'd already booked you guys. I love what you do on stage. Big fan here."

It's like getting the seal of approval from one of the most popular people on the planet. I've never been one of the cool kids but I feel like one now.

"Okay, I gotta share this," Ellen moves on before any of us can respond to her last statement. "Can we put the picture up?" A heartbeat later the big screen behind us is filled with our fourth grade class picture that is featured on our website. I blurred out all the non-Onions faces in the photo before posting it on the site out of respect for our classmates' privacy. "Was your class all in the witness protection program?" Raucous laughter from the audience as they see the only faces not blurred out are ours. It makes for a bizarre photo to be sure.

I pipe up. "We weren't just an elementary school, we were a *made* school." Ellen lurches forward and laughs along with the audience.

"Sounds like a tough school," Ellen plays along. "Recess must have been an adventure just not to get whacked." The four of us clap with appreciation at her cheekiness.

"How are you taking being an overnight sensation? Did you expect any of this?" she inquires eyes wide with curiosity. As Ellen asks the question the images on the screen behind us turn into rotating tweets and Instagram images since our Saturday night show. It's as unnerving seeing them on the big screen as it was first seeing them online.

"Not at all," Laurel answers. "This is a complete shock. Honestly, we hoped to not play in front of an empty room."

"When Eric told us about this idea I thought it was the dumbest thing ever. I didn't want any part of it," Todd says. "This is the most unbelievable thing I've ever seen. And we've just done one show."

"Yeah, your next shows are in St. Louis and Chicago, correct?" Ellen seeks to confirm.

"That's correct," I answer. "Tickets still available for both shows," I turn to the audience and grin. The audience chuckles and claps at my shameless plug.

"I have a feeling there won't be tickets for much longer," Ellen says. "The thing that confuses me is the reunion tour aspect. How does that work when this is the first time you've played together?"

My bandmates all look at me. "Well, I guess I'll take this question," I tease. "The reunion isn't in reference to the band getting back together; it's about reuniting four friends and making a dream become reality."

"But why only three shows?" Ellen follows up. "I would think you'd want to do more than that."

"This was never about being a long-term touring band," I clarify. "We have jobs, lives, and responsibilities so taking a few months to play some gigs seemed like something the others could get behind," I say gesturing with an arm sweep in my friends' direction. "They did." Three nods follow my assertion.

"How are your friends and family reacting to this? Did they ask you if you were having a midlife crisis?" Ellen asks tongue in cheek.

"We thought Eric was having a midlife crisis when he brought us together to tell us about his plan," Todd says. "But that hasn't been the reaction we've gotten from others."

"We did a friends and family show at the Surf Ballroom and the response was off the charts," Lori says. "We made it into a class reunion and family reunion all in one. Playing a friendly audience was fantastic but their excitement clued us in that we might be on to something."

"Our kids have been terrific," Laurel chimes in. "My three boys have been super supportive. After all, Mom's not supposed to be a rock star. But they've embraced our tour without question." Laurel pauses a few beats before continuing as the crowd claps in support. "My husband Seth and Eric's wife Julie are our management team, Lori's daughters handle our social media, and Eric's daughters handle merchandise and order fulfillment." Laurel nods to her own comments. "It's been fun to share this experience with our kids."

"Lorelei," Ellen addresses our keyboardist, "I see all these hashtags and quotes that state 'Embrace the Good' and I hear you came up with that. Where did that come from?"

Lori smiles a little self-consciously now being the center of attention. "It goes back to the time in my life after my husband Dominic died." She looks at us, then the crowd, then back to Ellen before continuing. "It's easy to see the darkness around us especially when we face our challenges in life. Sometimes we can take the good things for granted and forget to take time to celebrate them."

Ellen asks, "Because people are so used to seeing the bad they don't recognize the good?"

"Right," Lori replies. "Or believing we're not worthy enough to have good things happen. "People should embrace the good, large or small, in their lives. That was a life philosophy I adopted and we adopted it for our band and for the tour."

"Love that," Ellen approves. More applause.

"Now, Eric," Ellen shifts, "I was on the band's website and watched the video of you talking to the class about your band teacher telling you that drums weren't your thing. It got me to thinking about a friend of mine who encountered something similar..." I'm so focused on Ellen speaking directly to me the sudden applause and euphoria of the audience escapes my notice.

"It's Joan Jett!" Ellen exclaims as she stands and claps.

"What? Where?" I ask suddenly searching for an image or video or something on a screen. By the time I look over my shoulder, the person who has caused the commotion is next to me. I feel my face go white as a wave of cold surges through my body. I'm standing but am not sure how or when that happened.

"Ahhhh!" I cry out giving the impression a ghost suddenly appeared next to me. She's only five feet, five inches tall but she is a giant to yours truly. She's wearing black leather pants, black tank top with the words "Bad Reputation" on it, with black studded wristbands and a silver chain necklace with the symbol of her astrological sign - Virgo - hanging from it.

"Hey, man, I'm Joan. Great meeting you," she extends her right hand to me. I shake it out of reflex. *It'sJoanJett It'sJoanJett It'sJoanJett It'sJoanJett It'sJoanJett It'sJoanJett* the voice in my head tells me, trying to comprehend what my eyes and ears are reporting and the brain is not catching up. "Mind if I sit down?" she asks.

"Oh, yes, yes, please," I come to my senses. I motion her to sit next to me on the couch. My friends slide to their left so there's enough room for my rock and roll idol.

"I have all your albums, I've seen you in concert twice, I used to listen to your Bad Reputation and I Love Rock and Roll albums over and over while playing Atari in my room," I rattle on as the 15-year-old me is in control of my brain not the 50-year-old.

"So you're saying you're a fan," Ellen deadpans. Raucous laughter. Being the butt of her joke is fine with me. Joan Jett is sitting next to me. She just shook my hand!

"Listen, guys," Joan Jett says to us, "I have a lot of respect for what you're doing. When Ellen called me and told me to check out your band's music..."

Oh my God, Joan Jett just said our music. The Onions have music!

"...and I watched your video about that band teacher. That spoke to me, man. When I wanted to learn how to play guitar, I told my guitar teacher I wanted to play rock and roll. He told me, 'Girls don't play rock and roll'. I said 'bull' and walked out. People like to tear you down. People are always going to take shots. You've just got to go for it. If you believe in yourself, you cannot listen to other people."

Audience applause interrupts her thought. She swivels to face the crowd and nods, acknowledging their understanding.

After a brief pause, she continues. "I'm just really glad you guys had the guts to do something new at this stage of life, man. I've been doing this for a long time and I'm promoting the documentary about my career and I ask myself 'Am I still enjoying what I'm doing? I need to find the fire again'," she finishes her thought. I think the four of us are so star struck we feel like we've become the audience not the guests.

"So what keeps you doing this, Joan?" Ellen asks. "You've been playing rock and roll since you were a teenager. What keeps you going? Why keep doing it?"

"I've been thinking about that a lot," Joan begins. "I've been thinking about rock in general. It's always been a young person's game, writing about sex, love, and partying. As rock and rollers get older, what do they write about? I'm not sure there's an answer but we're looking for it."

Everyone in the room ponders what the rock and roll Hall of Famer has shared. "That's why I respect what you guys are doing, what your songs are about, what they stand for. It's inspiring to me."

My inner me puts a finger in his ear rattling it as if to clear some sort of obstruction that causes a questioning of whether I just heard what I thought I just heard. Did Joan Jett just say she's inspired by us? The hell?

"I like your song *Take the Day*," she continues. "Ellen tells me you're going to play that song today. I took some time to learn it. Mind if I jam with you?"

It's tough for any of us to reply with our jaws lying on the floor. Joan Jett learned our song and wants to play with us? What? WHAT? This isn't happening. This can't be happening. No way. NO WAY.

Laurel comes to her senses first. "It would be an honor if you'd play with us." All I can do is nod vigorously.

"Wait a minute," a voice belonging to no one on the set stops us. "No performing yet." Everyone is looking for the owner of the voice telling us we can't perform with Joan Jett. The audience sees her before we do and they erupt in applause and cheers once more.

Ellen delays no longer to announce the next guest to her show, "Hey, everybody, it's Sheila E!" Striding toward us in a long, flowing flowered dress is Sheila E. Long, dark hair cascades down over shoulders past her collarbone. She's wearing tan, wedge sandals. Sheila waves vigorously in all directions as a hello to everyone.

"Aw, damn," I respond shoulders slumping, not realizing my microphone is still on. The show just stops when my comments are heard by all assembled. Dismay runs rampant. *Why on earth would this guy say that?* is what they must be thinking. "I was hoping this was real," I say dejectedly. "But it's just a dream." My chin hits my chest like Charlie Brown after the tree ate his kite again.

"You dummy, this is real!" Lorelei yells at me as she, Laurel, and Todd pinch me as one.

"OW! Hey!" I yelp at the pinch attack. "Holy moley, it's Sheila E and Joan Jett!" I say like they snuck in and I'm the first to notice.

"Are you having some sort of medical emergency?" Ellen asks. I'm not sure if she's kidding or not.

"Hey, Eric, nice meeting you," Sheila E greets, extending her hand. I shake her hand and think this is the best day ever for my right hand. If I didn't need it to play drums, I'd cut the dang thing off and bronze it. In the meantime, the studio gets humid and my legs get wibbly-wobbly. This is getting a bit much for me to take.

Todd hooks me under my left arm and holds me up. He leans in and whispers, "Can you at least try to keep your shit together?"

"Hey, if that were Gene Simmons and Paul Stanley standing there I'd be hooking you under the arm," I defend, hoping our exchange is quiet enough not to be picked up by the microphones.

"Joan and I were talking back stage and agree how amazing what you're doing is. I mean, wow. That's great stuff," Sheila E begins. "When Ellen called me and pointed me to your website I saw the post about my performance at the American Music Awards and I definitely saw the video of you using the light up drumsticks."

The scene on the screen shifts to show the video of me using the light up sticks at last Saturday's show. It is a bizarre feeling to watch myself performing in concert on the set of Ellen standing next to Joan Jett and Sheila E. If it weren't for the triple pinch I'd just received from my bandmates, I'd swear I was dreaming.

"Now you know I've spent a lot of time in Minnesota, that I've played First Avenue, and the lit drumsticks are my thing, right?" Sheila E states to me. "You don't think I'm going to let you play drums and steal my move, do you?" she finishes the thought causing me to deflate. I knew this was all too good to be true.

"Hey, tiger, chin up," she says to me, lifting my chin with her left index finger. "You don't think I'm going to let you steal my move without using my drumsticks, do you?" Sheila E finishes. My heart goes from my feet to my throat in one beat. *What did she just say to me?*

Before I can process any further, Sheila E raises her right hand that had been holding a small bag. In all the commotion, I hadn't noticed she brought anything with her. Sheila E unzips the top of what almost looks like an old doctor's medicine bag and pulls out two drumsticks.

"These are the drumsticks I used at the AMAs in '85," she says. "I want you to use these when you play now." Sheila E punctuates her thought with, "I want a true fan to have these." She extends the sticks to me, my trembling hands accepting them.

"Thank you so much," I say sincerely and reverently. "This is so generous. I don't know what to say."

"We should thank Sheila E just for shutting this guy up," Todd says. We all snicker.

"Y'know, this show is only an hour long," Ellen ribs us. "Think it's time to play. Oh, and one more thing, Sheila E brought her bongos so she's going to join Eric on percussion as Joan Jett plays rhythm guitar while Laurel plays lead guitar and Todd plays bass with Lorelei on keyboard."

The four of us jump at the realization we have a song to perform and two legends are joining us. We go into Onions At A Crime Scene mode and move as quickly as we can to our instruments, off to the stage area to the audience's right.

Joan Jett and Sheila E follow us and take their places. Ellen's crew had been very sly because we never noticed they had set up the rock and roll legends' instruments with ours.

"Ladies and gentlemen, Onions At A Crime Scene with Joan Jett and Sheila E!!!!" Ellen introduces us. Geez, that sounds weird but it's a wonderful weird.

All the people playing this song are looking at me waiting for the count. "One," gets out but my voice cracks like I'm going through a second puberty causing gut-busting guffaws. I blush and give my throat a vigorous clearing.

"One, two...one, two, three, four!" I proclaim with authority and we begin an amazing rock and roll fantasy come reality. Concentrating is challenging as I'm trying to focus on my playing while being a fan and watching Joan Jett and Sheila E go about their business. I'm so glad I set my DVR to record the show. I know I'll need it as evidence this actually happened when we get back to the Midwest. Plus, I want to see what it looks like when we play with Joan Jett and Sheila E from the other side of the camera.

Take the Day has never sounded so impressive. Maybe it is the playing of our guest artists but also because their presence has inspired us to take our music to the next level. There is power in our instruments and in our voices. This is the second time I've thought people will remember where they were when the Onions came to town. I know I'll never forget it.

The song arrives to the part where the drum solo comes in and at that instant the lights go out and the studio goes pitch black. Sheila covers me long enough with her bongos for me to flip the switch on the sticks. They light up neon green to start and I know they'll cycle through colors as I rock the solo. Soon my drums are the only instrument being played. All eyes and ears are on me. This is freaking amazeballs.

I hear the bongos to my right once again but something's different. I glance over and see that Sheila E has put on light up gloves! Her hands are flying around and their track is matching my drumsticks beat for beat. As if I thought this moment couldn't get any more epic, she just made it so. The solo - or is it a duet now? - finishes, the lights come back on, and all my current and guest bandmates jump back in.

Ellen is on her feet dancing. No one in the audience is sitting. Phones are out. Oh, hell yeah, we are so gonna be trending. I don't know what Faith, Hope, Nicole, and Ashley are going to think about all this. They're going to have a lot to handle with social media and order fulfillment.

I wonder if our remaining shows will be sold out this week. Wouldn't that be a hoot? The song comes to its end though I don't want it to be so. This tour has gone from impossible to improbable to incredible. It's gone from the sublime to the ridiculous. This makes no sense. None. And, yet, it's happening.

The Onions and our guests receive a standing ovation. It's loud and wild and the biggest rush I've ever felt. I carefully lay my new drumsticks on my kit, dismount my drummer's perch, walk over to Sheila E and give her a big hug. "You did me proud, man. Did me proud," she says.

"Thank you for the most amazing gift ever," I reply. "I'm not just talking about the drumsticks." She gives me a little extra squeeze before letting me give my regards to everyone else.

High fives are exchanged with the Onions. We are jubilant. Ellen has sent the show to break and the crowd still stands showering us with a continuous ovation. We are grinning ear to ear. The last person in the greeting line is Joan Jett.

"Man, keep rockin'," she tells me. "Don't compromise yourself or your music ever. No matter where the journey takes you, keep being you." I nod taking my musical idol's words to heart. "I want you to have this," Joan says handing me her guitar. "It's autographed to you. Thanks for being a fan and thanks for having the guts to grab your dream by the nuts."

"But I don't play guitar," my brain is so overloaced it's being too literal. The guitar isn't for me because I also play guitar; it's her showing respect for me as a fan and as an artist. I catch myself quickly. "No, I get it now," accepting the guitar she has extended to me.

"It's a head trip, isn't it?" Joan Jett smiles at me.

"Is it ever," I agree admiring my new guitar. "I'm so grateful to you and Sheila E for being here and doing what you've done for us. You didn't have to come to meet us or play with us." I pause for a second to catch my breath. "I hope you know how much this means to me and to my friends. I will never forget this. Thank you. Thank you so much."

She gives me a bonafide rock and roll badass glare. "Damn straight." She smiles and smacks me on the shoulder like an old friend.

Ellen approaches us applauding. "Embrace the good!" she exclaims. The audience – the entire audience – echoes Ellen's exclamation. I shoot a glance at Lori. Her mouth is agape. Well, that was eight shades of freaking awesome.

Ellen bounces over our way looking more like a pogo stick than a talk show host. "That was fantastic! Great television," she tells

Lights, Camera, Onions | 255

us. "Joan, Sheila, Onions, thanks so much for coming on the show and playing. This is my highlight of the season."

Yup, should have gotten the Depends sponsorship, I think to myself.

CHAPTER SEVEN

WILD SCALLIONS

August 25, 2018

"I'm going to quit if this doesn't stop."

All eyes divert themselves to Faith as her fingers dash over the keyboard of her Mac. "Seriously, you guys, this is redonkulous. Hope, Nicole, Ashley, and I could work this full time and never keep up."

It's easy to believe that. Visits to our website, activity on our social media, incoming emails, and media interview requests now number in the absurd. Our daughters are struggling to keep their heads above the tidal wave.

Julie says from her post in the corner, "Come on, ladies, it's a lot of work but it's not forever. Do the best you can. We all are."

The point is not lost on the daughters of the Onions. They know how overwhelmed Julie has been after stepping in for Laurel and keeping a handle on our finances especially as money is cascading into our coffers.

It is a fact that everyone's job has gotten bigger since Onions At A Crime Scene officially became a thing following our performances at First Avenue and on Ellen.

Faith's outburst came just as we finished our practice for the St. Louis show next weekend. Practices are aces because they are truly about fine tuning and not hoping we make the cut.

While we let the girls handle the social media Laurel, Lorelei, Todd, and I believe we should answer emails personally. Answering fan's emails is the item currently on the Onions' post-practice agenda.

Our emails are not about the usual groupie or fan asking for something. The majority of our emails are actually thank you emails. Young adults – the children of our peers – are saying thanks for either inspiring them to pursue a dream they thought, or were told, wasn't realistic. Some thank us because one or both of their parents shared with them an unfulfilled dream they now decided they were going to give a try.

Other emails are from our peers who are grateful for what we're doing because it caused them to stop making excuses why it was too late to do that which was left undone.

Emails we have received from our next two venues present the band with an interesting dilemma. The booking agents at the Atomic Cowboy in St. Louis and Bottom Lounge in Chicago informed us that not only are our shows already sold out but there is a waiting list. Both booking agents are asking us to add shows at their venues.

"Do you think we should add shows to St. Louis and Chicago?" I ask my bandmates.

The other three sigh. "I'm not so sure," Laurel says, adjusting her leather wristbands. "Listen, I'm having fun but we're not a full-time touring band and we're trying to balance life with all this insanity. I'd prefer to stick with the three."

"Oh, I don't know," Lorelei counters. "If we added afternoon shows at each venue, would that work? I mean, we're not adding any dates. We'll already be there."

Todd grunts in a way that conveys Lori has thought of something he hadn't. "Well, when you put it like that, maybe we should add shows. Big difference between shows and dates." He throws a thumb my way and says, "You're the one that started all this. What do you say?"

My shoulders slump slightly at the great burden Todd has just tossed upon them. I consider the words of my friends and put them against the requests from our venues. Moments of silence pass as I ponder. Todd starts fidgeting with impatience. He thinks it's an easier question to answer than it is. After a few more moments of contemplation, I am ready to share my thought.

"When we gathered together at Applebee's and I pitched the reunion tour idea I promised you three shows. If this tour, if our getting back together, was about fame or money then I would say let's add the shows. But this is about us and the promise I made if you'd take this journey with me. I'd like to keep that promise to you."

Now the silence that hangs in the room is from the other three. Our daughters' fingers continue to fly across physical and virtual keyboards. They've tuned us out for the moment, focused on the issue at hand not whether or not the world gets more Onions At A Crime Scene. I look down at my shoes almost shy about looking at Todd, Laurel, and Lorelei while they ponder.

I have to look up finally because it's so quiet I question whether they've left me in the garage. A fly buzzes past my head and I flail at it wildly. The intruder settles on my lap long enough for me to slap my hand on it, smooshing the fly in-between. The loud crack startles my friends from their silent consideration. My cheeks get red at the accidental commotion.

Lorelei sweeps a rogue strand of hair from her face. She collects herself and says, "We're in agreement. Three shows it is."

"What is it you've said, Eric?" Laurel chimes in. "Always leave them wanting more."

"How sad is it that I was the one who almost took your head off and didn't want to do this and I'm sort of disappointed we're not doing more shows," Todd shakes his head at himself. "But I agree. Let's keep it as is."

A quiet settles over the four of us. The only sound is a tappity-tappity-tappity tap of the keyboard as Faith and Ashley are busy posting pictures from our just-completed practice. We are content to let the computer keyboards be our soundtrack for the moment.

We've only played one show but based on that, our appearance on Ellen, and viral nature of our journey, the Onions are beginning to feel like a household name which itself is bizarre. I was hoping venues wouldn't be empty and we just finished deciding we weren't going to add shows. I never envisioned this.

Ashley breaks the silence. "Dad?"

"Yeah, kiddo?"

"I respect what you just said but I think Lorelei is right. If you did two additional shows wouldn't that be more money to donate to fight human trafficking?" she asks and then looks at me.

The question smacks me like a frying pan in the face. It was an angle missed upon focusing only on a promise made to friends. When eye contact with Ash is broken it is quickly apparent that all eyes in the room are on me. My bandmates are looking at me with folded arms and heads cocked to the left silently saying to me, *Yeah, what about that?*

"Well, when you put it that way," I respond sardonically "maybe we want to do a couple more shows."

"Uh-huh," the other Onions agree in unison. And on key.

"Nice catch," Nicole says to her sister punctuating with a fist bump.

"Julie," my thought being directed to my wife sitting in the corner, "please let the folks at Atomic Cowboy and Bottom Lounge know that they can add second shows. With the night shows starting at 7:30, let's see if we can do something early afternoon."

"Can do," Julie replies with a nod. "I'll reach out to Something Resembling Responsible as well to make sure a second show works for them."

"Settled. Two shows," Lori confirms brushing that rogue strand of hair away from her face once more.

The vibe of the room changes instantly. Minutes ago there was a sense of disappointment about turning down the additional shows. The body language across the board has changed. There is almost a bounce in the step of people who are standing still. No comment is needed to convey the Onions are happy to carry on, even if it's not more dates but more people to play in front of in our remaining cities. Now it's my turn to silently celebrate. It was a lot less difficult to add two shows than it was to convince them to do shows in the first place. A guffaw nearly escapes me as the thought crosses my mind.

"Holy crap!" Hope blurts out. "Our song downloads are cray-cray."

"*Our* downloads?" Lorelei questions with more than a hint of teasing in her voice.

"Hey, you may be part of the hottest band in the known universe, Mom," Faith jumps in to defend her twin, "but we're managing and automating downloads and social media for the hottest band in the known universe." Faith and Hope stick their tongues out at their mother and say together, "So there."

They go back to typing and compiling. Ashley picks up their point. "Ninety four thousand downloads a week. The special mix of the song you did on Ellen has ex-PUH-loded. Have you checked the PayPal balance lately? Buttloads of money."

Joan Jett and Sheila E gave us permission to release the live version of our performance on Ellen on our streaming platforms, especially when they learned we are donating all our proceeds to fight human trafficking.

"You know, people are walking in my business asking if I have CDs they can buy," Todd snorts like an angry bull. "I'm an implement dealer not a Sam Goody, for cryin' out loud. My employees ask me if I'm planning on selling the business to tour full-time now that I'm a rock and roll star." He throws his hands in the air in exasperation. "We've played one freaking show!"

"Oh, calm down, Todd," Laurel lightly chides. "This is a lot better than if we got ignored and were begging for people to notice us." She pauses to take a sip of her iced tea. "Yeah, it's weird having co-workers, friends, and strangers ask for autographs or make comments but what we're doing is resonating with people."

Todd's head does this sort of head shake/bob where his right ear dips toward his shoulder as his left eyebrow raises slightly as a signal to concede the point.

"We are resonating, we are making a difference," Lorelei adds almost pleading for us to believe her.

It's my turn to cock my head sideways; not to concede a point but to ask for elaboration. "Care to expand on that thought?"

Lorelei looks a bit embarrassed, her statement a bit more urgent than she meant it to be. Lorelei comes out from behind her keyboard to get closer to us before sharing. She takes a slow, deep breath. "Well...I got a letter the other day." Lori looks down at the ground and then looks back up at us. "It was a letter from Unity Health Center in Des Moines. Someone in the grief support services department is a fan and saw an article in the Des Moines Register a couple weeks ago. Y'know, local woman does something out of the ordinary." Lori brushes the stubborn strand away from her face again.

"Anyway, the article mentioned my husband dying and the song my situation inspired. The person showed it around the department and the staff agreed that I'd be someone who'd fit in well with helping people to pick up the pieces after losing a spouse."

Laurel puts up her hand, palm to Lori, evidently directing verbal traffic. "Hang on. Are you saying they offered you a job?"

"Yes!" Lori answers. "Can you believe it?" She takes a deep breath. "I think I'm going to accept it, guys."

"Oh my gosh," Laurel responds her hands coming up to her cheeks. "That's excellent! Oh I'm so happy for you!"

"That is stupendous," Todd nods. "You'll be great."

"When do you start?" I inquire.

"Not till November," Lori says. "Too much going on plus I wanted to give my current employer time to hire my replacement. Didn't want to leave them in a bind."

"You nervous?" Todd asks.

"Not yet. I probably will be when I start. The tour and our experience so far has made me realize that life is still somewhat in a holding pattern. If a change is going to be made, now's the time to do it." She removes a hair band from around her wrist and pulls her hair back into a pony taking care of the rogue strands.

"I can't think of a better person to do this than you," Laurel encourages.

"Going through the loss of Dominic was a huge factor in accepting the offer. Not the loss itself but wishing I had someone to help walk me through the grieving process. No one is to blame. I had so much to figure out on my own. I want to help others to not feel that way from someone who has been on that path is walking along with them on theirs."

"Mom is the bomb," Faith states proudly.

"Oh, gawd," Nicole rolls her eyes, "how '90s of you. I used to think my parents were the lamest people here."

"Oh, no you didn't!" Faith protests. "Don't even go there! Don't even."

"And tomorrow, everyone, complete sentences," I board the mocking train.

"Why are they yelling at each other?" Todd joins in. "Don't these kids just argue via text and blast one another on social media? I didn't know they actually talk."

I snort with surprise at Todd's piling on. Laurel and Lorelei delight in Todd's unexpected sarcasm.

"Now look what you've done," Hope scolds Nicole. "Now the old people are mocking us. Lovely."

"I wouldn't worry about it," Ashley reassures looking down at her cell phone. "It's getting late in the afternoon. Won't be long now till nap time for them."

"Woah!" The other three young women exclaim. "Burn!"

I look at my bandmates and say, "I guess that would have been funny if we had our hearing aids on." A sliver of silence before the Onions plus Julie start laughing.

"They do get that we're making fun of them, don't they?" Faith puts out there.

Ashley rolls her eyes at us. "Yes. Dad poking fun at them is his way of defusing our burn while at the same time boomeranging the teasing back at us. Classic Dad move."

"Did you hear that?" I exclaim in over the top wonderment. "My daughter just said I'm a classic!"

"Turn up the hearing aid, old man," Nicole stands up for her sister. "She's just diagramming the lame."

"Diagramming the lame?" I parry. "Sure, it's no Embrace the Good but I'm sure it would be fitting on a millennial t-shirt."

"Now we've come full circle," Laurel shakes her head in amusement.

"I'm dizzy," Lori holds her head. "Too many zingers swirling around. Can we change the subject?"

"Ooh! Pick me!" I jump up and down.

"Wait," Laurel says in the voice of a press secretary answering questions from the media, pointing at me. "It seems Eric might have something for us." She nods. "Go ahead and share."

"Thinking back on the First Avenue show," I begin, "the word 'community' crossed my mind." I pause to take a drink from my water bottle. "When we're on stage and the lights are on us we can only see about – what – maybe ten rows deep of people? Got me thinking about my girl Taylor Swift…"

"No!" four young women turn and yell at me.

"Eww," Hope recoils. "That's just gross."

"Yeah, creeper," Faith echoes.

"Girls," Lori chides her daughters, "some respect, please."

"Just because you've been to one Taylor Swift concert doesn't suddenly make her 'your girl'," goes Ashley's mini-lecture. "I've been a fan since her first song." She waggles a finger at me. "No bandwagon jumping."

"Have you actually been to a Taylor Swift concert?" Laurel wonders not knowing if this is real or not.

"Yes," Julie confirms. "Eric got us tickets to one of her stadium shows and we went as a family. She was terrific. I only knew a couple of songs but, wow, can that woman put on a show."

Todd shakes his head in disdain. "Hand it over, dude," he demands extending his right hand toward me.

"Hand what over?" I ask.

"Your guy card," Todd says pushing his hand closer to me. "You go see Taylor Swift, you lose your card."

Making the motion of putting my hand in my back pocket I seemingly remove an invisible guy card, halfway extending it toward my friend before yanking my hand back.

"Psych!" I taunt. "I'll have you know, just before the show started Joan Jett's 'Bad Reputation' blared from the speakers so I get instant cool cred."

"Is that true?" Todd asks looking over at my Taylor superfan daughter.

"That 'Bad Reputation' played just before Taylor came out, yes. That my dad has any cool cred, not a chance," Ashley replies with a punctuating eye roll.

"Haters gonna hate, hate, hate, hate, hate," is my response with a disappointed head shake.

"No!" four young women protest once more.

"Isn't this where we started?" Lorelei asks rhetorically.

"Anyway," Laurel tries to get us back on track, "what is it you learned from Taylor Swift?"

"When we went to the Taylor Swift concert we were given electronic wristbands that lit up. The LED wristbands were controlled by a computer program to change color to match the mood of the song," I explain.

"Isn't that a bit fancy for us?" Todd scoffs.

"Hang on, there's a point," Julie jumps in. "He's just taking his time getting there."

"My stories don't get as long if people don't interrupt," comes from me as a melody.

Laurel makes a rolling motion with her hand. "Keep it moving."

"Certainly. At one point during the show, Taylor was on stage alone behind her piano. She referenced the wristbands and mentioned that in a large stadium with the lighting as it is she has trouble seeing her fans. But if everyone holds up their wristbands she can see us just as we can see her," I finish.

"Oh!" Lori completes the circuit. "We wouldn't need to get those elaborate ones but we could order wristbands that just light up. That would be so fun!"

"It would be safer than people holding up lighters and less annoying than people holding up their cell phones to create the same effect," Todd acknowledges rubbing his chin.

"Sounds like we have a consensus," Laurel announces sounding parliamentarian. "Julie, since you're familiar with these wristbands, would you handle ordering them for the next two shows?"

Julie throws a thumb in the air. "Consider them ordered."

"Stop," Todd's disdain seems never ending. "Are we literally doing something inspired by Taylor Swift?"

"Shake it off, Todd. Shake it off," I tease, doubling over in gut-busting glee at the tomfoolery.

Faith looks over at Ashley and comments, "Your dad cracks himself up."

"You can't even imagine, Faith," Ash says face palming. "You just have to experience it for yourself."

* * *

September 1, 2018

St. Louis in late summer can be sweltering, featuring a one-two punch of heat and humidity. On this September Saturday night the temperature is in the high 80s but the humidity is not horrible. It's more comfortable outside than one would reasonably expect. This is to our advantage because the Atomic Cowboy is our first outdoor venue.

The Atomic Cowboy Pavilion on Manchester Avenue in St. Louis is the entertainment extension of an exposed-brick emporium of art, alcohol and eats, planetary in size for what is basically a bar. The Atomic Cowboy is housed in an all-brick building straight out of the 1800s. If you saw it in a black and white or sepia photograph, you'd swear it still was...except for the mural on the side of the building that looks like it's a story high. The mural is that of a cowgirl in denim shorts, tank top, and cowboy hat riding a rather large missile. Atomic Cowboy is in cursive.

The afternoon show was bonkers. People were definitely in a party mood and the beer was flowing. What's impressive to us is that the afternoon show was the added show. We knew the 7:30 show was already sold out but to sell out a second show where ticket sales began about a week before the event is sensational.

We asked Something Resembling Responsible to be our opening act for all shows after the great job they did in Minneapolis. They got the crowd rowdy and ready before we hit the stage. We hit the stage and more than lived up to our post-Ellen hype.

We are relaxing in the green room before the night show. The Atomic Cowboy's green room is unreal. It's an event space with private lounge area, dinner area, bathroom, private entrance to and from stage with use of security escort and 20 feet of exposure to a public street. It's like a studio apartment with all the amenities and Onions At A Crime Scene is making the most of it.

Faith and Ashley are set up at a long table near the window handling our Instagram and Twitter accounts, reviewing posts from the first show. Our social media is a sea of photos of us and our fans in front of our Onions and Centrum Silver backdrop.

Hope and Nicole are at the next table going over merchandise sales and inventory. Julie and Seth are out in the pavilion working to make sure all is set for the second show, including the local video company we hired to record the evening concert. Why not have a live concert video we can sell on DVD and as a download?

For all the positivity of the first show, a pensive mood is upon the Onions. It's not long before the second show and we are pondering our first show and the meet-and-greet afterward. It is still astounding how this concert tour impacts those who attend. This was meant to be a nostalgic journey but it has manifested to be much more than that.

We four are gathered around the fireplace that is merely there for ambiance. Todd and I are in high back chairs bookending the hearth, backs to the outside wall. Laurel and Lorelei are sitting in side-by-side leather love seats. Laurel sits across from Todd curled up in her seat. Lorelei is opposite me with her legs stretched out on the matching foot rest.

Laurel stares at the fireplace with a letter in her hand she's just finished reading. Clearly the content of the letter is having an emotional impact. Her index finger is over her lips, thumb under her chin. Her finger and thumb seem to be working to keep her thoughts from becoming verbal.

"Eric," she says, one name escaping through her digits' defenses. Our eyes meet. "You've never been averse to flying in the face of convention, have you?" Laurel's assertion comes from nowhere and its intent is unclear and a little unsettling.

"That's a fair characterization," is my reply.

"Remember when you took shorthand?" Laurel asks shifting to better see me without having to crank her neck.

"Of course," comes out of me without hesitation; continuing in a voice that sounds like a narrator. "The ancient art of shorthand. An abbreviated symbolic writing method that increases speed and brevity of writing as compared to longhand," I finish and then revert back to my normal speaking voice. "I remember it very well."

A slight smile comes to Laurel's lips. Then she nods.

Todd who also had been staring into space while downing a beer snaps to attention in a heartbeat. "Stop. Are you telling me you actually took shorthand?"

"Sure did. I was the first and only guy in my high school's history to take shorthand or ever will be. It's not offered anymore." Shorthand went the way of the manual typewriter, the abacus, and – pretty soon – cursive. No one will ever equal my accomplishment but only because it is now obsolete.

"That has got to be the dumbest thing I've ever heard," Todd remarks with no shortage of disgust. "Why would you do that?"

"Oh, I don't know, Todd," Laurel interjects not hiding her annoyance at Todd's insinuating himself into this particular conversation. "One guy in the middle of a class of 13 very attractive girls; me, Randee, Cindy, Kathy, Leslie, Nancy, Dee, Becky...among others."

"Wow," Lorelei whistles, "sounds kind of genius to me." A huge smile forms on her face as she looks at me. "Kudos to you, sir."

"Thank you," I respond bowing from a seated position. "That was a fun year. The teacher was so flattered that a guy took her class."

"Oh, you got away with stuff the rest of us never could have," Laurel says almost in protest. "Mrs. Hinman loved you."

"My charm is a superpower I can't control," I respond to Laurel's assertion. "But what takes you down this particular path?"

Laurel holds up the piece of paper she's been contemplating. "My son Cole left a letter for me in my handbag. I'm not sure he meant for me to find it between shows tonight." She carefully sets the letter on the small end table next to the chair. "It's no secret that

I've been struggling with the prospect of being an empty nester. Cole is suggesting Seth and I become foster parents."

The room is quiet. Things just took a turn in a direction none of us anticipated. Todd lowers his beer so that it is resting on his right thigh. Lorelei sits up a little straighter.

"How does that fit with what you said about me?" is the only question I can think to ask.

"You've never shied away from the unconventional," Laurel answers. "Why is that?"

My shoulders shrug quickly. "The question I don't want to ask at the end of my life is 'what if'? I would rather know how the story ends in taking a risk or a chance – even if it doesn't turn out well." I pause to ponder if my answer is complete and end with, "Sometimes that means carving a new path just to see where it leads," I punctuate with a sweep of my right hand that gathers the Onions in its wave.

"How do you feel about Cole's suggestion?" Lorelei asks.

"Not sure. It's never crossed my mind before. Once the boys are all out of the house it would seem to be the end of my child raising days," Laurel admits her eyebrows rising. "But does it have to be? Perhaps not."

"Not to sound like a dick..." Todd starts.

"Never stopped you before," I zing.

"Fair enough," Todd nods then flips me off with his left hand as he returns his attention to Laurel. "Are you sure you want to raise someone else's kids? Someone else's troubles?"

"Todd!" Lorelei exclaims. "That's a horrible thing to say. They're kids for God's sake!"

Laurel holds up a hand to Lori. "No. It's okay. I know what he means. Not proud to admit it but the same thoughts crossed my mind. It's one thing when I know how my kids were raised but another thing entirely to come into the middle of another child's life. Would I even know how to do that?"

"Oh stop," Lori scoffs. "You won't suddenly forget how to be a great mom just because the youngest of yours leaves home. I'm sure you've been a mom figure to your sons' friends over the years."

A look of surprise appears on Laurels' face. "Yes! Yes, I have. Hadn't thought about that."

"Kids are kids," I add. "Each one comes with his or her own challenges but, regardless their circumstances, kids just want to be loved, to know someone gives a damn about them. I daresay those are things that are well within your skill set."

"What do you think Seth will say?" Todd wonders aloud.

"I don't think it'll take any convincing," Laurel admits. "It'll make him smile. A few years ago he suggested we adopt." A chuckle comes forth. "Seth will love the irony. He's such a wonderful father. I can see him being a foster dad in a heartbeat."

Todd turns away from us and stares at the wall. He returns to his beer taking a swig before lowering the bottle once more to rest on his right thigh. "Eric gets the band he's always wanted, Lorelei gets to help others through grief counseling, and Laurel will get new purpose as a foster mom." A heavy sigh, another swig, and then with more than a note of bitterness, "What the hell do I get out of this?"

It's a question left hanging in the air that none of us has any clue how to answer.

* * *

The sun has long since set by the time we take the stage at 8:30. The heat is still with us but with the sun and humidity out of the picture it is a gorgeous evening to rock St. Louis.

The stage is about four feet off the ground and is not very deep, making it very close quarters for us. We need to be mindful where we are when moving onstage so we don't trip over equipment or knock it over. It is the epitome of an intimate setting that has the feel of a summer street dance. The crowd is close and standing room only.

It is dark enough for us to see the wristbands in their full glory. It was fun to see the crowd wearing them during the afternoon show but there wasn't much point in them lighting up in broad daylight. Now, however, the wristbands are in full effect. And they are exquisite. There's not a person we can't see. Shout out to my girl Taylor Swift.

The four of us have large bottles of water to keep us hydrated taking drinks after every song. We have dressed for the occasion.

Todd looks very Springsteen with a sleeveless denim vest that has the top two buttons unbuttoned, black board shorts, and sneakers with no socks. An American flag bandana completes his look.

Laurel sports a grey tank with a deep scoop, white shorts, and flats.

Lorelei wears a green cotton blouse showing a hint of cleavage, a white cotton skirt, and sandals. She has her hair pulled back in a pony to keep her hair away from her face.

I'm in a blue Onions shirt, khaki shorts, and strap on sandals. I look over to make sure the set list is where I put it in the first place and hasn't accidentally been taken down. It's exactly where it needs to be.

St. Louis Set list:
Take The Day
1986
Happy Ever After
All Those Ones and Zeroes
California Dreamin'
Everything Changed
No Way Back Today
Talk Dirty to Me
Innovation Generation
Encore: It's Our Time Now

The assembled are in their concert groove by the time we hit *All Those Ones and Zeroes*. It might be they had all day to get psyched up or they've had a tough week and need to blow off steam or maybe they're excited because the Onions are in their town and it's a big-ass celebration. I like to think they're excited to see us.

Lori and I come out from behind our instruments to join Todd and Laurel at the front of the stage. Jake, the sound tech, brings out two wireless hand mics on stands and places them where Lori and I will be positioned. Todd and Laurel bring their mic stands over to where we line up. From the audience's perspective it's Todd, Eric, Lorelei, and Laurel.

"You're probably familiar with our story," Laurel begins once we're in place. "One of the deciding factors in us doing this reunion tour was, frankly, how we sounded together. It was at a bar in Des Moines that we did some karaoke and realized we had something special. This was the first song we ever did together. It's called

California Dreamin'. The crowd applauds with gusto. We look at one another and smile. Precious memories.

All is as it should be until midway through the song when, for an instant, it seems like Todd dropped a note. Nothing drastic but the three of us notice it only because we've sung this song many times with Todd and we know this is not how he usually sings it. Something's off. The crowd doesn't know it but I can't help wonder what happened. While playing to the crowd I scan it and our surroundings. Nothing out of the norm. No disturbances. No accidents. No nothing.

The last note fades away as we look out into the audience. Cheers and clapping. We bow and clap back at the fans before moving to return to our instruments. Todd suddenly intercepts us putting his body in Lori's and my path. Laurel moves our way when she notices her bandmates are in an impromptu tight formation. We look at Todd quizzically.

"She's here," Todd says with a panic I have never heard from him before. Never.

"Who's here?" I ask.

"Meredith!" Todd replies with an expression that conveys his world is crumbling in front of him.

Lori's eyes get as wide as dinner plates. "You mean 'Meredith, the one that got away Meredith'?"

"Yes!" he exclaims. "For God's sake, it's Meredith!"

"Where is she exactly?" Laurel inquires rotating her left leather wristband as she does.

"Redhead, second row, directly in front of where I'm standing," he informs us then adds, "do not turn around and look. Just go back and act normal."

My head cocks to one side as I give him a look that asks him if he's okay.

"Don't say anything, Eric. Just go back to your drum kit and let's move on," Todd orders.

Laurel looks over at Lori and me. "You know our next song, right? *Right?*"

"Oh shit," comes out of me just louder than a whisper.

"*Everything Changed*," Lori finishes the thought. "Oh my God."

Laurel nods and we do the only thing we can do - go back to our places and see where this development takes us. Our exchange takes a handful of moments but it seems like a lot longer. The fans continue to cheer and think what we're doing is just part of making sure the Onions are offering a crisp performance. On a normal night that would be the case. But normal now is a tiny dot in our rear view mirror.

I climb back behind my drums picking up my sticks about the same time my butt hits the seat. In that sliver of time I sneak a peak in the direction Todd described to us. I see her – an extremely attractive redhead standing in front of Todd in the second row. She's wearing a red tank top with jean shorts. She is stunning.

My friends look back at me ready - as much as we can be - to count us down to start the song. Using my sticks to count, afraid my voice might crack, it's four, three, two, one then the drums come to life and we've begun. Since this is Todd's song he's got the heavy vocal lifting to do. I'm his backup.

"Too apprehensive for my world to change..." Todd begins and the crowd goes up in a cheer of recognition. "Naively thinking I could control my own fate," his voice cracks on the last couple of words. "When she left everything changed anyway."

I can barely keep from throwing up. I am playing and watching the concert simultaneously. There are nearly two thousand people here and all I can see is Todd and Meredith. He's singing to her. Never takes his eyes off of her and, now, neither can I. She's not my lost love. She's not the woman I never got over. She doesn't haunt my dreams.

BUT. But this is the song that I co-wrote. But this is the song that got me kicked out of an Applebee's. But this is the song that my former childhood best friend nearly kicked my ass over when he read it. So, yeah, I'm emotionally invested.

As we play our second tour stop Todd is singing this song to the woman he loved more than anyone ever. As I sit here drumming in the middle of a St. Louis late summer evening I cannot get warm. I am freezing from the inside out. My blood runs cold and my stomach is like a pinwheel. Glancing quickly I see Lorelei and Laurel doing what I'm doing - forgetting there's a crowd and never taking their eyes off of Todd and Meredith.

As Todd sings to his true love I'm echoing his words to confirm to Meredith every word, every note is meant for her. Tears are flowing down Lori's and Laurel's cheeks. This has gone way beyond a concert performance and life just got insanely real and we don't know where the hell we go from here. We just follow the notes and hope for the best.

Todd's back is to me so I can't see his face but I can hear his voice and it sounds like my guts feel. Tears are streaking down Meredith's face. She's taken a tissue out of her back pocket and is dabbing it under her eyes. How did she end up here? Where did she come from? Why?

"Can I turn the hourglass upside down? Let me go back and be the man I am now. The sun and the moon will soar in rewind... back to the moment her hand was in mine," is the chorus I sing and it's damn near more than I can take. How the hell is Todd keeping it together?

No one gathered here tonight understands the significance of what is unfolding in front of them. Maybe when the biography of the Onions is written they'll find out. What I do know is that the three of us behind Todd have never played this song or - in my case - sung this song with the passion and depth we do tonight. We may never again. But tonight, for Todd, we are going to help him express to Meredith feelings he could never express years ago. We can only hope that counts for something.

"Under the stars no fears, no regrets..." the last words trail off as I finish the last chorus and the song. I still can't get warm.

"I love you, Meredith," Todd says like it's part of the song. "And I always will."

Laurel's, Lorelei's, and my mouths nearly bounce off the stage at the same moment Meredith's hands cover hers. She looks up at Todd and nods as the tears come faster now. Part of me just wants to stop the show, wish the people of Atomic Cowboy goodnight, and go home. Let those two have time together to catch up or whatever. My eyes glaze over, lost in thought, until Todd's voice comes in to fill the band's silence.

"*Everything Changed*," he announces like the crowd has no clue what song they've just heard. "Thank you," he lifts his right arm, guitar pick in hand, to acknowledge his appreciation of the crowd's indulging him in a special moment.

The rest of us are still so stunned about what just unfolded we're momentarily paralyzed. Somehow Todd is functioning better than the rest of us and he realizes it's up to him to get us jump started.

"The next song is the title track to our album and our tour...*No Way Back Today!*" Cheers and wild applause rise from the crowd which snaps me back to attention.

When Todd continues with a "one, two, one, two, three, four..." the count causes a reflexive action of striking the drums on my part allowing me to start playing on cue and on time. The ladies join in and we proceed with the next song. I can't help but wonder if there is as much turmoil in the women's heads as there is in mine. What is Todd thinking? What happens with those two after the show?

Talk Dirty to Me and *Innovation Generation* are the last two songs of the night as we bring our performance in for a landing. We nail the landing and thank our St. Louis fans for making us feel at home and then leave the stage. A few moments from now we'll be back for the encore song *It's Our Time Now*.

Making the most of those minutes, I dash from the Onions and find Jamaal who is Atomic Cowboy's main security guy.

"Jamaal, Jamaal," I call out jogging up to him. He is a mass of humanity in and of himself. He's nearly six-six and built like a brick you-know-what. Dude is powerful and one of the nicest guys I've ever met.

"What's good?" he asks.

As discreetly as possible I direct his attention to Meredith. "See that redhead over there, second row in front of where Todd sings?" Jamaal nods.

"During our encore song please ease your way over to her and let her know we'd like to meet with her after the show. Please escort her to the green room and have one of the staff members keep her comfortable till we get there. Anything she wants. On us."

"No problem, brother." He motions to one of the other security guys behind me. "Yo! Donnie! Can you cover for me? Got to do a thing for the band." Jamaal looks back to me and says, "Go finish your show, man. We got you."

A smile, a pat on the shoulder, and I'm off. I can focus on the last song of the night now that I know Todd and Meredith will get a chance to renew acquaintances in a somewhat private location after the show. The crowd has lost none of its energy when we reappear on stage for the encore and we leave any remaining energy we have with them. It's been a truly unforgettable day.

The four of us depart the stage and head for the dressing room after the encore. None of us say a word. We're tired and sweaty and jubilant yet apprehensive, still reeling from the unexpected appearance of Todd's lost love. We make our way back to the green room. Two steps before we get to the door I throw myself between my friends and our destination. They look at me like I'm trying to hide something from them. It's completely the opposite.

"Todd," I begin. "Remember when I promised you I'd never blindside you again?" My heart is in my throat because I'm not entirely sure how he's going to react when I share with him who is waiting behind door number one.

"Yes," Todd says warily. "Yes, I do. What have you done now?"

"Listen," I continue with urgency. "We were all shocked to see Meredith in the audience. I don't know about any of the rest of you but my heart is still in my throat and I didn't want to take a chance on Meredith slipping away..."

"What. Did. You. Do?" Todd presses.

"Before the encore I told Jamaal to go to Meredith and let her know we wanted her to be our guest in the green room." I toss a thumb to the door behind me. "She's behind that door waiting for you." At this moment I don't know if Todd's going to bear hug me or bury me. I exhale hard.

Todd's expression softens. "Really?" he asks. "Meredith is for sure behind that door?"

"With God as my witness," I confirm. "Would you like to say hello?"

"Damn right I would," Todd nods.

"Don't keep the lady waiting," Lorelei urges. "Go!" She and Laurel put their hands on Todd's back and gently push him forward toward me and the door. I pivot, open the door, and walk in. Alone in the corner on the other side of the room stands a solitary figure. I lead Todd there with the ladies behind him so he keeps advancing.

"You must be Meredith," I greet extending my hand which she hesitantly shakes. "I'm Eric. Thank you for coming to our show tonight." I point to the ladies. "That's Laurel and Lorelei, respectively. I believe you know Todd."

She grins at my stating the obvious. "Nice to meet you all," she says warmly.

"Okay, so, I think the ladies and I will go over there and freshen up a bit before the meet-and-greet while you two catch up," I state. "Take your time getting reacquainted. We'll cover the meet-and-greet till Todd can join us. No hurry." I put myself between Laurel and Lorelei and usher them to the opposite side of the room.

"So that's her," Laurel whispers.

"Yup. Meredith." I confirm in a matching whisper, acting like her first name only is sufficient for Meredith to be identified like celebrities such as Madonna, Cher, Prince, or Alf.

"That's Meredith. The woman who nearly got your ass kicked at Applebee's. Wow. She's gorgeous." Lorelei adds.

I nod. "Wonder what her story is. Don't see a ring on her finger," I interject. "Who knows what tonight leads to?"

"Wouldn't that be a fairytale ending?" Laurel ponders.

"Do you think they'll ask us to play at their wedding dance?" Lorelei giggles.

"Do I have a speech already written in my head to toast the couple," I add.

"What, now you're looking to get your ass kicked at a wedding reception?" Laurel teases.

The three of us scurry away barely able to hold back the snickering at Laurel's comeback.

* * *

It's late on a Saturday night but you wouldn't know it from the raw energy that crackles around us. About half of the 2000 people at the night show have stayed to be part of the meet-and-greet. Our four millennials were busy selling memorabilia to our fans who a few months ago didn't even know we existed while we were doing the quick change thing in the green room.

The intensity of their draw to us remains a joyful mystery. The folks in line for their concert memento are greater than those in queue for an autograph or picture. The three of us buy as much time as we can for Todd. Fans came to see all four of us so they should get all four of us.

Todd is not missed early on. Most people aren't interested in an autograph or a photo opportunity; they just want to tell us their stories. Stories of how the Onions have changed their lives in whatever way. Each person's affinity to the group depends on whose personal story – Laurel's, Lorelei's, Todd's or mine – he or she associates with or which song resonates most. That seems fair. We've shared our stories through songs and interviews, why shouldn't they get to share in return?

The line keeps moving and a young woman who looks to be in her early 30s appears before me. She's wearing a low cut, sleeveless, white blouse that showcases her girls exquisitely along with tight blue denim shorts and tan ankle boots. Extending a black sharpie in my direction, while pulling back her blouse with her right hand, she exposes her right breast not covered by her bra and asks, "Would you please sign my breast?"

Here is every rock and roller's dream scenario. And, as much as I would like to accommodate her request, it just doesn't seem the proper thing to do so my reply is, "I'd like to but I don't think my wife would appreciate it."

The woman looks at me with a semi-scowl. "So? I don't want your autograph. I want *hers*."

Lorelei is on my right standing shoulder to shoulder with me. The marker is as close to her as it is to me. "Me?" Lori responds with as much surprise outwardly as me inwardly. "I'd be honored." Lorelei accepts the marker and leans forward meeting her fan halfway. "What's your name, hon?"

"Leighann," the fan replies then spells her name for Lorelei. Leighann tells Lori, "I've seen all your performances on YouTube. The way you play keyboard is spectacular. And you always wear the cutest boots," she says.

"You *are* a fan. That is so sweet. I'm thrilled you like our songs," Lori replies as she finishes her signature.

"Oh my gawd," Leighann admires, "I *love* that. Thank you! I'm going to have this tattooed so it will always be with me. Keep rockin'!" She takes back the Sharpie from Lorelei, stashes it in her pocket, and leans in a little further so she can give my friend a hug.

"Such a pleasure to meet you, Leighann," Lorelei says in the embrace. "Once you get that tattooed, post a picture will you? I'd love to see how it turns out."

Leighann lights up at the suggestion. "Oh yes! I will! What a thrill meeting you, Lorelei."

"Hold up," Lori stops her fan and reaches into her back pocket for her phone and hands it to me. "Eric, would you take a picture of me and Leighann?" I take Lori's phone and get it ready to take the picture.

"Oh, oh, oh! Me too!" Leighann removes her phone from her pocket and hands it over to me. Lori steps over a few feet to be in front of our selfie station with the Onions and Centrum Silver logo on the backdrop. Leighann bounces with anticipation as she moves to stand next to her favorite Onion.

I snap the photos with both women's cameras and return each to the rightful owner. Both women are satisfied with my photographic skills and hug one more time before Leighann squeals with glee as she wades through the crowd. As Lori and I return to our previous positions she notices my look of dissatisfaction. "Why the frowny face, Eric?"

"I don't know whether to be relieved or insulted," I explain.

"Are you kidding me?" Lori asks her head tilted left and her hands on her hips.

"Come on, Lori, I am so much prettier than you," I say my voice dripping with a smart aleck tone.

She slaps me on the shoulder. "You're such a jerk," she responds.

"Geez, talk about a plot twist," I chuckle over the recent development. "Did not see that coming."

"Julie's going to tease you when she hears about this," Lori observes.

"Yes she will," I smile. Just then Todd appears from the green room. Meredith's hand is in his as he leads her through the mass of humanity to help get Meredith on her way. If my perception is correct, there is an aura of comfort, of contentment between them. It seems at first glance the reunion is a welcome one for both.

Meredith smiles at us. It's a smile of not knowing what else to do in this tremendously odd situation.

"Great concert, guys," she tells us. "Love what you do," Meredith says. With that she turns to Todd and adds, "I'll talk to you later. Call me when you get in."

Laurel, Lorelei, and I thank her and say so long as she quickly disappears. We take a moment to disengage from our fans to look at Todd. The look on our faces is a request for an immediate update.

Todd shakes his head, stupefied. "It's like no time has passed." He looks down at the ground for a brief instant. Then he looks at us once more. "She's divorced. Turns out he wasn't the one." He shrugs his shoulders. "Not sure where this goes from here but I'm meeting her for drinks and to talk when I get back to the hotel."

"Ooh, how exciting!" Lorelei exclaims. "What a wonderful part of our story. I'm so happy for you!"

"Don't get ahead of things, it's just a conversation. A happy coincidence," he cautions.

"Not a coincidence," I counter. "Meredith didn't end up here by accident. She bought a ticket to see us, to see you. That's significant."

"Reunions. Second chances," Laurel ponders aloud.

"What's that?" I ask.

"Reunions. Second chances," Laurel repeats. "Maybe that's what this is all about. Maybe this is what we all get of out this."

The four of us are allowed only a heartbeat to consider Laurel's words before being snapped back to reality and more fans who want to say hello, take pictures, or have their body parts signed.

CHAPTER EIGHT

THANKS, SHALLOT!

October 13, 2018

"So, tell me, what's the thing you remember most about each other from 4th grade?"

The question comes as my Onions compatriots and I sit on the stage at the Bottom Lounge in Chicago chilling after the first show and meet and greet session. My friend Jen DeSalvo is standing on the floor facing us at eye level. Over Jen's right shoulder is a video camera on a tripod. Her cameraman has headphones on to make sure the incoming audio is clean. He gives Jen the okay sign.

Jen – like me – is a fan of all things superhero. She and I met at the Chicago Comic and Entertainment Expo a couple years ago. We followed one another on Twitter shortly thereafter and have been friends ever since.

Jen stands about five-seven with shoulder-length brown hair providing a frame for her smile, one that could power several city blocks. Jen is the epitome of fitness, which makes sense since she's an avid marathoner and ultra-marathon runner.

Jen is not only a friend who knows the owner of the Bottom Lounge and helped get us booked here; she is a reporter for WGN AM radio and WMAQ television. Jen also serves as a contributor for the show Nude Hippo which is an around-town show in Chicago that features interviews and sketches. Once an episodic show, these days Nude Hippo does the occasional reunion show. Today Jen is doing a segment on Onions At A Crime Scene for such an episode. The irony of a reunion episode about a reunion tour is not lost on me.

Jen loves a unique story and has certainly found one in us. We had carved out some time for Jen in between shows to share thoughts on this journey that has brought us here and ends at the Bottom Lounge.

The Bottom Lounge is located on Chicago's West Side. The environment has a clean but industrial energy that resonates from its cement and steel construction. The Bottom Lounge is known for bringing in aspiring bands from all over the country and featuring some great local talent as well, which was welcome news to me when I began the search for possible Onion venues. The Bottom Lounge's main concert hall capacity is 700 which is an excellent fit for us.

The Bottom Lounge's music set up positions it to be one of the best places to see a show. It's almost like you're seeing a band in a friend's oversized garage that also happens to have a stellar bar inside. Great intimate venue and the perfect amount of space for the band. Cement floor, cement walls, small bar to the side.

The room is kind of wide but not terribly deep. The cavernous music space reminds me of being in a public school gymnasium back when I was 11 at a middle school dance. The stage isn't very high at all.

When you go to a concert at Bottom Lounge you'll find it is standing room only. The best part about The Bottom Lounge is there's not a bad place to stand. It's one of those great venues where you can see the band no matter where you are. Trust me, I checked.

The four of us – along with the packed house – were dripping wet after the first show. The joint was jumping and we fed off the crowd's energy. Almost half of those in attendance at the first show came to see us afterward to buy something, get an autograph, or take photos. Or all of the above. Faith, Hope, Nicole, Ashley, Julie, and Seth ran a smooth meet and greet with everyone who came to see us walking away with smiling faces.

Jen's addition to her initial question brings me back to the interview at hand. "Let's start with Eric. What do you remember most about him from 4th grade?" Her eyebrows rise with anticipation. A pregnant pause and then my three friends respond in unison, "Viking." My head dips and nods as my shoulders slump. Of all the things to remember me for, they remember Viking.

"What's Viking?" Jen follows up.

Todd picks up. "Viking was Eric's lucky pet rock. It was this polished, misshapen rock about three inches long. He always had it in his back pocket. Always."

"No kidding," Laurel continues. "He was so superstitious. Eric would take out that rock and rub it before a test, before recess...anytime he believed he needed a little extra luck...out came Viking."

"Do you still have that lucky rock?" Lorelei turns to me and asks.

"It's in my pocket as we speak," I answer reaching for my pocket. Three jaws drop and eyes widen. "Kidding!" The three plus Jen shake their heads at my hijinx. "Viking is resting comfortably in the attic at home in a box of treasured items. After 4th grade I put Viking away for safekeeping. Going to junior high I was afraid the older kids would take him away from me."

"That's sweet and a little sad," Jen says then moves on to the next Onion. "What about Lorelei?"

"The time she took flight," I say immediately. Todd and Laurel both groan.

"Kickball. Oh how I thought she was going to break something. Like an arm," Laurel shudders.

"What the heck happened?" Jen leans in.

It's up to me to provide the 4-1-1. "Our homeroom had taken a walking field trip to the library during the last class period one Spring afternoon. We got back early so we had time to play a quick game of kickball. At one point Lorelei was trying to score on someone else's kick. Troy got the relay and, from just behind second base, he uncorked a throw to get Lori out."

"Oof," Todd shakes his head in reverence. "That guy had cannon."

"Yeah," I nod along with his head shake. "Lori tries jumping midway between third and home to avoid the throw and the ball hits her in the ankle..."

"...and Lori goes airborne and flew home. Mind you, the playground is all asphalt so there's not a soft spot to land and she skids in," Laurel finishes. "Miracle she didn't get hurt."

"Wow," Jen's blue eyes go wide. "Were you okay?" she looks intently at our keyboardist.

Lori chuckles. "Yeah. Couple of scrapes but nothing major. I was lucky...and that was the end of my playing kickball."

"Totally get that," Jen sympathizes. "How about Laurel? What do you remember about her from that year?"

"Queen of the swingset!" Lori exclaims so fervently she almost goes pop like the weasel.

"Oh! And how!" Todd jumps in.

"Still don't know how you did it," I whistle to provide punctuation.

"Did what?" Jen asks. "Spill!"

"No one could swing like Laurel," Lori asserts. "We had this giant industrial swing set on the playground at school. Laurel was the first person I ever saw who went so high that she looped over the swing set."

"No way!" Jen exclaims in disbelief. "Honestly?"

"I was running up to kick a pitch during kickball," says Todd. "Laurel was in my sightline over the pitcher's shoulder and I saw her do the loop a split-second before swinging my leg. The sight of her going over the top distracted me so much that I tripped over the ball and face-planted." Todd removes his glasses and extends them toward our interviewer. "My glasses went flying. Luckily, not broken. She just kept going up, up, up."

Jen eyes go wide in amazement. "Incredible."

"Ohhh, it was," I echo. "It was the talk of school for a week. I think Laurel just did it because she could but wasn't trying to, if that makes sense. All of us were trying to duplicate her feat the rest of the week." I shake my head with admiration. "No one could. Laurel was the only one who could do it."

"Yeah, then she did it just to show off," Lori says with mock disdain. "She just had to rub it in."

"The boys had been telling me a girl shouldn't be able to do it so I just reminded them a girl was the only one who could," Laurel fills in the blanks. "They straight up ticked me off. So I kept doing it to spite them."

"Why did you stop?" I turn to her and ask before Jen could, not knowing part of the story.

"The principal took me aside and told me to knock it off. He was afraid I was going to get hurt," Laurel tells me.

Todd sniffs in the air. "I smell a lawsuit."

She smiles and nods. "I'm sure that's exactly what he was smelling."

"Girl power," Jen exclaims raising her left fist. "So glorious." She then gestures toward Todd. "What memory stands out about Todd?"

The girls look at me to take the lead on this interrogative. "Hmmm..." I start to buy time and then the obvious hits me. "Oh, of course. Number one KISS fan over here." Todd beams with pride. His chest puffs up and his posture straightens.

"He was such a fanboy," Lorelei continues. "He brought in their album *Destroyer* when school started up after Christmas break. Showed it to everyone."

"Don't forget all the KISS t-shirts and the essays he wrote when we had to do writing assignments for Mrs. Johnson," Laurel adds. "It was almost like a religion with him."

"What do you mean 'was'?" Todd jokes.

"You're still a fan all these years later? Sensational," Jen admires his continued passion. She utilizes a pregnant pause to signal a change in questioning then asks, "What's been the biggest surprise for you on this reunion tour?"

"How much of this tour isn't about music or the past," Laurel jumps in first. "This is about how we have linked with one another and established a rapport with people we don't even know."

"For me," Lorelei picks up the question, "it's how many people share or are inspired by our experiences. The responses and the comments have been astounding."

"Meredith," Todd says matter-of-factly.

Jen stares blankly at Todd. "Do I know who that is?"

Todd pauses to contemplate how exactly he wants to answer. "Meredith is the woman in the song *Everything Changed*."

"What was surprising about her?" Jen follows up.

"She showed up at the St. Louis show out of the blue and I ended up singing the song directly to her," Todd clears up the mystery.

Jen's eyebrows nearly clear her forehead. "You did *what* now?"

"Yeah, took me completely by surprise," Todd acknowledges. "Had no clue she would be at the show or even knew about us. But there she was."

"Took us all by surprise," I insert. The ladies nod.

"We hadn't seen each other since we broke up. Then she appears at our show and we've started talking again," he finishes.

"That's crazy," Jen shakes her head trying to wrap her mind around it all. "How are things going?"

"Slowly. Which is just the way we want it," Todd answers.

"There's a story all by itself," Jen suggests. "What about you, Eric? You're the one who started all this...what's been the biggest surprise for you?"

My eyes go skyward trying to find one answer in a multitude of possibilities. "I guess the biggest surprise in a tour of surprises is that this reunion tour happened at all. From learning how to play drums, to finding the others, to putting a tour together on the fly...there's no way this should have been possible and, yet, here we are. And it is such a wonderful gift."

"As wicked a gift as light up drum sticks from Sheila E, a signed guitar from Joan Jett, and performing with them both on Ellen?" Jen asks with a sparkle in her eye.

"Almost," I grin.

Jen pivots to the camera and says, "From the Bottom Lounge on Chicago's West Side, here with Onions At A Crime Scene, I'm Jen DeSalvo for Nude Hippo." She holds her pose and her smile. The cameraman gives the clear signal and she becomes just Jen again.

"Great! You four are old pros at this interview stuff," Jen turns and tells us. "We'll get that edited into a package that includes footage from the first show, meet-and-greet, plus some sound bites from fans." She's almost bouncing in place with excitement knowing she's sitting on a fun story.

The four of us dismount from our positions on the stage to thank Jen and say so long. Jen wraps a big hug around me and says, "Thanks for the story tip, Eric. I'm so happy for you and your friends. What a treat!"

"Hey, we appreciate you coming down and doing a story on us," I express. I look at Jen as we pull back from our hug and say, "You were working during the first show so I hope you're able to stay and join with us for the last show."

"Are you kidding?" Jen throws her hands in the air like she's tossing confetti. "Of course I'm staying. This girl loves a party!"

Jen hugs the other Onions trading best wishes and thanks. "I just have to run back to the station quickly to log footage and such. I'll be back before the next show starts. Seeya soon." With that she and her colleague are on their way.

The four of us watch them make their way toward the exit and we realize everyone is gone. No family, no technical guys, no bar staff, no nobody...just the Onions in the middle of the small arena. We stand silent taking in the calm.

Soon the Bottom Lounge will again rock to the rafters with a new group of concertgoers to witness our final performance. This silence reminds us the final curtain at the end of the evening is indeed the final curtain for the Onions. It's the finality we're struggling with.

After tonight's show there will be no more practices, no more interviews, no more concerts, no meet-and-greets, no merch, no hashtagging, no Onions. Life returns to normal tomorrow and normal just doesn't have much appeal at this moment.

Todd lifts his wrist to get a view of his watch. "We should probably get ready for the last supper." The three of us turn to him and look at him with an expression of *did you just say that?* noting the Biblical implications of his comment. He waves his hands about a foot in front of his chest somehow trying to erase what he said. "Sorry. Came out wrong," he continues. "But we do have our family supper to get to."

Indeed we do. Julie negotiated with the Bottom Lounge to reserve their banquet room for us. She thought it would be a nice touch for us to share a family meal here to celebrate a successful tour and what all of us accomplished together. Aniko and Jared,

Christopher, Colin, and Cole, plus Meredith are joining us as special guests.

Todd invited Meredith to join us for the show and for our family meal too. She accepted and we are thrilled. This will be the first opportunity for us to get to know Meredith. We only had the abbreviated interaction following the St. Louis show so tonight we'll get quality time with her.

Lorelei puts her hand on Todd's forearm. "Yes, we do but can I ask you something?"

Todd furrows his brow as one corner of his mouth moves out in sort of a half-smile while the other corner stays put. "Of course. What's on your mind?"

"Well," Lori starts tentatively, "we're wondering how things are with her and what her story is. We've been wondering but have been afraid to ask."

Todd nods understanding the trepidation. "Ah. Got it." He pats Lori's hand. "We've been talking and texting since St. Louis. She's divorced. About ten years in they realized it wasn't meant to be till death do them part. She's been on her own since."

"Kids?" Laurel asks.

"No," Todd shakes his head. "They were both career first people and had put off having kids and split before they ever did."

"What does she do?" I inquire.

"Bank president," Todd says with more than a hint of pride.

"Nice!" I respond.

"Yeah," Todd agrees. "We're on equal footing. She doesn't need my money and I don't need hers. We'll see where we go from here."

Lori leans in. "But you're hoping this relationship goes the distance, aren't you?" Her smile is ear to ear.

My throat clears loudly and conspicuously bringing everyone's attention my way. The others are bemused by this display. Todd observes, "I get the feeling you have something to say. Out with it."

"I accept your lavish gratitude and praise for a song that brought about you and Meredith reuniting..." is what comes out only for Lori to interrupt me as I am in mid-bow.

"...and almost got you killed, I might add."

"Yes," I acknowledge. "That too."

Todd lunges at me and grabs my untucked, navy blue, short-sleeved shirt, pulling me nose to nose with a speed that catches me off guard. My eyes go wide as the girls gasp. No one says a word wondering if I've gone too far.

Todd roars, releases my shirt, and proceeds to throw a bear hug on me that I'm pretty sure is about to break a few ribs. He starts laughing with a joy I can't remember him ever showing.

"Ha! Got me there," Todd guffaws. "I so wanted to deck you. But it all turned out okay, didn't it?"

"I guess so," barely squeaks out. Did I mention I think my ribs are about to go? Todd releases the embrace and air is allowed to enter my lungs again. The girls are laughing themselves silly at the spectacle. "Oh my goodness!" Laurel exclaims hugging herself, nearly doubled over. "You should have seen Eric's eyes..."

"...they were like this big," Lori continues making her eyes as wide as humanly possible then framing her face with both hands to signify how big my eyes looked. Her fingers wipe a continuous flow of tears from her face.

"You big lummox!" I smack Todd on the arm. "You trying to cripple me before our last show? Geez!" I am full of melodrama and everyone knows it. Todd puts a hand out and we shake on it. An acknowledgment of a friendship not just re-formed but re-forged.

"What's going on out here?" Julie appears from behind the door that separates the hall from our event room where we'll be eating. "We can hear you all the way across the ballroom. Is everything okay?"

"More than okay," Lori replies.

"Good," Julie says. "Let's eat so we don't have to rush before we have to take places for the night show," she waves us in. The four of us smile at one another and turn to make our way toward the dining area. Todd slaps me on the back and I'm still wondering if my ribs are intact. We enter the room and before we know what's happening...

"SURPRISE!!!"

The four of us flinch hard startled by the exclamation. Then we notice it. Helium balloons and streamers everywhere. Two large balloons - one in the shape of a five and the other a zero - are at the end of the room. Smaller balloons have phrases on them such as "Over the Hill" and "50 is Nifty". All our family and friends plus our warm-up band Something Resembling Responsible are wearing those little cone-shaped party hats with the elastic chin straps.

Everyone in the room is wearing "Embrace the Good" t-shirts and blue jeans. About half are wearing Onions wristbands. Meredith walks up to Todd and puts a party hat on him. "Here," she says. "This is yours." Once the hat is on, Meredith gives him a peck on the cheek. Seth and Julie put hats on Laurel and me respectively. Faith and Hope each put one on Lorelei. She looks like she has pointy ears.

"Whaaaaat?" I finally respond.

"Well, come on," Julie says. "Now that you're all 50 we figured tonight would be our best chance to throw all of you a surprise 50th birthday party, especially since Lorelei finally joined the club a few days ago. Surprise!" she gestures around the room. "You had no idea, did you?"

"None," Laurel answers taking in the decorations. "When did all of this happen?"

"When you four were out there being interviewed," Seth says. "We had to scramble but I think we did ourselves proud."

Jen walks in the room before another word can be said.

"Jen! Were you in on this?" I question.

"Sure was. Told you this girl likes a party!" Jen points to Seth and Julie. "These two clued me in about the surprise party after we scheduled the interview and I was in. They wanted to make sure I gave them enough time to get the room decorated. I guess with all these hands to help, I gave them all the time they needed."

The four of us become statues still stunned by the surprise. It's just now I notice the four, custom-made canes awaiting us. Each one is light blue, has our name on it, and have the Onions and Centrum Silver logos adorning them. Nice touch.

Once our brains have begun processing the scene we are delighted by the spectacle. It's funny to me that this journey began, in part, because our 50th birthdays were approaching. Now we're all 50, we've shared a meaningful experience, and walked a path completed here.

"Don't just stand there," Julie urges us. "Get something to eat. Celebrate!"

The four sudden guests of honor do as we're told and make our way to the buffet table. No sooner than we grab our plates and tableware we notice that the spread is the same as what we had at our practices - brats and burgers with all the fixings. We all look at each other and smile.

Laurel leans in to Lorelei and says just above a whisper, "Remember, brat to mouth" and we all share a fond memory of Lori's wisecrack. Our family and friends make their way through the line once we've moved through. We move to our predetermined seats as noted by the place cards directing us to sit together.

"This is so wild," Lorelei says. "Did not see this coming. You guys?" The rest of us shake our heads as our mouths are full of food.

"Whoa," Todd alerts us, "what is that?" he points to the back corner of the room. The ladies and I turn to see what has Todd's attention. "Is that some sort of shrine?"

Julie leans in toward us taking her seat next to Lorelei then points to Seth, all the Onions' kids, and Meredith. "We created a memorabilia display of the tour along with photo displays of you four through the years. It was a side project we all worked on the last month or so. Finish eating so you can go over and check it out. The kids are especially proud of it."

The four of us eat as quickly as we can without being rude or piggish and then move swiftly to the beginning of the display.

The "This Is Your Life - Onions Edition" begins with a "Timeline of the Onions"...a long line of construction paper that stretches twenty feet in length. The timeline begins with 1977 and a copy of our class picture. Following it is a stretch of paper labeled "The Dormant Years".

"Dormant," I say aloud. "That's an understatement." There are pictures in this section of the timeline of us graduating college, getting married, having kids, and professional successes.

The timeline picks up again in January 2018 and there is mark after mark, date after date plus pictures and news clippings noting important happenings from our reunion journey. The Surf ballroom. Practices. The Jason Show. Mall of America. First Avenue. Ellen. Joan Jett. Sheila E. St. Louis. Selfies with fans. Candid shots behind stage and during the show and all the moments in-between. It is marvelous.

"I don't get it," Laurel points. "Why is there a picture of a messy counter?" All of our attention is focused on a picture from earlier this year. When I see it I almost fall over.

"Julie! Nicole! Ashley!" I exclaim. "Who took this picture?"

Ashley's hand shoots straight up with pride. "This one girl, Dad!"

"How on earth did you get this photo?" I ask in wonderment.

"It wasn't that difficult," my youngest asserts. "You were so mesmerized by what was on the counter it was pretty easy to take a picture of it. I'm not sure why I took it but it just seemed like something I should do."

"Kiddo, you are one fast thinker," I tell her. "Thank you for doing so."

"Someone mind filling us in what we're looking at?" Todd asks impatiently. I walk my bandmates through the inspiration for our group's name. Laurel and Lorelei are in spasm over the origin of our band's name. Todd less so.

"Are you shitting me?" he says hands on hips. "We were named after a messy supper?"

"Hey," Nicole pipes up not thrilled with Todd's apparent diss. "After a messy *family* supper. Like tonight."

"Oh," Todd responds relaxing a bit. "I guess that's okay then. This started with a family supper and ends with a family supper. Appropriate."

"That's our Eric," Lorelei chimes in. "Always likes things tied up in a nice, neat bow." Everyone in attendance nods at Lori's observation.

A tremendous amount of work went in to this. A lifetime of living done by a band that's lived less than a year. A lifetime of memories created. My mom always said that no matter what happens in life - good or bad - we're just making memories. And we have created so many. Not just for the four of us. For our families. For our fans. This was such a blast.

"Whoa," Laurel marvels as we move to the next stop down the line. The wall is covered - every square inch - with emails, tweets, IG posts, and Facebook posts from fans that the girls printed out and taped to the wall.

The messages are a testimony of the true impact of Onions At A Crime Scene. It is incredible. A sniff comes from over my shoulder. Lori grabs a tissue and wipes her nose. I notice we all have tears in our eyes.

The Onions exhale in unison. Sometimes there truly are no words. This reunion started out being about the four of us getting back together. None of us could have ever envisioned this. Certainly not me.

"We're so proud of you all," Seth says coming up behind his wife and putting his hand on her shoulder. They are then joined by

Christopher, Colin, and Cole. Julie, Nicole, and Ashley come up behind me, Meredith to Todd, Faith and Hope to Lori.

Emotion overcomes us all and we weep. Not sure why. Maybe it's how meaningful this tour is to us. Maybe it's how meaningful this tour has been to others. We wanted to connect with people through our music and, wow, what a connection it is.

"Damn allergies," Todd says with a loud sniff, wiping tears from his eyes. The rest of us curse our allergies as well followed by four hard exhales.

"The next part is my favorite," Meredith announces.

"There's more?" Todd asks his true love. She smiles at him and points him to the table a few feet down the line. Resting on top of the table are four tri-fold display boards. We each have an individual board containing photos from childhood up to just before the Onions formed.

We move sideways and lean in to check each other's boards. We delight in seeing all the moments in one another's lives through the years that led us here. I stop and take stock of where we are. The boards are in order - and now so are we - Todd, Eric, Laurel, and Lorelei. T.E.L.L.

"I see what you did there," I say loud enough for all to hear. "Who did it?"

"Over here!" my sister Ani's hand goes up. "Circle of life, big brother." The four of us shake our heads and smile. The only thing I can think to do is to start singing the chorus of *All Those Ones and Zeroes*.

"All those ones and zeroes," I begin.

"Traveling through time," the other three jump in and we proceed to sing our song acapella.

"Who'd have thought that digital code would reunite us down the line?" Lorelei grabs Laurel's hand who grabs my hand then I grab Todd's hand. He's okay with holding my hand in this moment.

"With all those little bits across cyberspace, all our prayers are answered. Our childhood dreams are taking place."

Then we just stand here holding hands keeping our own thoughts. I look over my shoulder as I hear a roomful of sniffles. Our impromptu song has moved anyone in the room with a pulse. I become aware that my friend Jen didn't come by herself. Her cameraman is with her.

"Um, Jen," I say, releasing my hand holds so I can turn to face her. "I thought you'd shot all of your video for Nude Hippo."

Jen beams. "I did," she confirms and then sweeps her arm like she's showcasing a new car on a game show. "But WMAQ TV wants to do a larger feature story on the band and when Julie told me about the surprise party, I knew I wanted to get some video from this as well. Plus, I had to be here for the next part of the surprise."

My three bandmates turn to face the assembled once more. "Next part of the surprise?" Laurel repeats as a question.

Stepping forward as if on cue is someone we recognize instantly. It's Ian Read the CEO of the company that makes Centrum Silver. What on earth is he doing here?

Jen steps next to Todd as her cameraman moves in closer to get the best shot. "Everyone, I'd like to welcome a very special guest who flew in especially for this event. Ladies and gentlemen, Mr. Ian Read, CEO of the company that makes Centrum Silver."

Welcoming applause as Mr. Read approaches us and stands next to Lorelei. He looks to his right so he can make eye contact with us all down the line. He stands about five inches taller than Lori.

Mr. Read looks to be in his mid-60s with a Roman emperor wreath of gray hair from ear to ear with round wire-rimmed glasses. He is dressed in a sport coat with a light blue shirt with a button-down collar, pants that match his sport coat, and brown Italian shoes.

"Lorelei, Laurel, Eric, and Todd," Mr. Read begins, "never has Centrum Silver sponsored a project like this before. We found the idea of this reunion tour so intriguing we couldn't resist being part of it. Our sponsorship of Onions At A Crime Scene has been one of the best things we have ever done. Sales of our products have increased since your tour began and the only thing we've done differently in our marketing this year has been sponsoring your tour. You four have exceeded our expectations."

Hearty clapping and cheers interrupt Mr. Read. The four of us smile and nod. I can't help but think back to the moment at the Surf Ballroom when we pulled that big-ass check out of the priority envelope. We really have come a long way since that night.

"As one of my final acts before stepping down as CEO," Mr. Read picks up his thought, "it is my pleasure to express our gratitude by presenting you this check for one hundred thousand dollars."

Mr. Read moves to his left, leaving Lori's side, to hand the check to me. I accept it simply because that's what one does when another person extends something to you. But things aren't tracking for me and, by observation, the others as well.

"Thank you, Mr. Read, but I'm confused. The money you gave us originally paid for everything. There's nothing left for us to purchase. Why are you giving us more?"

"Oh," Mr. Read says, "my apologies for not finishing my thought. The money isn't for you. We're so grateful for what you've done and for what you stand for that this check is for you to donate on Centrum Silver's behalf to fight human trafficking."

My legs give out and find myself kneeling on the floor. This was the last emotional straw and I break down. My bandmates join me as we huddle in one puddle. "You people are killing us," I squeak as we four are overcome by the outpouring of generosity and goodwill. Those are the only words any of us can get out.

Julie steps between us and the CEO who has literally brought us to our knees, reaches out, and shakes his hand.

"Mr. Read, on behalf of the band, we'd like to thank you for your belief in Onions At A Crime Scene when it was just an idea and for your generous contribution to fight human trafficking," Julie tells him. "They are proud to have represented your product, your company, and your team."

Mr. Read smiles and then Jen ushers him to a corner to get some additional comments for her story but also to give us time to pull ourselves together. Julie and Seth come over with boxes of tissues so we can wipe away tears and clear our sinuses.

"Well, surprise party certainly did live up to the name," I say followed by a long honk into my tissue.

"It's all so overwhelming," Laurel adds dabbing away tears. "What a way to end the tour."

"No more surprises, right?" Todd asks with a tone that sounds more challenge than question.

"Please?" Lori pleads.

* * *

We are all pacing. We never pace. We're restless, nervous, and impatient. What we're about to do isn't new to us but what is new is that this is the last time we'll do this. We're pumped to put on a show for the fans who are wound up and ready to go. Something Resembling Responsible again did their usual excellent job of lathering up the crowd. It's our time now – see what I did there? – to give the people what they came to see.

The Onions are riding an emotional high from our surprise birthday party which was so life affirming. I think our birthday party also increased our apprehension because we're putting pressure on ourselves to make this last show our best show.

Peeking out from behind the curtain I see our family and friends all lined up in the front row.

Our team is usually working their usual support roles but not tonight. For our last effort we want each of them to be able to enjoy the show as a concert goer not a staff person. We all should be able to enjoy ourselves for this last performance.

I smile catching sight of Jen DeSalvo and her husband with my family. Julie said she was going to have them escorted to the front and that she did. Jen is rocking a little black dress that flares out slightly as it gets close to her knees. Her husband stands about six inches above Jen. He is sporting an untucked black, short-sleeved shirt with blue jeans and red hightops.

A room full of fists punches the air as the chants continue. On those wrists are the Taylor Swift-inspired light up wristbands. There are "Embrace the Good" t-shirts everywhere. Again a crowd of strangers proves to me how we have bonded with them and them us. The blessings never seem to end.

"Two minutes to show time," Rob the stage manager alerts us.

As time ticks away and the curtains are about to part one last time I think of something Sheila E said to me as we said goodbye on the Ellen set.

"When I first picked up a set of sticks and got behind a kit, I didn't know where this road would take me. You never do. There's no way you can plan for the highs, the lows, the incomparable successes and unforgettable losses. Even now, all I can be is thankful to keep doing what I love, and for this journey that has never, and will never, give you all the answers at once. One thing's clear...there's no place I'd rather be."

Those words ring true as the crowd chants, "Onions, Onions!" My breathing gets fast and shallow. I exhale hard to calm myself down with a conscious effort to slow my breathing. The Onions' concert tonight will be remembered for many things but the drummer hyperventilating will not be one of them. I become aware of how clammy my hands feel and wipe my sweaty palms on my pants. Can't have Sheila E's best drumsticks fly out of my hands, can I?

Normally we'd be a bit chattier but we'd decided to not say anything before this last performance. We wanted to give each other the opportunity to have his or her own experience, to be present for ourselves and no one else, to soak in all around us, to soak in all that has blessed us...tonight and all through this ride together. This one time we're not in our normal positions on stage before the show begins. We'll take our places after we've been announced.

An aroma of whisky, sweat, and jubilation moves through the air. The hair on the back of my neck seems to be jumping in time with the crowd. Chills roll through my body starting at my feet and working their way up. My friends and I just stand here with goofy smiles on our faces. We're ready.

"Seems like Chicago is kinda your town," Garrett, the Bottom Lounge's house announcer teases us as he moves past us. He continues his way onto the stage and then knifes between the curtains. A roar comes forth from the floor.

Garrett waves to those assembled and then moves his arms in a motion to encourage the crowd to get louder. Trying to be heard over the crowd he yells, "Ladies and gentlemen, welcome to Chicago's Bottom Lounge! You've been waiting for them and here they are! Please welcome for the final performance of their No Way Back Today reunion tour...Onions At A Crime Scene!" The crowd erupts with near deafening cheers, whistles, and clapping.

"One more time," Todd says breaking our silence.

"One more time," the rest of us repeat, grinning.

"Let's give 'em the show they came here for!" Lorelei exhorts.

The curtains part on cue and the four of us jog on stage and wave to the mass of humanity as we take our places. Spotlights are on us. Crowd's manic and we haven't played a note yet. On my left is the set list. On my right is a hand-drawn picture of a band I drew in 4th grade. Stomach calms. The smile on my face is almost as bright as the lights shining on the band.

Todd, Laurel, and Lorelei turn to me and we have one last beat to take measure of an odyssey filled with the improbable, the inspirational, and the incredible. We smile, nod, and stick out our tongues at each other. Then we return our attention to the fans. In a split second before beginning the count and bringing down the drumsticks to begin *Take The Day* a thought flashes in my mind:

Is this the end of Onions At A Crime Scene?

If KISS, REO Speedwagon, .38 Special, Van Halen, and all the other bands we grew up with have taught us anything it's that you can have more than one reunion tour and that it's never over till the Farewell Tour is done. And tonight is goodbye but not farewell.

* * *

NO WAY BACK TODAY

LYRICS

"TAKE THE DAY"

(Intro line) How could we forget?

VERSE 1

Those sweet childhood days

Naivety and carefree fun

In the schoolyard, as we played

We go back to yesterday

Reminisce of good times

So glad, that this day came

CHORUS

Old friends, we can't let this dream end

God only knows what's around the bend

Seize the moment, take the day

Sing and laugh and dance and play

VERSE 2

You know we had this rock dream

That we'd become a band

we'd rock out all night

our name up there in lights

microphones in our hands

Moms and Dads didn't understand

CHORUS

Old friends, we can't let this dream end

God only knows what's around the bend

Seize the moment, take the day

Let's sing and laugh and dance and play

VERSE 3

Never let go of your dream

No matter how crazy it seems

That child's still inside you

begging to be set free

Feel the passion in your heart

That's where you'll find the key

BRIDGE

Now it's time

Let's make the soundtrack

to the rest of our lives

Let our inner children thrive

And really feel alive

FINAL CHORUS

Old friends, we can't let this dream end

God only knows what's around the bend

Seize the moment, take the day

Sing and laugh and dance and play

Repeat chorus to end

"1986"

VERSE 1

Longing for the day we'd be free to go

Rolling through winter

Riding that big yellow bus in the snow

Our rolling prison

fingertips etched 86

in the windows

CHORUS

86, 86

The year that we longed for so hard

86, 86

The year when our lives could finally start

86, 86

Etched with our fingers in the frost on the glass

VERSE 2

Many long years waiting for that great day

How time has changed us

We used plastic to play now we use it to pay

We found our freedom

We lived by their rules

but now we make our own

CHORUS

86, 86

The year that we longed for so hard

86, 86

The year when our lives could finally start

86, 86

Etched with our fingers in the frost on the glass

BRIDGE

Our futures, our freedom

In frosted panes of winter

Our futures, our freedom

86 was our beginning

CHORUS

86, 86

The year that we longed for so hard

86, 86

The year when our lives could finally start

86, 86

Etched with our fingers in the frost on the glass

Repeat chorus to end

"ALL THOSE ONES AND ZEROES"

VERSE 1

Remember when, we had to wait, for everything?
Parents taught, patience virtuous, as a good thing.
Six-week long deliveries, now two days with prime
Favorite shows, took months to watch, now kids
    binge all night
Delayed rewards, just dinosaurs; in the Smithsonian
The life we knew, to kids today, it's alien

CHORUS

All the ones and zeroes
Travelling through time
Who'd have thought, that digital code, would
    reunite us down the line
With all those little bits
Across the cyberspace
All our prayers are answered, our childhood dreams
    are taking place

VERSE 2

The world once far and wide, now at our fingertips
Log on, plan a trip, find a new relationship
Navigate, renovate, communicate, or date
Seeya snail mail post, wait a moment at the most
Lost friends, make amends, reunited in a weekend
Everything you can dream, you can find in
    that screen

CHORUS

All the ones and zeroes

Travelling through time

Who'd have thought, that digital code, would
    reunite us down the line

Without those little bits

Across the cyberspace

All our prayers are answered, our childhood dreams
    are taking place

VERSE 3

The world now comes to us, in an instant, a blink

Be kind, rewind, sit back, chill, spend some
    quiet time

Listen to the ticking of a clock with hands

Play you vinyl records, the old familiar sound

Of that old world through music, and our
    favorite bands

They're now obsolete, like an hourglass out of sand

CHORUS

All the ones and zeroes

Travelling through time

Who'd have thought, that digital code, would
    reunite us down the line

Without those little bits

Across the cyberspace

All our prayers are answered, our childhood dreams
    are taking place

BRIDGE

Thank the ones and zeroes for bringing us together

Life and times have changed forever

CHORUS

All the ones and zeroes

Travelling through time

Who'd have thought, that digital code, would
    reunite us down the line

Without those little bits

Across the cyberspace

All our prayers are answered, and our childhood
    dreams are taking place

"HAPPY EVER AFTER"

VERSE 1

Sitting in your chair

The old one that reclines

Your coffee mug, warms my cold hands

hands you once held so tight

this sweater holds the scent of you

I think of time gone by

I cry no tears, the river's dry

CHORUS

You were meant to be

The one who held me eternally

Who made my sad all right

I don't know how long I can fight

Without your joy your laughter

I've lost my happy ever after

VERSE 2

Sunshine through the window

Cutting through my dark

this cold grey house is silent

no happy yelling daughters

playing hopscotch in the yard

They've both flown, too grown to be at home

I cry no tears, the river's dry

CHORUS

You were meant to be

The one who held me eternally

Who made my sad all right

I don't know how long I can fight

In this big world alone

Without your joy your laughter

I 've lost my happy ever after

VERSE 3

They say you live forever

As an angel in my heart

What use is this when it's you I miss

Please love, return, for one last kiss

I can't breathe now we're apart

No breath to say goodbye

I cry no tears, the river's dry

BRIDGE

Somehow, I'm supposed to move on with my life

Everybody leaves you, but you have to survive

Wait for me darling, one day I'll be back by
    your side

CHORUS

You were meant to be

The one who held me eternally

Who made my sad all right

I don't know how long I can fight

Without your joy your laughter

Farewell, my happy ever after

"EVERYTHING CHANGED"

VERSE 1

Too apprehensive for my world to change

Naively thinking I could control my own fate

When she left, everything changed anyway

CHORUS

Can I turn the hourglass upside down?

Let me go back and be the man I am now

The sun and the moon will soar in rewind

back to that moment her hand was in mine

When we were so young, our whole lives ahead

Under the stars, no fears or regrets

telling her things that need to be said

VERSE 2

The last time we kissed she had tears in her eyes

I couldn't be him, I just couldn't be that guy

The one that she needed to be by her side

CHORUS

Can I turn the hourglass upside down?

Let me go back and be the man I am now

The sun and the moon will soar in rewind

back to that moment her hand was in mine

When we were so young, our whole lives ahead

Under the stars, no fears or regrets

telling her things that need to be said

BRIDGE

Shun trepidation

Live each day as your last

There's no gain in time wasted

dwelling on the regrets of the past

VERSE 3

The joy in her eyes, as he spins her around

With his ring on her finger, she's happier now

I could have been him, but I didn't know how

CHORUS

Can I turn the hourglass upside down?

    (Upside down)

Let me go back, be the man I am now

    (The man I am now)

Let the sun and the moon soar in rewind

Back to that moment her hand was in mine

    (hand in mine)

When we were so young, our whole lives ahead

    (lives ahead)

telling her things that need to be said

Under the stars, no fears, no regrets

    (no regrets)

Can I turn the hourglass back to the start?

    (Back to the start)

Let me go back, be the man of her heart

    (her heart)

Let the sun and the moon soar in rewind

Kissing her lips, our young lives entwined
    (lives entwined)
We were so young, our whole lives ahead
    (lives ahead)
She's hear the words that needed to be said
Under the stars, no fears, no regrets (no regrets)

"NO WAY BACK TODAY"

VERSE 1

Feeding the babies, ironing days

Picking up Legos, messy floor plays

Packing their lunches, a kiss on a graze

Toddlers, tears, tantrums, sweet yesterdays

All of a sudden, too big for Mom

video games and thrash metal drums

Sneaking up late, midnight snack crumbs

Teenage defiance, cheap booze and bubblegum

And she raises them strong, so they won't succumb

To the pressures of life; to know they are loved

But now they have flown

CHORUS

She's lost and alone

In her own familiar home

Now it's silent, empty and grey

She's lost her way

There's no finding her way back today (no way)

There's no finding her way back today

La da, da da da, la la, da da da, la la,
    (she can't find her way)

La da, da da da, la la, da da da, la la,
    (no way back today)

VERSE 2

Her babies have flown, she raised them well
She waits for the phone calls, picks up her cell
Hi Mom, I still love you, still need you as well
Look at how good I take care of myself?
Like a ragdoll abandoned, alone on the shelf
or wallflower yearning for her dancefloor fairytale
This is so new, no clue what to do
Who to be. This wife who lacks purpose
fulfils her husband's needs. So why does her heart
    still bleed?
Inside she's empty, she lost her joie de vivre
Searching for direction, a little meaningful intention

CHORUS

She's lost and alone
In her own familiar home
Now it's silent, empty and grey
She's lost her way
There's no finding her way back today (no way)
There's no finding her way back today
La da, da da da, la la, da da da, la la,
    (she can't find her way)
La da, da da da, la la, da da da, la la,
    (no way back today)

BRIDGE

An empty room
An empty house
An empty town

A lost angel on earth

Waiting to be found

DOUBLE CHORUS

She's lost and alone

In her own familiar home

Now it's silent, empty and grey

She's lost her way

There's no finding her way back today (no way)

There's no finding her way back today

La da, da da da, la la, da da da, la la,
    (she can't find her way)

La da, da da da, la la, da da da, la la,
    (no way back today)

She's lost and alone

In her own familiar home

Now it's silent, empty and grey

She's lost her way

There's no finding her way back today (no way)

There's no finding her way back today

La da, da da da, la la, da da da, la la,
    (she can't find her way)

La da, da da da, la la, da da da, la la,
    (no way back today)

La da, da da da, la la, da da da, la la,
    (she can't find her way)

La da, da da da, la la, da da da, la la,
    (no way back today)

"IT'S OUR TIME NOW"

VERSE 1

We're the first generation that nobody wanted
The ones that the Boomers, tried to abort
Latchkeys kids, all alone, unsupported
Those of us who made it, we were ignored
But now it's our time to step up and shine bright
Be a beacon of hope for the future
You don't have to sit back and shrug helplessly
You can make changes, you have all you need

CHORUS

It's our time now
We're gonna make it no matter what
We're gonna give it all we've got
Join us you'll see that we won't give up
It's our time now
Together we'll make all the change we need
Have faith you'll be, who you wanna be
Be the change in the world that you wanna see
It's our time now

VERSE 2

If you don't choose your story, they will dictate
Step up and narrate your own future
Life it won't be handed to you on a plate
These days it's us taking care of our Boomers
Shaping a world for the future's our promise
As we take care of those, that once took care of us

We won't sit back, and trust in destiny

Let's make some changes, we've got all we need

CHORUS

It's our time now

We're gonna make it no matter what

We're gonna give it all we've got

Join us you'll see that we won't give up

It's our time now

Together we'll make all the change we need

Have faith you'll be, who you wanna be

Be the change in the world that you wanna see

It's our time now

BRIDGE

We have the power to make a better tomorrow.

No fear, no hate, no sorrow

Join with us, it's out time now

It's our time now

It's our time now

CHORUS

It's our time now

We're gonna make it no matter what

We're gonna give it all we've got

Join us you'll see that we won't give up

It's our time now

Together we'll make all the change we need

Have faith you'll be, who you wanna be

Be the change in the world that you wanna see

It's our time now

"INNOVATION GENERATION"

VERSE 1

Generation X, would never miss a show

With VHS recorders, they were in the know

On demand culture, they began to see

The rise of cable TV

Round the clock news, rocking out to MTV

CHORUS

A digital revolution, Gen-Xers with solutions

The babies of the boomers, and their modern
    age plans

With video games in the palms of their hands

And society expands, to the beat of a new sound

It's the innovation generation. Our
    forgotten inspiration.

VERSE 2

Generation X, found the world outside

Confided in strangers, bared their souls online

Blogged and shopped and dated in a way they
    never knew

The online community grew

Finding long lost friends, catching up,
    making amends

CHORUS

A digital revolution, Gen-Xers with solutions

The babies of the boomers, and their modern
    age plans

With video games in the palms of their hands

And society expands, to the beat of a new sound

It's the innovation generation. Our
    forgotten inspiration.

BRIDGE

Innovation generation

Youth, experience, drive

Innovation generation

We're so glad that you arrived

Innovation generation

With your help, we grew, and we thrive

CHORUS

A digital revolution, Gen-Xers with solutions

The babies of the boomers, and their modern
    age plans

With video games in the palms of their hands

And society expands, to the beat of a new sound

It's the innovation generation. Our
    forgotten inspiration.

With your help, we grew and we thrive.

AND NOW FOR THE LEGAL STUFF...

This is a work of fiction. Although its form is that of an autobiography, it is not one. Space and time have been rearranged to suit the convenience of the book. The characters in this book are fictitious representations inspired by real people who are or have been family, friends, classmates, or professional colleagues of the author at one time or another during the author's life. Other than the events described on October 18, 1977, and on January 18, 2018, all scenes, events, actions, and dialogue are a result of the author's imagination.

The roles played by Ellen DeGeneres, Joan Jett, Sheila E., Jason Matheson, and Ian Read in this narrative are entirely fictional. My imagined interactions with them are based upon research from public interviews and comments. However, passages relating to their actions in this work have no factual basis. The appearances on The Ellen Show and The Jason Show are based upon watching their programs and writing a narrative about what the fictionalized account of the characters' experiences would have been on those respective television shows.

Centrum Silver is a registered trademark of the Pfizer Corporation and is used without permission. The product's use in this fictional work is merely a plot device to better ground the characters and make their fictional experience more real for you the reader. Centrum Silver and Pfizer Corporation are NOT endorsers of this book's content in any way including financial.

Rockstar is owned by Russell Weiner and is distributed by Pepsico and is used without permission. The product's use in this fictional work is merely a plot device to better ground the characters and make their account more real for you the reader. Rockstar and Pepsico are NOT endorsers of this book's content in any way including financial.

Liquid Ice is a registered trademark of Liquid Management Partners and is used without permission. The product's use in this fictional work is merely a plot device to better ground the characters and make their account more real for you the reader. Liquid Ice is NOT an endorser of this book's content in any way including financial.

Depends is a registered trademark of Kimberly-Clark and is used without permission. The product's use in this fictional work is merely a plot device to better ground the characters and make their account more real for you the reader. Depends is NOT an endorser of this book's content in any way including financial.

Applebees is a registered trademark of Dine Brands Global and is used without permission. The restaurant's use in this fictional work is merely a plot device to better ground the characters and make their account more real for you the reader. Applebees is NOT an endorser of this book's content in any way including financial.

The song Innovation Generation was inspired by a story on The Hartford's website The Extra Mile as seen here: https://extramile.thehartford.com/transitions/generation-x-contributions/

The story about Eric's family attending the Taylor Swift stadium tour concert and her light up wristbands actually happened. And, no, you cannot have his guy card.

No animals were harmed in the writing of this book. In truth, Bixby was given copious tummy rubs.

For all things Onions At A Crime Scene: www.OnionsReunion.com

ABOUT THE AUTHOR

Eric Shoars is a serial storyteller who considers the English language his playground and who never met a pun he didn't like. Eric is a modern day Walter Mitty with a serious twist. His writing style is best described as "fly on the wall" putting the reader in the shoes of the lead character experiencing what he does as he does. His heart's desire is to have a personal narrator for his daily life. It works in comic books so why not in the real world?

No Way Back Today is Shoars' first foray into fiction. His non-fiction works include *Women Under Glass: The Secret Nature of Glass Ceilings and The Steps to Overcome Them* and *Evil Does Not Have The Last Word*.

Follow Eric on Twitter @eric_shoars and on Instagram at eric_shoars